OUR LAST FIRST KISS

THE COMPLETE SPENCER BROOKS COLLECTION

S.L. STERLING

Our Last First Kiss: The Complete Spencer Brooks Collection

Copyright © 2025 by S.L. Sterling

Editor: Brandi Aquino, Editing Done Write

Cover Design: Thunderstruck Cover Design

OUR LITTLE SECRET

Spencer Brooks was the most attractive man I'd ever laid eyes on.

He was not only our neighbor and the father to the little girl I babysat for, but he was also my father's best friend.

All of those reasons combined should have said he was totally off-limits, but my desire for him was too strong.

After all, What could one night really hurt?

AINSLEY

I STARED out of my bedroom window down into my next-door neighbor's backyard and watched as he walked behind his mower, cutting his lawn. I looked forward to every Saturday morning, because that was the day that Spencer would appear shirtless and do all his yard work. Spencer and his little girl, Nikki, had moved in almost a year ago now, and from the time I'd laid eyes on him, I'd wanted him. Problem was, he was a good twenty years older, divorced, and a father, and I had only turned twenty a few months ago. Not that any of that mattered, except for the fact that he was also my father's best friend.

"Still staring at your god?" Carly questioned.

"How did you guess?"

"Well, you were actually in mid-sentence, and you

just stopped talking." Carly giggled. "That was the only logical reason I could come up with. Unless, of course, you were having a stroke."

I rolled my eyes. "I'm sorry, but how is it even possible that he can look just as sexy in grubby sweats, covered in sweat, as he does every weekday morning when he leaves for the office dressed to the nines in a suit and tie?" I questioned. "I mean, it doesn't help that the man is beautiful. Thick, dark hair I'd love to run my fingers through, blue eyes anyone with half a pulse could get lost in, 6'2" and a solid wall of pure muscle that I'd love to lay under. God, how I'd love to lay under him." I grew quiet envisioning that image. "But in all seriousness, he looks dynamite dressed in a suit, and he looks just as amazing now."

"God, I know what the man looks like, Ainsley. His picture is plastered on every bus stop and major billboard all over the damn city." She sighed with irritation. The topic of Spencer Brooks had dominated every conversation we'd had for the past year.

"I think he makes the city look better. You can't honestly tell me that you don't agree?"

The phone was silent for a moment, and then I heard a huge sigh. "Is Spencer Brooks all we are going to talk about today?"

"I'm sorry...it's just..."

"It's just you're obsessed with an older man," Carly

bit out. "One who just happens to be the same age as your father, which is just gross. He's also, in case you've forgotten, your soon-to-be boss! Did you forget about that? It's seriously quite a predicament you've gotten yourself into."

I glanced out the window again, hoping to catch a glimpse of Spencer one more time, but he had disappeared, leaving the lawn mower in the middle of the yard. I frowned as I did a quick search around the back yard but couldn't see him anywhere.

"Well, it's my predicament isn't it," I mumbled.

"You know, girl, I was thinking, Craig really likes you. Perhaps you should go for him. He will be there with us tonight. That is, if you are coming," Carly said.

"I'm...I'm not sure if I am going just yet," I mumbled, distracted by a voice coming from downstairs. I could hear my father speaking with someone and I strained to hear who it was.

"Come on, how do you not know yet? It's Jon's birthday. He is really looking forward to partying, and I don't think I need to remind you that you did, in fact, promise him you would be there the other day when we had coffee together! You can't back out now."

I heard a rumble of laughter from downstairs, followed by our neighbor's deep voice. A surge of excitement ran through me.

"How about I call you back in five. He's here," I sighed into the phone.

"Who's there? Ainsley, come on. I'm trying to get final numbers for reservations, that is why I called you over a half hour ago, not to talk about Spencer. I just need to know if you are in or out."

"The one, the only, Spencer Brooks," I whispered, ignoring what she had asked me. I heard Carly groan her displeasure into the phone as I opened my bedroom door a little farther just to catch the sound of his deep, sexy voice. I was sure she was tired of listening to me go on and on about Spencer, but I couldn't help myself.

"Girl, you've got it bad. Seriously, I think you should go for Craig. If not him then perhaps someone at school has turned your head."

"The guys at school are dull," I whined. "None of them are mature like Spencer." Another burst of laughter came from downstairs, catching my attention, followed by his deep, sexy voice that gave me chills.

"Spencer should be mature he owns his own company and has a daughter."

"I'll call you back in ten minutes. Oh, and Craig isn't my type," I said.

"Ainsley, he's the captain of your university football team. How the hell is that not your type? He's almost six feet, with dark hair and blue eyes and what was it...a wall of pure muscle." Carly giggled. "Sounds exactly like a younger Spencer."

"You are impossible. I'll call you back."

"Oh, Ains...come on. I just need a yes or no. The reservations—"

"Got to go," I whispered, cutting her off and hanging up the phone. I wandered over to my dresser, checking out my reflection in the mirror and fluffing my hair. I pulled my bulky sweatshirt over my head and smiled as I looked at myself in my fitted tank top and jean shorts. That's much better, I thought to myself. I grabbed my glass from my desk, opened my bedroom door, and headed down toward the kitchen.

I stopped in the hallway just outside the kitchen door and took a deep breath. I needed to gather myself before I walked into that kitchen.

"Spencer, what you really need is a hot twenty-year-old to fuck the shit out of," I heard my father say.

Immediately, at my father's words, I imagined Spencer placing me up against a wall and having his way with me. My body heated at the very thought. I was twenty and I would more than happily allow him to have his way with me, I thought to myself. I took a deep breath, pulled my tank top down, then took a step forward.

"That will help you get Brittany out of your system," my father said as I rounded the corner.

Almost instantly, I met Spencer's blue eyes. I swallowed hard as I saw them quickly roam over my body before they came back up to my face. I looked down at his large, muscular hands, instantly wondering what they would feel like as they gripped my hips. I swallowed hard, smiled, and did my best to keep the heat from rising to my face.

"Good morning, Ainsley," Spencer said, clearing his throat, his eyes skimming over my chest again. "Any plans for tonight?"

"Hey, Ains!" Dad said, taking a sip of his beer.

"Hey, Dad. Hey, Mr. Brooks. No, not yet. Carly wants me to go out," I replied as I reached for the orange juice in the fridge and poured myself a glass, then turned and leaned against the counter.

"Ahhh to be young again." My father chuckled.

"Ainsley, I told you, call me Spencer. This Mr. Brooks nonsense can stop. It will just be a formality when you start at the office." He winked, picking up his beer and taking a swig.

I was going to be interning at his office over the summer as his executive assistant, while his regular assistant was off on medical leave. "Of course, Spencer," I replied. His name felt thick on my tongue, and as I looked at him, his eyes once again roamed over my body.

"Oh gosh, excuse me for a minute. I'll get that drill

you wanted to borrow, Spencer," Dad said, getting up off his chair and leaving the two of us alone together in the room.

The air suddenly felt thick as Spencer's eyes met mine. My eyes burned as the nervous flutter in my stomach began again. The longer we stared at one another, the more the heat grew within me and the more intense it became. I was glad when a loud ring finally pulled his eyes from mine and he began checking something on his cell phone that sat on the table in front of him.

While he was reading, I couldn't help but let my eyes roam over his muscular arms and broad, strong chest and shoulders. I was completely lost in thought as to what he must feel like when he cleared his throat and my eyes flashed to his face. I had no idea how long he had been watching me watch him, but the smirk he wore told me it had been long enough. I wanted to die. How embarrassing. I could feel the heat in my cheeks as I met his eyes.

"Here it is!" Dad said, coming back into the kitchen and placing the drill on the counter. He was completely oblivious to the way Spencer looked at me.

I cleared my throat and reached for something in the cupboard so my father couldn't see my flushed cheeks. As I let out a breath and turned back to them, my father sat back down, grabbed his beer, and took a swig, and then began talking with Spencer again as if I weren't even in the room.

I slowly faded out of the conversation as I watched Spencer grip the neck of his beer bottle, bring it to his lips, and tip his head back, emptying the bottle's contents. I couldn't help but watch the taught muscles in his throat as he swallowed. Then my eyes traveled to his large, muscular hands once again. *God he hand nice hands.* A pulse of excitement ran through me as I wondered what it would feel like if they were on my body, touching me in places that I'd only ever imagined being touched in. *Carly was right, this had to stop. There was no way I could spend my summer in this state, nor be like this while I worked under him, I mean beside him.* Spencer placed the bottle on the table and his eyes wandered back over to me, and then he flashed that sexy smirk in my direction.

"Oh, Ainsley, before I forget, do you think you could watch Nikki for Spencer on the twelfth next month?"

I looked to my father and then over to Spencer who waited for my reply.

"I have that Valentine's Day function I'm hosting for my clients, and it's my weekend to have her," Spencer replied.

Nikki was Spencer's three-year-old daughter. He shared custody of her after he and his wife separated a year ago. When Spencer had Nikki, I usually always babysat for her when he had a work function.

"Yep, sure thing. I'd better go call Carly back." I pushed myself off the counter and left the kitchen, turning quickly to look back at Spencer one last time. I noticed his gaze was firmly planted on my ass, and he quickly averted his eyes as soon as he knew I had caught him. I waited one second, and as his eyes met mine, I smiled at him over my shoulder and continued down the hall, stopping halfway once again to listen to their conversation.

"So, like I said before Ains came in, you need a hot twenty-year-old to fuck her from your mind."

"Where the hell am I going to find that? I'm over the hill. Besides, I'm over Brittany, I just think I'm having a hard time with the loneliness."

I swallowed hard as I listened. One thing Spencer Brooks was not was over the hill.

"Surely you could find a girl at one of these functions of yours," my father responded.

"No, I don't think so. However, you should come with me to this function on the twelfth, that way you can see what my company can do for you," he said to my father.

"You want me to go, but tell me this, why don't you use your own company to find your twenty-year-old then if it's so great?"

"My company isn't for hookups. It's for long-term, meaningful relationships, which is something I'm not sure I'm looking for right now. It's been a hard year for me. I think I just want to have some fun, you know, no strings."

"I understand. I remember how it was for me after Ain's mom left. However, like you, I don't know what I want." I heard my father say, "I'm not sure I want to get involved with someone long term. I've barely dated since Ainsley's mother left."

"I totally understand, but you won't know until you try something. I'll send you over a trial pass, that way you can look around, and if you don't like what you see, no hard feelings. I'll send over a couple extras for some of your friends at work too."

"Sounds good, Spencer. I've got to get going. It's grocery day. I also have errands to run in the city."

"Okay, see you later then. I'll drop off those passes later this afternoon. I'll leave them in the mailbox if you aren't home."

"I look forward to it."

I listened as the chairs scraped across the floor and went back into my room, shutting the door.

AINSLEY

A TRIAL FOR MY FATHER. I let out a breath, not sure if I was ready for him to start dating. I leaned against the cool door, trying to cool myself off. I grabbed my phone and dialed Carly's number. While waiting for her to answer, I grabbed the magazine I had purchased, flopped down on my bed, and began flipping through the pages.

"It's about time you called me back. What the hell took so long?"

"Yeah, sorry about that," I said, continuing to flip through the pages. "Spencer asked me to babysit."

"Tonight?"

"No, not tonight," I bit out as I slowly flipped the page.

"So then you are coming with us tonight right?"

I flipped to the next page and instantly all the air

left the room. In front of me was an ad for *Finding Forever* with Spencer on it. He sat at a table, a coffee in front of him, looking into the camera, those blue eyes of his sparkling. Spencer Brooks owned *Finding Forever*; it was one of the top, elite matchmaking companies in the world, and I would soon be working side-by-side with that hunk of a man. "Holy shit!" I exclaimed.

"What?" Carly asked with excitement.

"You're never going to believe this. Do you have the new *Cosmo* mag that came out last week?" I questioned, looking over the ad and all the manly goodness that was Spencer in the photo.

"Yeah, I think so, why?"

"Get it and look at page twenty-five."

"Ainsley, really, I just need to know if you are coming tonight. Seriously, babe, I need to get the reservations placed. The place fills up so fast, and if I don't, my head will be on the chopping block."

"Get the magazine!" I gritted out between clenched teeth. "Page twenty-five."

I studied the page, and that was when I noticed in small letters, in the upper right-hand corner of the page, what appeared to be an ID handle for his dating site.

"What am I supposed to be looking for?" Carly huffed.

"My God, just go to page twenty-five. You'll see." I

could hear Carly frantically flipping through the pages, and finally she stopped.

"Yeah, so, it's your Greek god, so what."

"Look up in the corner. Looks like it could be his ID handle, RomanticAlpha42."

"Oh, Ainsley!! You're crazy. As if the man is going to post his real handle to the world. Get a freaking grip. Now are you coming with us tonight or not?"

I slid off my bed and wandered over to my desk and opened my laptop, quickly typing in *Finding Forever* in the search bar. Within seconds, the page had loaded. "Um, sure, I guess."

"All right got to go. Oh, and, Ains, don't do anything stupid, okay."

"What is that supposed to mean?"

"Exactly what I said. Don't do anything stupid. Promise me."

I rolled my eyes. "I thought you had to place the reservation?"

"I do, just don't do anything stupid."

"Go call," I said and hung up the phone, burying my face back into the computer.

I turned my attention to the website. I'd been meaning to check it out for a while, especially after I'd been hired. I read through the FAQ page and noticed they offered a free two-week trial. I bit my bottom lip as Carly's words floated through my mind not to do anything stupid. I looked over at the magazine sitting beside me, staring at his handle. *Could it really be his?*

Two weeks, that would be all I would need to find out if it was really him, I thought to myself. I could sign up, contact him, and I wouldn't mention a single word to Carly about it. It would be my secret.

I clicked on "signup" and began setting up my profile, quickly creating a username, and hit next. My stomach sank when the next screen loaded. They wanted credit card information.

"Fuck," I muttered under my breath. I nervously tapped my finger on the mouse, trying to decide what I should do. Then I closed the laptop, there was no way I could give my credit card information to the company. What if Spencer had access to that information.

I got up off my chair and ran my fingers through my hair, feeling completely unsettled. I flipped my stereo on, one of my favorite songs blaring through the speakers, then turned around to see the magazine open to the advertisement. I pulled it closer, studying the handle once again, then looked to my laptop. I blew out a frustrated sigh and then grabbed my purse. "What could it hurt? I'll just make sure I cancel before the free trial period is over," I mumbled, curiosity getting the best of me.

I sat back down at my desk and opened my laptop again and typed in my credit card details. A few more clicks and I was in, staring at a bunch of questions that needed to be answered before they would let me start searching. I used most of my real facts that way I wouldn't have to remember any lies, and forty-five minutes later, BabyGirl89 had been born.

I hit search and typed in RomanticAlpha42, and within seconds, I was faced with a picture-less profile. My stomach churned with excitement that I could barely contain, as I read over the profile, which barely contained anything that would lead me to believe this was Spencer.

I hovered my mouse over the contact button, my stomach flopping with nerves. What if it wasn't him? My hand shook at the thought. I sat there staring at the screen, almost sure I was going to be sick. I grabbed my phone and dialed Carly.

"Let me guess, you've changed your mind and you aren't coming with us after all."

"No, I'll be there. But you won't believe this, but it was real."

"What was real? Ainsley, what are you talking about?"

"RomanticAlpha42."

"Ainsley!"

"What?"

"Tell me you didn't sign up. Tell me you didn't send a message to that profile."

I was quiet as I listened to my friend panic on the other end of the phone. "Ainsley, please tell me you didn't."

"I haven't messaged it. Not yet anyways. But I did create myself a profile," I said as I hit the connect button below RomanticAlpha's name and began typing.

"Oh, Ainsley, do not message that profile. It could be anybody. Besides, you need to get ready for dinner. I'll be picking you up in an hour."

"Too late!"

"Too late? What do you mean too late?"

"I just sent my first connection email!" I giggled into the phone.

"What???" Girl, you are impossible, and you are going to get yourself into trouble."

"I know and I know, but that is why you love me."

I GRABBED my purse and followed Carly out to the car. Tonight, had been fun, until Craig had shown up. He'd slid into the booth beside me and hadn't let me move. The only reprieve I'd gotten was when he had headed to the men's room.

"I can take Ainsley home if you like, Carly," Craig called, as he and Jon hurried to catch up to us.

"It's okay, Carly has to get something from my house that she forgot the other day," I lied.

"Oh, what did I forget?" Carly said, looking at me with confusion.

All three of them looked at me as I struggled to come up with something that Carly had forgotten. "You know...that thing," I bit out, meeting her eyes.

"Ainsley, I'm sure I haven't forgotten anything."

"Yes, you did. Remember, I told you earlier," I said, grabbing her arm and whispering in her ear to just go along with it.

"Oh, that's right. I know what it is."

Jon and Craig both looked at us as we approached Carly's car. I went around to the passenger's side and waited for Carly to open the door when Craig came up beside me.

"How about I call you tomorrow? Perhaps we could go out to a movie or something."

I nodded. "Sure, if you like." I smiled, looking in Carly's direction. "Can you unlock the door."

"Talk to you tomorrow," Craig said as he leaned in and placed a kiss on my cheek just as the locks on the door opened.

I climbed into the front seat and pulled my phone from my pocket. I'd promised Carly I wouldn't check it at dinner tonight, but as soon as I checked my email, I'd wished I'd stayed home.

Carly climbed in the front seat beside me and shoved the key into the ignition, turning the car on. She adjusted the radio and put on her seatbelt, while I sat there staring at my screen.

"Well, that went well. See, I told you Craig likes you. You really need to give him a chance. Oh, and the next time you want to use me for a lie, just tell me ahead of time okay."

"Um..."

"Um what? What are you looking at? Did Craig message you already? Is there love in the air between you two?"

I sat there staring down at my phone, at the email I'd received almost one hour after I'd left the house.

"Ainsley, what is it?" Carly asked, her voice full of concern.

I looked at her, a smile creeping onto my face, and slowly turned my phone for her to see. RomanticAlpha42 had responded to my contact email. I swallowed hard as she read his words.

"What are you going to do about that?" she questioned, looking from the screen then up to me.

"What do you think I'm going to do? I'm going to respond to him," I said. "Now what should I say." I pulled my phone back and hit reply.

"Honestly? I think you should leave it alone, Ainsley. You're playing with fire," Carly said as she put the car in reverse and backed out of the parking spot.

I read the response from him one more time as Carly's words floated through my mind. I blew out a breath, shut the phone off, and shoved it into my purse. I'd sleep on it, and if I still felt I needed to respond in the morning I would, but for now, I was going to follow her advice.

AINSLEY

RomanticAlpha42: I'd love to bury my face between those creamy thighs of yours, make you scream for hours.

I FELT my cheeks heat as I smiled to myself. My fingers tapped quietly against the keyboard as I typed out a response to yet another message from RomanticAlpha42. We had been messaging now for a solid two months. We'd barely missed a day. I hit send and relaxed back against my bed's headboard while I waited for a reply.

I flipped through the channels on the TV, and I'd just settled into an episode of *Outlander* when my phone rang.

"Hello," I whispered into the phone, trying to be quiet, so I didn't disturb my father who was sure to be asleep by now.

"So has the love of your life, Mr. Spencer Brooks, or should I say RomanticAlpha42, confessed his love for you yet?" Carly giggled into the phone.

I rolled my eyes as I checked to see if I had any new messages but was quickly disappointed when I saw that nothing had come through. In fact, he hadn't even read what I'd sent back yet.

"It's just harmless fun. Plus, I don't even know if it's really him!" I replied as I watched the three little dots bounce on the screen letting me know he was typing something. Suddenly, a little check mark appeared on our chat, and I clicked to open the new message and read the words on my screen.

"I can't believe you're actually engaging with people on there." She laughed. "If you ask me, it's kind of creepy, talking to people you don't know."

Truth was, when my trial had expired, I'd let it lapse for two days, but then I was so curious to see if he would continue speaking with me that I ended up paying for a month, followed by another, and yet another because I was enjoying speaking with whoever it was I was speaking to so much. Deep down I'd prayed it was Spencer, but of course, I wouldn't ever know until I met the person—if I ever met the person.

"Not people," I corrected. "I'm only interacting with one person."

Carly let out a loud laugh. "Yeah, sorry about that. One person you believe to be Spencer. So, what does Mr. Romance have to say? Is he as smooth as you'd hoped?"

I had barely heard a word Carly had said as I read the message that sat on my screen. "Oh my God, you're not going to believe this."

"What? Trouble in paradise already?" Carly laughed.

"He's asked me to go on a date with him this coming weekend!" I answered.

"This weekend? As in Valentine's weekend?"

"Yes. Which, if this is Spencer, it would be to the Valentine's thing he is hosting, the one my father is going to be at." I kept reading his words repeatedly. "What do I do?"

"Ask him what he has in mind."

I quickly typed out what Carly told me to type and hit send. I only waited for a couple of seconds before a response came in. "He says not to worry, I would be perfectly safe, it would be a public event, nothing private."

"Interesting," Carly responded.

"What do I do now?"

"Well, since you are babysitting his daughter, you'll have to tell him no, or you could cancel on the little girl and explain to the real Spencer why it is you are canceling. However, I am sure it will be very uncomfortable when you give him your address, or perhaps when you meet up with him and you have to explain all over again. But you're a big girl. I am sure you will figure it out."

I swallowed hard as I tapped my fingers on the keyboard, debating what to respond with. "That isn't helpful, Carly."

"That's true. However, you haven't needed my help to get you this far, so I am sure you will figure it out." She giggled.

SPENCER

THIS WOMAN HAD ME SPINNING, and I had no clue what she even looked like. I sat behind my desk awaiting a response from BabyGirl98. This was the exact reason why I loved the company I had created. It gave people the chance to get to know the real person without any outside judgment. I flipped between my email and back to my profile. I had sent off the date request almost forty minutes ago, and I knew that she had read it. It had never taken so long for a response from her to come through. Perhaps she wasn't interested.

I'd been out of the game so long I feared I might be losing my touch; although I had kept her online the past three nights engaged in some very heavy dirty talk, enough to even get a couple gratuitous photos sent my way, which while I waited for her response, I opened up.

I leaned back in my chair and stared at my screen, my cock throbbing as I flipped between the photos, when my phone rang. "Spencer Brooks."

"Hey, Spencer, what time are we leaving tonight?"

"Hey, Jon! Ainsley is coming by around seven, so I figure after I get Nikki settled with her, I guess we could leave around eight."

"Great!"

"Did you look at the package I dropped off for you?"

"I glanced at it but haven't had a chance to sit down and log into the computer or anything."

"Well, make sure you do. As I said, these aren't your run-of-the-mill women just looking to get laid. They are looking for meaningful relationships, and I have implemented a very rigorous screening process. Also to ease your mind, every account is 100% private. No one can see what you talk about."

"I'll check it out before we leave. Are you bringing a date tonight?"

"Hopefully a date with a very sexy twenty-year-old!"

"That sounds promising. I'll see you tonight then!"

"You got it."

I hung up the phone in time to see a message from BabyGirl89. I clicked open the message, excitement building in me, and leaned back in my chair.

> **BabyGirl89: RomanticAlpha42, I would love nothing more than to accompany you tonight.**
>
> **However, I have a prior engagement that, unfortunately, I cannot get out of. Until then, I will dream of you, BabyGirl89**

> **RomanticAlpha42: To say I am disappointed is an understatement. Perhaps another time?**

THE THREE DOTS bounced around on the page, and before I knew it, a message appeared.

BabyGirl89: Absolutely. It's just bad timing.

I LEANED BACK, disappointment filling me. After three months of talking, I was just a bit shocked at the answer I'd received, but it was really a last-minute thing and perhaps she was telling me the truth. Perhaps she really was busy.

I flipped from the chat screen over to my email and sent off a few end-of-the-day emails, then I began shutting things down and getting ready to head home. I was just about to log out of our chat screen when I noticed another message, titled 'Just for You'. I clicked it open and my jaw dropped.

I had to blink to make sure I wasn't seeing things, but when I opened my eyes, the picture was still there. She stood before the camera, almost naked, wearing only a sexy bra and panty set, but once again, there wasn't a picture of her face. My cock ached, and I reached down and placed my hand over it, squeezing it as I willed it to go down.

SPENCER

I GROANED out loud as shots of cum sprayed over my abs. This was the seventh time in twelve hours that I had jerked off thanks to BabyGirl89. We'd chatted late into the night, and the string of pictures she had sent to me once I'd gotten into bed had been permanently burned into my memory.

I reached for a tissue and had just finished cleaning up the sticky mess I had made when the doorbell rang. I grabbed another tissue, swiped it across my stomach, and reached for my T-shirt that was lying on the back of the desk chair, throwing it over my head. I tied the string on my gym shorts and pulled open my bedroom door, as I listened to Nikki scream for me.

"I got it, Nikki, don't worry," I called as I climbed down the three steps to the front door and pulled it open to see Ainsley standing there, a bag slung over her shoulder.

"Hey, Ains, come on in." She awkwardly smiled at me and stepped through the door. "Here, give me these," I said, reaching for her bags and setting them down on the upper step. "Oh and let me take your coat."

She turned, allowing me to slip her coat from her shoulders. I couldn't help but look down at her breasts, as they spilled out of the top of her low-cut shirt. I swallowed hard as she turned around to face me, and I took her coat and grabbed a hanger from the closet.

She wore a snug black T-shirt and tight jeans that perfectly molded to her tight, round ass. I couldn't help it, my eyes ran the length of her body, her long, shapely legs, perky tits that I'd love to bury my face in, and nipples hard enough that they called to me through her T-shirt. They'd been calling to me since last summer, every time I saw her sunbathing in her backyard.

I remembered the first time I had seen her sprawled out in her backyard. I had sat in the kitchen across from her father that same afternoon with a rock-hard cock as she came into the kitchen in that skimpy little bikini to get a drink. It was all I could do then to keep my eyes off her. That was the exact moment that I had begun this descent into imagining what it would be like to fuck Ainsley Matthews senseless. I imagined on more than one occasion what it would be like to have her legs wrapped around my neck, panting my name as I pounded relentlessly into her. It hadn't gotten any better either because after a year, I still imagined it. I imagined it was Ainsley every single time I spoke to BabyGirl89.

"Hey, Mr. ummm...Spencer. Where's Nikki?"

"In the kitchen coloring. Come on in. I'm just trying to finish getting ready. Nikki has been demanding today."

She toed her shoes off before she climbed the stairs and stopped beside me in the hallway. The smell of vanilla invaded my senses. "I see you brought a night bag."

"I did. I hope that's all right. I know I am just next door, but I figured it would be best in case you are late. I'll just sleep in the room attached to Nikki's, like I've done before. Oh, and I also brought some craft supplies, movies, and snacks for us ladies. I'll make sure that crafts stay in the kitchen, that way we won't get glue on anything." She looked up at me innocently.

"That's fine." I smiled, even though I instantly wanted to bend down and remove that look of innocence off her face. "I've got to finish getting ready."

"All right, we will be in the kitchen." Ainsley smiled, bent down, and picked up her bag and wandered toward the kitchen.

I couldn't help but watch as she walked away from me, taking that hot, sexy body with her. My eyes were glued to that perfect ass as it swayed back and forth. I felt my cock start to stir, and I knew in that instant that I had to tear my eyes from her. I began to make my way down to my bedroom when I heard Nikki's little voice filled with excitement.

"OH, SPENCER, THAT IS JUST HILARIOUS," Jenelle said as she ran her hand down my arm.

Jenelle had been after me all night. She had sat with me through dinner, approached me for a dance, and had hung on to my every word as I mingled with all the clients of *Finding Forever*.

"Please, excuse me for a few moments. I need to check on a private business matter," I lied and excused myself from the group. I was tired of being pawed. Women like Jenelle only took interest in me for one thing, and that was my wallet. I knew it, and they knew it as well.

I made a graceful exit, pretending I had seen someone off in the crowd, and quickly escaped the party. I snuck out of the conference room door and made my way up to my office where I closed the door and relished in the quiet. Sitting down at my desk, I removed my phone from my breast pocket, immediately pulling up my conversation with BabyGirl89, and sent out a message.

RomanticAlpha42: Wish you were here tonight. I would love nothing more than to have you on my arm.

BabyGirl89: I'd love nothing more also, but as I said, I have a previous engagement.

RomanticAlpha42: You're making me jealous; do you have a boyfriend?

BabyGirl89: If you must know, I am helping a friend out.

RomanticAlpha42: Is it a male friend

BabyGirl89: Yes

RomanticAlpha42: Why don't you send me something naughty

I smiled as I hit send. Minutes went by, and then an image populated my screen. My cock instantly hardened at the sight of her fingers inching their way into her black lace panties. I licked my lips and ran my hand over the thick, hard ridge that sat behind my suit pants. I felt like I was going to bust when another image populated my screen. This time I was faced with a panty-less, fully-shaven BabyGirl89. I swallowed hard and groaned as I squeezed my cock. As I studied the picture, I froze, noticing something familiar about the blanket that lay underneath her. I looked harder at the pattern in the blanket, instantly recognizing it as the blanket my great aunt had made me that lay on the bed in my spare guest room. I swallowed hard, only to see another message.

BabyGirl89: Are you there? Do you not like me?

I dropped my phone and turned on my computer, logging into the confidential client information area. I quickly searched for BabyGirl89, and within seconds, I was faced with every drop of her personal information. I scanned through it looking for anything that might be familiar. I didn't see anything that would lead me to believe it was, in fact, Ainsley, so I clicked over to the payment information and froze. Ainsley Matthews was the credit card holder. I swallowed hard, panic filling me for a second as I looked down at my phone at the pictures that had been sent. I picked up my phone and looked back up to the screen in front of me and thought for a second of what to reply.

BabyGirl89: Well?

I swallowed hard and closed my eyes. I picked up my phone, looking back to the computer screen and staring at Ainsley's name. All the things I'd said to her, all the dirty, dirty things I'd said… What was worse was the fact that I had meant every single one of them. I took in a deep breath, then I slowly typed out my response.

RomanticAlpha42: I like you very much.

SPENCER

AFTER FINDING out it was indeed Ainsley I'd been talking to, I hadn't been able to look Jon in the face after I'd returned from my office. I'd seen him watching for me as I made my way through the crowd of people, but I ignored the fact and kept busy mingling with clients.

After everyone had left and the cleanup crew started, I made my way over to a bar down the street. I made my way in and sat down at the bar and ordered a scotch on the rocks. As soon as the golden liquid was placed down in front of me, I picked up the glass and took a sip. I had to figure out how to end this with her.

I'd said things to her, she'd sent things to me—things that neither of us should have shown or said to one another. Hell, she shouldn't even know some of those things, I thought to myself as I downed my drink and nodded to the bartender for another one. Then I pulled my phone from my pocket and went over our conversations. There would be no way I would have guessed it had been her, she seemed so mature for her age. There was no need to figure it all out right now, I thought to myself. I downed my drink, paid my bill, and made my way back to the office where I'd left my car.

I slowly turned into the driveway, put the car in park, shut the engine off, and glanced down at my watch. It was shortly after two. I hadn't planned on being this late, and I was surprised to see the soft glow of the living room light on through the front window.

Ainsley was still awake. I felt my heart start to accelerate as I opened the car door. I'd hoped she would be asleep. I walked up to the front door, put my key in the lock, and turned it, pushing the door open. I was quiet, doing my best not to disturb her in case she was asleep. *I prayed she was asleep.* I quietly took my shoes off and had just shrugged out of my suit jacket when I heard Ainsley's tired voice.

"Hello, Mr... I mean, Spencer. Is that you?"

I smiled to myself. Her sleepy voice was sexy as fuck. "Yeah, it's just me, Ainsley," I said, hanging my suit jacket on the banister and climbing the stairs to the living room.

I stopped in my tracks. Ainsley lay curled up on the couch, under a blanket, watching TV. As her eyes met mine, she quickly sat up, shoving the blankets off her, and my eyes fell to her bare legs.

"How did everything go tonight?" I questioned, swallowing hard. "Nikki be-have herself?"

"Nikki went to bed with no problem. I let her stay up a little later than normal. We were watching *Lady and the Tramp*. I hope that's okay."

"Sure." I smiled.

"How did tonight go for you?" she asked, gathering the blanket and folding it back up.

"It went well."

She smiled at me. "That's fantastic. I'm happy to hear that. Perhaps next year I will get to go to this event."

Yes, you will get to go next year, but you will go as my date, I thought to myself.

"Well, I should get going, let you get some sleep. It's late and Nikki told me you guys are off to the zoo in the morning. I'll just grab my things and be on my way."

Shit, I'd forgotten about the zoo. I pinched the bridge of my nose and then looked over to Ainsley who had her back to me as she threw the blanket onto the back of the couch.

"Ainsley, there's no rush." I turned and walked into the kitchen. "I was going to have a glass of wine. Would you care for one?" Every single part of me knew that I was crossing a line by asking her to join me. Hell, I had crossed a line by even speaking with her for the past couple of months. Granted, I hadn't known it was her.

I pulled the bottle from the fridge and turned to see her leaning against the doorway. What was I doing? I had decided to end this with her, not invite her to have wine with me. I had to end it; this was ridiculous. After all, she was going to be working for me soon, and I had a strict no fraternization policy in my company.

I pulled at my tie, loosening it from my neck, and unbuttoned the top three buttons of my shirt as I watched her eyes wash over me, her cheeks flushed while she bit her bottom lip. *God I'd love to make her bite that bottom lip, better yet, I'd love to bite it.*

"Um...okay...I guess one glass won't hurt. Can I help you with anything?" I noticed she swallowed hard as she looked around the room.

"I'm fine. Why don't you go sit down? I will bring the wine in." I winked at her and watched as she left to go back into the living room. As soon as she left the room, I pulled my phone from my pocket and sent a message to BabyGirl89. I needed to know if, in fact, it was her, and there was no other way I would ever find out. I couldn't ask her. After all, I was sure there were other Ainsley Matthews in the world. I hit send and placed two glasses on the counter. I reached into the fridge and pulled the bottle of wine out, and that was when I heard her phone give off a notification.

AINSLEY

I WANDERED into the living room and took a seat in the same spot I'd been in when Spencer had come in. I curled my feet underneath me and relaxed into the plush cushions. I'd just gotten comfortable when my phone went off. I grabbed it from the table and stared at the screen, biting my bottom lip.

RomanticAlpha42: You busy?

"FUCK," I muttered. If RomanticAlpha42 truly was Spencer, I wondered if there was a way that he could find out that BabyGirl89 was me. I tapped the edge of my phone and bit my bottom lip while I listened to Spencer continue to bang around in the kitchen.

"Did you want anything to eat? Cheese and crackers perhaps?" he called out.

"Um...sure," I answered while I quickly typed my response. I'd hoped that would stall him until I could figure out if it truly was Spencer.

BabyGirl89: Just heading to bed.

As I HIT SEND, I listened hard and heard Spencer's ringtone go off. My stomach flipped with nerves, and suddenly the room got very warm. Almost instantly, my phone went off again.

RomanticAlpha42: Are you going to bed alone?

BabyGirl89: I wish I didn't have to say yes, but sadly yes.

I BIT MY BOTTOM LIP, and when I heard his phone go off again, I knew I had to get out of here. RomanticAlpha42 was Spencer. Carly was right, I'd played with fire, and I was about to get burned. Then, as if my brain hadn't registered what I had done, I recalled each picture I had sent him. Pictures of me that...well, pictures of me that should never have been sent, should never have been seen, and embarrassment flooded me. Shit, I should have listened to Carly.

I looked around the room, remembering that my bags were already in the spare room down the hall. "Fuck," I whispered under my breath, debating if I had time to make it to the spare room to get my stuff before I left. As panic built, I flew to the front door, my phone going off once again in my pocket. I fought to get one shoe on and pulled my phone from my pocket, looking down to see a message from RomanticAlpha42 on my screen.

RomanticAlpha42: That's too bad BabyGirl. I'd gladly join you if I were there.

I SLIPPED my phone back into my pocket and picked up my shoe, my hands shaking so bad that I immediately dropped it back to the floor. I bent to pick it up, and that was when I heard Spencer clear his throat.

I froze and slowly turned to see him leaning against the wall looking sexier than I'd ever seen him. He had completely removed his tie. His shirt was undone and hung open enough that I could see his chest. His shirt-sleeves were rolled up, exposing his muscular forearms. I felt that familiar ache beginning between my legs. An ache that I had felt so many other times seeing him like this. He stood there holding a glass of wine in one hand and his phone in the other, a sexy smirk on his face.

I turned back around and grabbed my shoe from the floor and went to put it on when I heard Spencer clear his throat again.

"Ainsley?"

I stopped moving and swallowed hard. "Yes?"

"Where are you going?"

I fought back my embarrassment and pulled the front door open. I still didn't have my other shoe on; I still held it in my hand as the cold night air hit my face, instantly cooling me. I was about to step out onto the stoop when I felt his strong hand grip my arm. Fire lit inside of me, and instantly, I could feel the heat coming off him as he stepped forward, closing the space between us. When I felt the puff of his breath on the back of my neck, chills ran through my body. I closed my eyes as he leaned into me and whispered in my ear, "It's okay, you don't need to run from me, BabyGirl."

I stood frozen. I couldn't speak, I couldn't move, every nerve in body was on overdrive as he slid his arm around my waist, his large hand resting on my abdomen as he pulled me back against him. I hadn't expected my body to respond to him this way.

He shut the front door, locking it. "You don't need to run from me," he whispered again, and that was when I felt his hard, rigid cock press into me from behind as his lips lightly danced over the side of my neck.

My hands shook as they ran over his forearms. I breathed in his scent, and I closed my eyes as his lips continued to caress over my skin, relishing in the fact that Spencer Brooks was kissing me.

SPENCER

I WAS INTOXICATED by her vanilla scent as my lips skimmed along her soft, sweet neck. I could feel her body tremor slightly the longer my lips grazed her neck. I placed my hand on the flat of her belly, and a soft moan escaped her lips. I turned her into me and pulled her against my chest, my hands gripping her hips. Once she was against me, I noticed she had finally stopped shaking.

I pushed her back up against the front door and pressed my body against hers. I ran my hand over her cheek and looked down into those sweet brown eyes and ran my thumb over her full, pouty, pink lips, her tongue jutting out to wet them. I bent slowly, taking her mouth with mine.

"I shouldn't have...I'm sorry," she murmured as my lips left hers.

"Shhhh, don't be sorry. I'm not. Do you not see the way I look at you, because I've seen the way you look at me, always full of want," I whispered, my hands gripping her ass and pulling her against me so she could feel just how not sorry I was. I met her lips and kissed her deeply, my tongue parting her lips.

In one swift motion, I picked her up, her legs quickly wrapping around my waist, and I pushed her against the wall, pinning her there, her arms around my neck, her fingers running through my hair.

"You know what I want to see," I whispered as I licked and sucked her earlobe and listened to that sexy little moan of hers.

"What?" she asked breathlessly as I continued kissing my way down her neck.

I looked at her, wanting to see her reaction. "That sweet pussy, the one you've been teasing me with for months."

Her cheeks reddened at my answer. "I haven't," she answered breathlessly between kisses.

She wrapped her fingers in my hair, gripping as she kissed me. When the next soft moan escaped her lips, I carried her upstairs and headed down the hall toward my bedroom.

I placed her gently down on the edge of my bed, and

she looked up at me with innocent eyes. I unbuttoned my shirt, her eyes washing over me, the flush on her cheeks beautiful as she bit her bottom lip. She sat there staring back at me, unsure of what she should do.

I grabbed the hem of her shirt and pulled it up and over her head, tossing it over in the corner. I was surprised when I felt her grab my belt and nervously fumble with the buckle. Once undone, she pulled at the button on my dress pants, which I finished undoing myself, my cock aching for her hands, her mouth, whatever she wanted to use.

There was something so innocent about the way she looked at me, at my erection. I placed my hand under her chin, bringing her eyes to mine. At first, I wasn't sure she was even going to touch me, and then I nearly came right on the spot as she brought her hand to my boxers and gripped my hardened shaft through the material.

I closed my eyes and steadied my breathing. There was no way I could embarrass myself in front of her by coming early. I pushed her back, ripping the cups of her bra down and exposing her perfect tits. Her nipples were already hard, calling to me. I knelt down onto the bed and sucked one into my mouth, gently teasing her with little nibbles. Her moan echoed loudly through the room.

"Ainsley, shhhh, you'll wake Nikki," I whispered.

I took the other in my mouth, doing the same thing and getting the same response. God I loved the way she sounded. I kissed my way down the flat of her stomach and gripped the waistband of her shorts, inching them off along with her panties, kissing every bare inch of her body as I went.

Finally, once those were gone, I spread her legs and kneeled on the floor. I spread them as far as they would go. She was already glistening, and I had barely touched her. I kept my hands firmly placed on the insides of her thighs so she couldn't close her legs and ran my tongue right through her center. Her hands gripped my duvet tightly as she struggled not to make a sound. I repeated what I had just done, this time my tongue flicking against her swollen clit. This time she couldn't contain it, and her cries went straight to my cock.

I reached into the drawer of my nightstand and pulled a condom out. "Fuck, I want to bury myself inside of you," I murmured as I ran my tongue through her again. I sat back, ripping the package open and rolling it down my cock.

I crawled up between her legs, kneeling on the bed. I slipped one finger then two deep inside of her, my thumb gently circling her clit. She was tight, and the more I circled her clit, the tighter she gripped my fingers as she began to whimper. Instantly, I kissed her to hush those cries that continued to send a shiver through my body.

I pulled my fingers from her and lined myself up at her entrance and pumped my hard, aching cock a couple of times, then I gripped her hips to hold her still and met her lips one more time.

I eased the head of my cock into her and heard her whimper as she dug her fingernails into my back. She was tighter than I imagined, and I had to take a breath before I continued.

"You okay, BabyGirl?" I whispered, waiting for her to adjust to me before I fully buried myself into her. It was all I could do to hold back and not come instantly as I pushed myself into her and she bit into my shoulder to keep from moaning too loud. As soon as I knew she had adjusted to me, I began pumping into her as I held her tightly.

I placed her legs on my shoulders and buried myself as deep as I could go, and she let out a loud moan. I pumped hard and deep, gripping her hips as she closed her eyes and bit her lip, trying hard to be quiet. I could feel her tightening around me. The tighter she got, the harder it was for me to hold back, and soon I could feel my balls tightening. She came first, hard and loud, and I followed, emptying myself into the condom.

I stayed deep inside of her until the pulsing stopped, and then I slipped from inside of her. As I walked across the room to the bathroom, I already missed her body. I got rid of the condom and then took a minute to heat a cloth. I carried it into the bedroom to find her laying spent on the bed.

I crawled in beside her, placing the warm cloth between her legs, gently cleaning her. Then I dropped the cloth beside the bed, pulled the covers back, and slipped my arm under her neck, pulling her close to me.

AINSLEY LAY IN MY ARMS, her head resting on my chest, her warm body against mine. I kissed her gently and ran my hand over her hip, relishing in the softness of her skin. I could already feel my cock starting to stir at the thought of how she fit so perfectly against me. I never wanted the night to end, and I glanced to the clock to see how much time we had left together.

She started to stir in my arms, and I placed a gentle kiss on her forehead and closed my eyes. We had plenty of time before morning. I'd almost drifted off to sleep when I heard a shrill scream from the other room.

"DAAAAAAADDDDDDYYYYY."

My heart thudded hard in my chest, as panic filled me at the thought of Nikki coming into this room to find us together.

"DDDDDAAAAAAADDDDDDDDYYYYYY," she cried out again.

I pulled my arm out from under Ainsley's body and

sat up, picking up my boxers from the floor and pulling them on. "Wha...What's going on? Where are you going?" Ainsley murmured, lifting her head from the pillow and looking at me with sleepy eyes.

"Shhhh....go to sleep. It's just Nikki. I've got to go check on her. I'll be right back."

I left Ainsley and went down the hall and into Nikki's room to find her crying in her bed. I picked her up and held her close to me, sitting down with her until she fell back asleep, then I made my way back to my bedroom.

I opened the door quietly, expecting to find Ainsley still asleep, but instead, I found her sitting on the edge of the bed, fully dressed. The second I closed the door, she stood up and turned away from me.

"Ainsley, is everything okay?" I swallowed hard as I walked up behind her and placed my hands on her arms. As soon as I touched her, she was flooded with emotion.

"What is it, what's wrong?" I questioned.

"This was not a wise choice." Her voice was thick with emotion.

"DAAAAADDDDDYYYY," Nikki cried out again from the other room.

"Fuck," I muttered under my breath. "Give me a minute."

"No, Spencer, I have to go," she cried, her eyes brimming with tears.

"Please. Don't go anywhere. Just give me a minute, please," I begged.

It took me ten minutes to get Nikki back to sleep before I could finally return to my bedroom. I was afraid she would have left, gone home to her bedroom where she would be out of my reach. However, when I opened the bedroom door, I was pleasantly surprised to see her sitting on opposite side of the bed, her back to me.

"Now, onto you," I said as I clicked the door shut and walked around the bed, kneeling between her legs. "What's going on in that pretty head of yours?" I asked, brushing a loose strand of hair from her face.

She avoided eye contact with me at first, looking everywhere but at me. Then she took in a deep breath and met my eyes. "It's just...we shouldn't have," she said, glancing back to the bed. "What if my father finds out?"

I looked at her and chuckled, then quit. I didn't want her to think I was making fun of her worries, because that wasn't what I was doing. She had every right to be worried, but she also needed to know that I wasn't about to go talking to her father about this. "This...what went on here tonight, is our little secret. If you want it to stop, it stops, no questions asked," I whispered, leaning in to kiss her. "If you want it to continue, then it continues. You say that word, BabyGirl. You're in control here, no one else, just you."

I could still see a lot of uncertainty in her eyes. "What is it?"

"What about you? Don't you have a say?"

I shook my head. I had no right to have a say. "You are in control. You say what you want," I repeated.

She studied my face, my eyes, my lips, and slowly she leaned in and kissed me, slowly at first, and then with a little more passion.

"I take it that means you want more?."

She nodded her head and smiled at me, wrapping her arms around my neck.

AINSLEY

I LAY CURLED up under my blankets watching TV. It was after ten, and I was exhausted from the night I'd spent with Spencer. I'd tried all day, but I hadn't been able to shut my head off. My mind continuously floated to what had happened between us. My father had asked me numerous times how the night had gone, and I had just shrugged and given him my usual answer: that Nikki had behaved, and Spencer had gotten home late, so I'd spent the night. Only, this was the first time I had noticed my father looked at me strangely.

I closed my eyes. I could still feel his hands on my body. I could feel myself getting aroused as I remembered how his lips felt against my neck.

"Ainsley, I'm heading to bed," my father said, poking his head into my room.

Alarm filled me for a moment as I opened my eyes, my father standing there watching me. I swallowed hard. "Okay, have a good night's sleep."

"You too, baby girl."

My body flooded with heat at the sound of my username on *Finding Forever*. My eyes opened wide, but my father was already gone, then something switched inside of me as I remembered my father had called me that since I'd been a little girl, and I giggled to myself at my moment of panic. *Why had I chosen that name for my username?* I lay back against my pile of pillows and reached for my remote control when my phone vibrated.

I smiled to myself as I looked at the screen.

RomanticAlpha42: I can't stop thinking of you.

I quickly hit reply and bit my bottom lip as I typed.

BabyGirl89: Same here, all I can think about is your hands, your lips, your tongue.

RomanticAlpha42: Is that all?

BabyGirl89: What?

RomanticAlpha42: Is that all you miss?

I sat there staring at his message, a smile on my face.

BabyGirl89: No

RomanticAlpha42: Tell me what else you miss?

I bit my bottom lip again as my body heated at the memory of him sliding his large, thick cock into me. I began typing and then quickly deleted what I'd typed. Then I tapped the side of my phone, retyping the words. I stared down at the message, then I hit send before I had time to think about it.

BabyGirl89: I miss your cock.

I sat biting on my thumb as I waited for his response, yet nothing came. Had I crossed a line by saying that, I wondered to myself. I had no idea how many times he had said those dirty things to me, but now my imagination was running wild, until I saw the three little dots begin to jump around as he typed.

RomaticAlpha42: You have no idea how much I miss that pussy of yours.

RomaticAlpha42: Want to have a little fun?

RomaticAlpha42: Hit the little call button down at the bottom of the chat area.

BabyGirl89: What does that do?

RomaticAlpha42: Press it and find out.

I pressed the call button and was shocked to see Spencer appear on my phone. He lay on his bed, shirtless, looking sexy as hell with his hand behind his head as he stared into the camera.

"I can't chat. I'll wake my dad," I whispered.

"Do you have headphones?"

I bit my bottom lip as I nodded.

"Get them."

I reached over to my nightstand and grabbed my headphones, quickly plugging them into the bottom of my phone. Then I slipped one of the ear pieces into my ear. That way I could listen for my dad.

"Can you hear me. Just nod if you can."

I nodded.

"Okay. I want you to do as I tell you, okay."

Once again, I nodded.

"I want you to get comfortable. What are you wearing?"

I kicked the covers off and ran the camera the length of my body so he could see my T-shirt and pajama pants.

"Remove your T-shirt and your pants, but if you have panties on, leave them on."

I swallowed hard and put the phone down beside me as I removed my shirt and quickly slid out of my pants. Throwing them on the floor, I quickly picked my phone back up, careful to keep any part of my body from the camera.

"I want you to imagine me being there with you. Take your free hand and slide your fingers over your right nipple."

I did as he asked, my nipples instantly getting hard at my touch. I opened my eyes and looked at the screen, at Spencer as he lay there.

"Now, slide your hand into your panties," his deep voice commanded.

At first, I hesitated, but then I slid my hand down the flat of my stomach to the waistband of my panties. I angled the camera lower so that Spencer could see as I slid my fingers inside of them.

"Now I want you to rub yourself for me, like I rubbed you. Just glide your fingers over yourself, teasing."

His voice was breathless as I did as he instructed. I angled my phone back up so I could see Spencer through what I was sure was lust-filled eyes.

"God, Ainsley, you're so hot," he murmured before flashing his camera down to his large, thick cock he held in his hand. He lay there stroking himself, which only turned me on more.

"Apply more pressure, Ainsley. Just enough, no more."

I did as he instructed. I could feel pressure beginning to build as I continued, first in slow, small, light circles, then harder and faster.

I watched as Spencer's muscles tightened in his chest and neck, as he continuously stroked himself. It would only be a matter of second before I would explode.

"Keep going, Ainsley. I want to hear you come."

I bit my bottom lip to keep myself from screaming as my orgasm ripped through me at the same time Spencer's ripped through him. I dropped my phone on my bed as I lay there breathing hard.

As soon as I had come down, I pulled my blankets over top of me and grabbed my phone, expecting to see Spencer's face, but the video call had gone dark. I was about to press it again when suddenly those three little familiar dots began to jump around.

RomaticAlpha42: That was hot as fuck. I wish I could have been there.

BabyGirl89: How about tomorrow night I leave my window open?

RomaticAlpha42: Don't tempt me. That might get me arrested ;) Good night BabyGirl.

Just like that, Spencer was gone, logged out for the night, leaving me all alone with my thoughts. I lay back on my bed, placed my phone on my nightstand, and took in a deep breath, trying to calm my beating heart. I had no idea what I had gotten myself into, but whatever it was, I was going to enjoy the ride.

AINSLEY: ONE WEEK LATER

It was midafternoon the following Sunday, I was on the phone with Carly, and I watched from my bedroom window as Spencer came walking up the walkway to our front door, carrying a box of beer and what appeared to be a bottle of wine. I'd barely heard from him the entire week, except for Thursday afternoon for five minutes when he'd messaged me to see if I could run next door and see if he had locked his front door.

I listened with half an ear as Carly went on and on about some guy she was seeing. When the doorbell rang, I jumped and listened hard at my bedroom door for my father to answer.

"Carly, I've got to go."

"No fair, I was just getting ready to ask you all about

RomanticAlpha42. You haven't spoken about him all week."

"There is nothing to tell, to be honest. I guess the fizzle wore out," I lied as I heard the doorbell ring and heard both my father's voice and Spencer's.

"That's too bad. I was seriously hoping for some Spencer stories."

"I'm sure you were, but considering it wasn't Spencer, I don't have any stories to tell," I lied. "I'll call you later, okay."

"Ainsley, are you okay?" Carly questioned.

"Yeah why?"

"Just making sure. I know how badly you wanted it to be Spencer."

I swallowed hard. I wanted to tell her all about it. I hated lying to my best friend, but it was something that had to be done for now. There was no way I could risk even her finding out what had happened between us.

"I'll talk to you later, okay." I hung up the phone and made my way downstairs. "Smells good, Dad," I said, stepping into the kitchen and coming face-to-face with Spencer. He smiled softly at me.

"Thanks. Roast beef tonight. I invited Spencer to join us for dinner. I hope you don't mind."

"Why would I mind," I questioned, looking over at him, my cheeks heating as his eyes ran over me.

"I just figured you might. After all, Sunday night dinner has always been our night together," Dad replied.

"It's fine," I replied and walked over to the cupboard as Dad and Spencer continued their conversation they'd been having before I'd arrived. I was about to reach for a water glass when I heard Spencer clear his throat.

"I brought a bottle of wine for you, Ainsley. It's in the fridge."

"Thank you," I said, looking over my shoulder in Spencer's direction. He got up and grabbed the bottle of wine from the fridge. I dug around in the drawer for our wine opener and switched out my water glass for one of my new stemless wine glasses.

"Shit, I forgot to get something from the car. I'll be right back" my dad said, placing the roast back in the oven and grabbing his car keys from the hook by the door.

Seconds after my father had left the house, I felt Spencer's hands on my arms and his lips at the back of my neck. I closed my eyes as he pressed his lips to my neck, and then I turned to meet them, and that was when the front door crashed.

He pulled away from me, letting out a low, frustrated growl, and tore the wine bottle from my hand and began shoving the corkscrew into the cork, opening the wine for me.

"Forgot dessert," Dad said, ignoring us both and opening the fridge to put the dessert inside.

"How's things going with that chick?" Spencer asked my father as he sat back down, not taking his eyes from me, but doing his best to keep my father distracted.

"Great, we have another date next week. You were right, Spencer. I don't know why it took me so long to sign up."

"What about you, Spence, how are things? You find anyone yet?" Dad asked while tending to the roast in the oven, once again ignoring the pair of us.

Spencer cleared his throat and looked over to where I stood, watching me as he brought his beer bottle to his lips. "Um, I think I have."

I glanced to Spencer, wondering what the hell he was doing.

"And?" my father asked.

"She is amazing, but I don't want to jinx it."

I felt the flush on my cheeks as he looked over at me, but I had to look away.

"That is great, Spencer, really. You'll have to show me a picture of her. Or better yet, perhaps we could set up a double date."

I picked up my cell phone and quickly typed out a message, giving him shit, and hit send, Spencer's phone going off a second later. "I don't have one on me right now. Perhaps later," he lied as he typed a reply on his phone.

I pulled my phone from my pocket and noticed a message from RomanticAlpha42 on my screen. I clicked it open and sucked in a full breath.

RomanticAlpha42: Perhaps you won't be so mad at me when I lick that sweet pussy later.

"Ainsley, everything okay?" Dad asked, taking a drink of his beer.

"What...Yep! Just Carly," I lied, taking a drink of my wine, almost chocking as it hit the back of my throat. I quickly typed out another message. Spencer's phone went off almost immediately. I had to get out of the kitchen before Dad caught on. "I'll be in my room," I murmured, taking my wine with me.

"Ainsley, we have company," my father gritted, annoyed with my behavior.

"Just let me deal with this. I'll be right down," I said, waving my hand at my father.

I walked into the living room and stood up against the wall in the hallway while I listened to my father as he rambled on to Spencer about Kate, the woman he had been seeing. I poked my head around the corner and watched Spencer read the message I had sent. As soon as he replied, my phone went off again, and I took off down the hall, pulling my phone out of my pocket as soon as I got into my room.

RomanticAlpha42: My place tonight, after your father has gone to bed. I'll make sure he is good and drunk by the time I leave, so you've got nothing to worry about!

I smiled to myself and typed out a response, agreeing to meet him. Then I quickly called Carly back then threw my phone down on my bed, grabbed my wine, and returned to join Dad and Spencer.

SPENCER - THREE MONTH'S LATER

To say I enjoyed working beside Ainsley more than my sixty-year-old assistant was an understatement. I leaned back in my chair and watched Ainsley through my partially opened office door, just like I'd done every night at this time. Today though was different. She looked absolutely amazing today. The dark sweater she wore clung to every curve, and paired with her black skirt, it took very little imagination on my part to picture her naked. She really needed to stop wearing office attire that made it hard for me to concentrate.

Suddenly, she looked up in my direction, and I quickly turned my attention back to the email I'd received early this morning. I was looking at expanding *Finding Forever* and was looking at opening a new office in Denver. I looked to the email I'd received earlier this morning from the real estate agent I'd contacted about office space; she could meet with me next week.

I tapped my fingers on the desk, fighting within myself. I figured this would be the perfect opportunity to get Ainsley alone for an entire weekend. I just needed to come up with a reason as to why I would need my assistant with me for such a thing. It wasn't because of a business decision. Hell, I ran the company. I could place funds wherever I needed. It was more because of Jon. He didn't understand the corporate world, and also didn't understand the need for me to keep Ainsley working so late most nights of the week. He had made more comments to me about her hours in the recent days.

I reached for the hot cup of coffee she had brought me ten minutes ago and took a sip, leaning back against my chair as I stared at her once again. The only thing on my mind was how I was going to convince her to come away with me.

I leaned forward and hit the extension for her desk. "Ainsley, could you come here for a moment please," I said, letting go of the intercom button on the phone.

Seconds later, she stood at my door. "Yes, Spencer?"

"Come in, close the door, please."

She shut the door behind her and approached my desk. "What did you need?" she questioned, giving me that innocent smile.

I couldn't take my eyes off her, my mind instantly

traveling back to two nights ago when I'd taken her on my desk. That night had started all because of that exact same smile. I smiled, picked up my mug, and took another sip.

"I heard back from that realtor in Denver. The one I had you contact about that office space."

"That is exciting. And..."

"Yes, and they have a few available spaces for me to check out, so I'll need a hotel booked. We have a corporate account at the Marriott. You should be able to find all the information in the binder Mary left for you, so, if possible, could you please book one for me for next Friday?"

She stepped forward, her eyes meeting mine as she leaned across my desk, the V-neck of her sweater falling open just enough for me to catch a glimpse of her full breasts. She grabbed the pad of sticky notes that sat in front of me then grabbed a pencil, met my eyes with a teasing glance, and smiled before scribbling a note down. "Anything else."

I clenched my jaw at the playfulness in her eyes.

"I'd like a king bed, jacuzzi room, and dinner reservations for Saturday night at a steak house near the hotel."

I watched as she made more notes on the small square note before glancing up at me. "How many people will be attending the dinner so I can make the appropriate reservation?"

"Make it for two people." Her eyes lifted from the paper, meeting mine, and I was sure I saw a hint of jealousy in them, but she proceeded to give me a soft smile.

"For two…" her voice hitched as she stared at the note. "Okay, I'll get that booked right away," she said, turning and heading to the door. She'd just pulled the door open then abruptly turned around.

"Oh, before I forget, you have a meeting with the IT department in thirty minutes. Shall I set up the boardroom and order in lunch?"

I quickly clicked over to my calendar and saw that my entire afternoon had been booked with this meeting, the only one I'd forgotten about. "Please, assorted wraps from Mario's is fine."

"Very well, I'll have them dropped in at twelve thirty."

"Thank you. Oh, and, Ainsley, this meeting is probably going to go into the early evening. Are you able to stay a little later tonight so I can go over a few things with you?"

Ainsley nodded, then smiled before pulling my door shut.

AINSLEY

It was a little after eight. The other two people who worked on this floor had already left for the night. I glanced down the hall at the boardroom door. It was still tightly shut. No one had come out of that room since I'd gone in at five with a fresh thermos of coffee, cookies, and muffins that I'd had delivered from the local bakery down the road.

I heard voices and the handle of the door to the boardroom jiggle, so I turned my attention back to my computer screen and went back to completing the booking for Denver. Once that was confirmed, I proceeded to book him a reservation at the closest steak house I could find. I'd just finalized that when the board-room door opened and out walked the members of the IT department, each of the men scattering toward the elevator.

It was only a matter of moments before Spencer came walking out of the room. He had already removed his tie, and his dress shirt was open at the collar. He appeared tense and on edge, and I bit my bottom lip as he met my eyes. He said nothing to me, so I quickly averted my eyes back down to the paperwork in front of me. Once he was inside his office, I looked up in time to see him place his paperwork on his desk.

I watched him as he stood at his desk, cell phone in hand, then reached for the phone on his desk. I couldn't help but admire him from afar; he was gorgeous. As my eyes climbed his body, he turned, our eyes meeting at the same time. Instead of smiling, he walked over to the door and kicked it closed. I jumped at the sound.

He'd asked me to stay, he'd said he wanted to talk to me, yet he hadn't said a single word. I'd been fielding calls from Brittany all afternoon, so no doubt he was in there calling her right now. Spencer rarely spoke of his ex to me; it wasn't my business, but I knew that suddenly there had been a lot of tension between the two of them. I decided that I wasn't waiting.

I began closing down all the programs I had opened, and then shut my monitor off. Anything he wanted to speak to me about could wait until tomorrow, I thought. If not, he could text me.

I'd just come back from the ladies room and was

putting on my coat when the phone rang on my desk. I glanced to his closed door, then to the phone, and decided I'd better answer it.

"Finding Forever, Spencer Brooks office, Ainsley speaking."

"Ains, it's Dad."

"Oh…Hey, Dad," I said, glancing to Spencer's door again.

"Ains, did you forget we had plans tonight? The ballgame, pizza, and wings?"

I blew out a breath and turned away to look out the window. My father had been begging me to spend time with him. Since I'd begun working for Spencer, I'd had a lot of late work nights. "No, Dad, I didn't forget. Spencer was in meetings all day, and my desk looked like a bomb went off," I lied as I looked out over the city.

"Ainsley, how many more late nights are you going to be putting in? I think this is a tad ridiculous, don't you?"

I turned around to see Spencer leaning up against the doorframe, his eyes skimming my body before they met mine.

It's my dad, I mouthed to Spencer. He hung his head, and I could see his chest rising and falling in a silent chuckle.

"I'm not sure, Dad. I'm just trying to do a good job."

"What time do you figure you'll be home tonight?"

I looked to Spencer and tapped the face of my watch. He smiled, thought for a minute, and then mouthed ten.

"Ah I should be done about ten," I replied.

"All right." My father huffed his disappointment. "Drive careful."

"I will. Love you." I placed the phone into the receiver and looked over to Spencer. I could barely take my eyes off him, he looked so deliciously sexy.

"He wants you home, doesn't he," Spencer questioned and looked to the floor.

I nodded. "Honestly, it was my fault. I agreed to watch the game with him tonight. I should have known better."

"Were you getting ready to leave?" Spencer asked, looking around at the items on my desk.

I'd closed my notebook and had arranged all the items for tomorrow morning.

"I was. I figured maybe you needed some time, perhaps to speak with Brittany. She's been calling all day," I said, holding up the stack of messages she'd left. "Besides, you've had a long day."

"Brittany can wait, and yes, I have had a long day, but I wanted to run something by you before you go. Why don't you come on in for a few minutes."

I could see the want flash in his eyes as he looked at me, waiting for my answer. It was only a matter of minutes before I stood in Spencer's office. He sat behind his computer, tapping his fingers on the keyboard. He stopped, looked up at me, and blew out a breath.

"I see you booked the room as I asked."

I nodded and smiled. "And the restaurant. It's only a couple of blocks from the hotel. I figured it was the most logical choice. It looks amazing, and I figured with it being so close, you wouldn't have to take a cab, you could walk."

Spencer nodded, his face serious. "Perfect."

"Spencer, is everything okay?" I couldn't help but feel that there was a note of unnecessary tension between the two of us. "You looked...stressed." It was the only word I had for the look on his face and the tension I could see in his shoulders.

Spencer looked at me, then got up from his chair and walked around the desk. He slid in front of me and leaned against his desk, then pulled me into his arms and against his chest. "I am. It's just been...a day. I'm glad you stayed," he murmured, meeting my lips with a tender kiss.

I placed my arms on his shoulders. "You asked, and since I'm new, I can't exactly go doing whatever I want now can I. I mean...the boss...he would get mad...perhaps punish me."

I felt Spencer's chest rise and fall in laughter, a little bit of tension falling from his face. "Perhaps you are right," he said, holding me tighter against him. "But not tonight. Tonight, I just want to take you."

"You want to take me where?" I questioned, completely missing what he'd truly said.

His eyes met mine. I could feel the heat rise in my body, my cheeks growing warmer the longer he looked at me. He placed his fingers below my chin, bringing my mouth to his, and he bent down and kissed me hard, backing me up and pressing me against the wall.

I gripped his shirt as his tongue assaulted my mouth, his hands roaming my body. He gripped the bottom of my sweater and swiftly lifted it up and over my head, discarding it to the ground. I pulled at his shirt, ripping it from his pants, then reached for his belt, quickly loosening the buckle as he kissed me harder and with more want than I'd ever felt.

His lips left mine as he knelt down in front of me. He placed a gentle kiss on stomach and looked up at me. I ran my fingers through his hair as he gently tugged at my skirt, pulling it down over my hips. I stood there in my matching bra and panties and was surprised when he buried his face between my legs.

I let out a moan when I felt the pressure of his tongue through my panties. I fisted his hair as he continued. I jumped at a sound out in the hall and placed my hand on his shoulder. "Spencer, there's someone..." I whispered, fighting to hold back my moan.

"It's the cleaning crew. You'll have to be quiet. I don't plan on stopping," he whispered as he began running his tongue over my panties again, teasing me with every lick.

"Spencer, they are right outside the door," I whispered breathlessly as he continued torturing me with his tongue.

"Door is shut, they won't come in. They know that rule well."

He didn't stop. Instead, he pushed my panties to the side and buried his tongue in me, licking and sucking. My breathing quickened and my legs began to shake so bad I could barely keep myself up. I slid my fingers into his hair, grasping as I tilted my head back against the wall, looking toward the ceiling, and bit my bottom lip fighting to keep quiet.

"Give me your leg," he gritted, and he grasped my calf, lifting my left leg over his shoulder, opening me up to him. It was all I could do to keep from screaming out as he slid two fingers inside of me and continued this mind-blowing form of torture with his tongue.

In a matter of seconds, I could feel wave after wave of pleasure beginning to run through my body. I gripped at the wall as my orgasm ripped through me as Spencer relentlessly lapped and sucked at my center. I brought my hand up to my mouth and bit the back of it to stifle my cries. My entire body went limp as I rested against the wall, breathing hard and fast.

Spencer kissed his way up my body, pulling me against him. "Come away with me, Ainsley. To Denver," he whispered.

Without even realizing what it was I was agreeing to, I nodded my head, my eyes closed as I tried to regain the part of myself I'd just lost. It was then I felt Spencer grip my arms, spin me around, and press me flat down onto his desk. I was still breathing hard as he sank his large, hot, throbbing cock into me, pumping hard.

SPENCER

RomanticAlpha42: You just about ready to head out?

I CLOSED the trunk of my car and leaned up against it. This was the third time I'd messaged Ainsley in the past hour, and I still didn't have a response from her.

I knew that Jon had been giving her a hard time over the last couple of weeks for working so much. She'd repeatedly told him that she was just trying her hardest to impress me enough for her to keep her job, but Jon wouldn't listen. He'd finally called me the other day and asked me not to keep her at the office so late, and I'd done as I'd been asked.

I ran back into the house to grab my laptop bag and felt my phone vibrate in my pocket. I quickly pulled it out and looked down at the message that sat on my screen.

BabyGirl89: Dad's pissed. Perhaps I shouldn't go.

I blew out a breath, picked up my laptop, and made my way out to the car where I placed it into the trunk and shut it. This was something I'd been anticipating; it was also something that I wasn't going to let happen. She was coming with me. I pocketed my phone and made my way over to Ainsley's.

I knocked on the door and waited, listening as Jon yelled from inside. I was about to knock again when the door was pulled open, and Jon stood there looking out at me with irritation.

"Spencer!"

"Hey, Jon, I just came by to pick up Ainsley."

Ainsley had shared with me numerous times over the last few nights how uneasy she felt about us going away together. She was afraid that her father suspected something was going on between us, but I assured her he didn't.

"We have a flight to catch at three," I said, looking down at my watch. "Is she ready?"

I could see the tension in Jon's jaw as he opened the door and stepped aside to let me in.

"Ainsley..." Jon yelled.

"Anything wrong?" I questioned. "You seem... tense."

"She's hiding something from me. She's been acting funny for the past few weeks. It's not like her not to talk to me, but no matter how much I ask, she just gets more closed off," Jon said, looking in the direction of Ainsley's room.

"Perhaps you're pushing too hard."

"I think I know my daughter," Jon gritted. "She's hiding something, I know it. I just hope it isn't drugs. Her mother got involved in drugs. It didn't end well for her."

I looked to the floor. Jon was a mess. "I can assure you it's not drugs. She hasn't missed work, Jon. She's very on the ball with everything. She isn't even late coming back from lunch, and I have seen no signs of alcohol abuse. Perhaps it's a woman's issue," I suggested.

Just then I heard a door open, and Ainsley stepped into the living room carrying a bag over her shoulder and her purse on the other. "Sorry, I'm ready."

I glanced at both bags and cleared my throat. "You have your laptop, right?"

Ainsley met my eyes, a look of unease on her face as she shook her head. "Oh gosh, how could I forget that." She laughed nervously as she dropped her bags and headed back down to her bedroom.

I looked to Jon, who squinted in Ainsley's direction.

"See what I mean?" Jon said, looking at me. "Business trip and she forgets her computer. She's been like this for weeks."

"In her defense, Jon, I almost forgot mine." I chuckled. "Give her a break. This is her first real job, and her first work-related trip. Surely, it's just nerves," I said, trying to cover for her. "She's very eager to impress."

"What's just nerves?" Ainsley said, stepping back into the living room, her laptop bag slung over her shoulder.

"Why you're acting so strange," I said, trying to hint at her to gather herself as I bent down and picked up her bags. "We've got to get going," I said, glancing at my watch.

"I'll see you Monday, Dad," Ainsley said, then leaned in to give him a hug. She stepped out onto the porch first, then I followed her, waiting until she was down the stairs, and then we proceeded to make our way to my car.

"See you later. See you, Spencer. I'll keep an eye on your house. What time do you think you'll be back on Monday?"

Ainsley continued walking, but I turned. "Our flight lands at nine in the morning. We will head to the office from the airport, so I will say dinnertime."

"Sounds good." Jon called out, "Love you, Ains."

Ainsley lifted her arm, waving good-bye, then she stopped outside of my car. I loaded her things into the trunk, and then together we climbed into the car. Once inside, I started the engine and backed out of the driveway, leaving our houses behind.

"Thank you for coming over. I couldn't take it. Seriously, I was about to cancel."

"Understandable. What was going on?"

"He just keeps telling me that I am acting strange. I've done nothing. I get up, I go to work, I call if I'm going to be late. Last night, however, he was all over me about it."

"He asked me the other day to stop working you so much. I of course told him I would, and then you probably went home and told him about this weekend." I chuckled.

"Yeah, he wasn't too thrilled about it, that much I can say."

I could see the stress all over Ainsley's face. I reached over and placed my hand on her thigh. "It's going to be okay, Ains."

She met my eyes, then looked down at my hand, her small hand coming down and resting on top of mine.

I'D SIGNED the papers for the new office space and sent a message to Ainsley asking her to begin listing job openings within the company directory while I waited for the cab.

Seconds later, I looked down to my phone to see a message from BabyGirl89. A smile landed on my lips as I opened it.

BabyGirl89: Congratulations! I'll have a surprise for you once you return, to celebrate.

I was standing on the sidewalk grinning like an idiot when my phone began to ring. Expecting it to be Ainsley, I didn't wait for the call display to populate before I answered it.

"So, Ains...I can't wait to see what you have in mind for my surprise."

"Spencer? What are you talking about?" Brittany's voice sounded in my ear.

The second I heard her voice, my body stiffened. "Brittany..."

"Yes, where the hell are you? I tried calling the house all weekend, but there was no answer."

"I'm in Denver, acquiring new office space. Not that you care."

"I see, and Ainsley's with you?"

"She's my assistant, Brittany. Of course, she is here with me," I bit out.

"Uh huh."

I rolled my eyes. "What is it you needed?" I questioned, just wanting to get rid of her.

"Spencer, I'd expect you to have a better assistant, honestly. I've been leaving messages for you at the office and you've never called me back. Has she been giving them to you?"

I blew out a breath. "Yes, Brittany, she has given them to me. I've been busy, and you never said it was an emergency. I planned to call you tomorrow when I get back into the office."

"Well how on earth would you know if it was an emergency or not. You never called me back."

"I'd assume that if it was an emergency that you would say that. Can you please just tell me what it is you want?"

"Why? Do you need to run off to Miss Twenty-Year-Old?"

"Brittany, what exactly are you insinuating?"

"I'm sure you can put two and two together, Spencer. Honestly."

The tone of her voice made me want to punch the brick wall I stood against. She wasn't being fair. Although it shouldn't have surprised me; she never was fair. She hadn't been fair during our separation or our divorce.

"If you must know, I am having dinner with a couple of clients. If it makes you feel better, Ainsley is not joining us. Now, if you'd like to tell me what it is you need..."

"Fine, Spencer, I am wondering if we can switch weekends with Nikki. Something has come up on my weekend."

"So, hire a sitter, Brittany. You know I have planned out every weekend I have with her. If you can't get a sitter, she can of course come and stay with me, but I'm not switching."

"It's just like you to be difficult. Shall I call the lawyer?" she threatened.

This was just like Brittany. Whenever she didn't get her way, she threatened me with legal action. I blew out a breath. "No need to get the lawyer involved. We can switch."

"Thank you. Now you aren't going to leave her with Ainsley are you? I mean, she did tell me you left her Valentine's weekend."

I rolled my eyes and looked up to the sky, then noticed the cab pull up to the sidewalk. "You knew that I had a prior engagement that weekend. It was a work-related event, and in case I need to remind you, it is the way I pay for child support, so yes, Ainsley stayed with Nikki."

"I will have to let the lawyer know that too."

I could feel the anger surge through my body. I could never win with her. "Listen, I have to go, my cab is here. I will call you tomorrow."

"Fine, Spencer."

I hung up the phone and opened the cab door and climbed in. The second the door shut, the cab driver pulled away from the curb and sped off toward the hotel.

AINSLEY

"WHAT TIME DO WE FLY?" I questioned, yawning, looking over to Spencer. He stared at the screen of his laptop, looking over the job postings I'd created. He studied them, a slight scowl on his face. "Seven," he bit out.

"So we have to be at the airport at what, three?" I asked, looking to the clock on the side table.

"Close to it," he mumbled.

I rolled back over onto my side and stared at the wall. When I had talked to Spencer at the end of his meeting with the realtor he'd been in a great mood. It had taken him longer than he expected to return. I didn't think anything of it until dinner. He was mostly silent, very distant, and closed off all the way through dinner, which had me worried.

We'd walked back to the hotel in silence, my arm laced through his. When we stepped inside the lobby, we could hear piano music coming from the lounge over. Spencer looked at me, then leaned into my ear. "Ainsley, do you mind if I take an hour, get a drink?"

His eyes were full of a sadness I'd never seen before. I simply nodded my head, raised up onto my toes, and placed a small, tender kiss on his lips. "Sure, Spencer, go ahead. I'll be upstairs."

"Thank you," he said, kissing my forehead.

I watched as he walked over to the lounge and entered. He took a seat just inside the door, and I stood there watching him for a few minutes. He pulled at the knot in his tie, then removed it, placing it on the table in front of him. Then he unbuttoned the top of his shirt, ran his fingers through his hair, and relaxed back in his chair. Perhaps the meeting hadn't gone well, and he hadn't wanted to say anything, I thought to myself. Whatever was bothering him was none of my business. I walked over to the elevator bank and hit the call button.

Once I was back in the room, I'd decided to have a hot bath. I filled the jacuzzi with hot water and a little bubble bath and climbed in, allowing the heat to sink into my muscles.

I kept an eye on the clock, and once I'd climbed out of the tub, I reached for the box that contained the gift Spencer had given me when we arrived. I lifted the lid and looked down at the prettiest lacey red-and-black teddy, remembering the way he'd growled in my ear how he couldn't wait to see me in it. I picked up the lacey material and held it up in front of me. Tonight, I would give him his wish.

Once I had gotten it on I glanced to the clock, I knew he'd be coming back any moment, so I sprawled across the bed. I'd just gotten comfortable, and like clockwork, I heard the click of the door. Except his reaction hadn't been what I'd expected.

He'd walked in, threw his tie down on the table, and walked right by me, mumbling something about needing to take a shower. He didn't even look my way; he just marched into the bathroom and shut the door behind him.

I rolled onto my back and stared up at the ceiling, my eyes burning. It had taken a lot for me to put myself out there like that, and he hadn't even noticed. I got up, slipped out of the teddy, folding it up neatly, and placed it into a secret pocket in my suitcase. Then I slipped into my usual T-shirt and shorts and crawled under the covers.

His response, or lack of, had been bothering me all night. After his shower, he'd grabbed his laptop and climbed into bed and buried himself in work, checking over all the listings I'd done. It was almost eleven. I never expected he'd still be working on them this late.

"Spencer, it's almost eleven."

"Yep, almost finished. If the light is bothering, you I can move to the desk. That way you can turn the lights off," he mumbled.

I blew out a breath, not saying anything, and rolled onto my back. "Is something wrong, Spencer?"

"No, why do you ask?"

I swallowed back the tears that threatened to fall. "You've been very distant. All through dinner, the walk back, you barely said anything. Then when you came back here you didn't even notice…." My throat burned, and I had to stop talking for fear I started crying.

"Didn't notice what?" he questioned, tearing his eyes away from the laptop for the first time in hours and looked down at me.

"Nothing, it's nothing," I said, swallowing hard, turning away from him.

I listened as I fought back tears. I heard the lid of laptop shut, felt the bed move, then the light was turned off and we were bathed in the light from the TV. I felt him slide his arm around my waist, the other move under my pillow as he gathered me in his arms.

"What didn't I notice?" he whispered.

When I didn't answer him right away, he placed a kiss on the side of my neck and pulled my body into his. I lay in his arms, trying to fight back tears as he tried to comfort me for an unknown reason.

We lay in silence for a few moments, then he cleared his throat. "I'm sorry I've been distant. Brittany called me before I arrived back here this afternoon. She wanted me to switch her weekends for Nikki. When I refused, she threatened me with a lawyer, like she always does. Then she started going on about you. Apparently, she must have a bit of a jealous streak in her. She doesn't seem to like you very much, and I guess you could say it threw me a bit."

I knew exactly how she could be. When she'd called for Spencer at the office, she'd passed some remarks my way that I hadn't appreciated. I hadn't told Spencer because I knew it would make him angry. I'd just taken her messages and passed them on like a good assistant would. Besides, it wasn't my place to talk to him about his ex.

"I'm sorry, Spencer."

"She said some things that rubbed me the wrong way. I guess you could say it took away all my focus."

"Were they things about me?" I questioned. I needed to know if she had bashed me to him.

"Why do you ask that?" Spencer frowned.

"No reason."

"Ainsley, has she said things to you?"

I swallowed hard, but the tears burned the corners of my eyes. I bit my bottom lip and nodded. "She's brutal," I cried. "At first, I barely paid attention to the things she'd said, but after the fifth call the other day, I couldn't anymore. Does she know about us?"

"No, Ainsley, she doesn't. She will try to convince you otherwise. She's a manipulator, and she will work to find out the information she wants, especially when she suspects something, but I swear to you, I haven't said a word."

I wiped at my eyes and nodded my head, then rolled onto my back to look up at Spencer. He studied me for a moment, then leaned down and took my mouth with his. I could already feel his growing arousal as he pulled me into him, allowing me to rest my head on his shoulder.

"I don't want you to worry about it, okay? I also want you to tell me when she gets out of line next time so I can stop it."

I looked at Spencer, not saying anything.

"Promise me, Ainsley."

I nodded my head. "I promise."

He shut the TV off and we lay in the dark in silence for a few moments. He cleared his throat. "So are you going to tell me what it was I missed?"

I bit my bottom lip, thankful he couldn't see how red my face was. "Maybe another time," I whispered.

I relaxed into his side, my head on his chest, the warmth of his body comforting me. I knew that come tomorrow night I would miss this, miss falling asleep in his arms, and because of that I didn't want the night to end. I rolled away from him, and I felt him roll onto his side, pulling me back against his chest. I closed my eyes, relishing in the warmth of his body, and felt his lips on the back of my neck, his breath tickling me. "I'm going to miss this tomorrow night," he whispered. "So much."

SPENCER

THE TRIP HOME had been a long one. Ainsley and I had returned a little after ten. From the airport we'd gone to the office, and while I spent most of my day in meetings with human resources going over the hiring for the new office, Ainsley worked away on some monthly reports for me.

When I'd returned from the meetings, I'd noticed Ainsley looked exhausted as she worked away. I'd gone into my office and gathered my things and then made my way over to her desk. She looked up at me from behind her computer screen and gave me a soft smile.

"I'm just about finished with those reports you'd asked for, except for two. I think I am going to need a little more time on those."

I didn't say anything. I just studied her gorgeous face and nodded.

"I mean, I can get them done for you before I go, but it may take me until eight."

I looked down the hall to the left, then to the right, before taking a step in behind her desk and placing my hands on her shoulders. I gently began massaging her and could feel her body stiffen at my touch. I bent down and placed a kiss on top of her head then leaned in and whispered into her ear, "No more work tonight. It's a good night to head home and get some rest."

She looked up at me, then smiled, placing her right hand onto mine. "You're right," she murmured. "This can wait until tomorrow then?"

"It can."

I reached in front of her and shut off her computer screen, then held my hand out for her to take. She hesitantly took it then stood up and reached for her purse and coat. It was only a matter of minutes before we were speeding off in my car.

I'd been home for a little over three hours. I'd eaten and showered and now stood in the kitchen in boxers and a T-shirt and reached for my favorite rock glass from the cupboard. I placed it onto the counter and listened as the ice I dropped into the glass jingled. I reached for my favorite bottle of scotch and poured myself three fingers, then I grabbed the remote and turned on the radio, jazz pouring out of the speaker.

This was my quiet time, the time I usually relished having, only tonight something felt different. I sat down and closed my eyes and thought about the kiss she'd given me before I'd shut the trunk of the car. The trunk had given us just enough privacy to keep her father from seeing anything out of his front window. That kiss had been soft, gentle, and firm, and one she had initiated herself for the first time. Then she took her bags and made her way home, while I watched.

I'd regretted not noticing her last night when she'd put herself out there. I'd known that had taken a lot for her to do. I'd walked in like an asshole, not even looking her way, completely consumed with the fact that my ex-wife was once again holding Nikki over my head. Even though I'd talked to her about it, it still was haunting me.

I blew out a breath, took a sip of my scotch, and then sat down at the table and pulled my laptop in front of me. I had paperwork that needed to get finished, yet I couldn't concentrate. Instead, I glanced down at my phone, hoping that Ainsley would have messaged me, but there was nothing.

I took another sip of my scotch and rested my head against the back of my chair, closing my eyes, allowing the music to invade me. I jumped at the sound of my phone vibrating against the table and smiled as I looked down at my screen.

BabyGirl89: Are you busy??

RomanticAlpha42: It depends on what you consider busy.

I smiled to myself as I watched the three dots jump around on the screen. I picked up my glass and took a mouthful of scotch and almost choked as an image of Ainsley in the bra and panty set appeared before me. Instantly, my cock hardened, and I very much wished I'd turned my attention to her our last night away.

RomanticAlpha42: Are you trying to kill me.

BabyGirl89: Not my intention ;)

RomanticAlpha42: What exactly is your intention?

BabyGirl89: I guess you could say that I'm feeling adventurous.

RomanticAlpha42: Feeling adventurous? I have an idea...my front door is open.

I watched as the three dots began jumping around, then went away, then began again, then went away for good. I left my phone on the table, adjusted my hard cock, and got up to pour another glass of scotch. I had a feeling I was going to need it. I set my glass down and plopped two ice cubes in the glass again, then heard someone clear their throat behind me.

I turned abruptly to find Ainsley, standing in the doorway of the room, leaning up against the doorframe. She wore her bathrobe, which now hung open just enough for me to catch a peak of her in the teddy I'd bought for her.

My eyes washed over her body. She looked good enough to eat. "My God, you look...."

"Tell me, tell me how I look," she said in a low, throaty growl as she grabbed the tie of her bathrobe and swung it around, her eyes giving off a playful glint.

I didn't wait. Instantly, I walked over to her, taking her in my arms as she wrapped her arms around my neck and met my mouth. I pushed her up against the wall, assaulting her mouth with my tongue as I pressed my body against hers. Then I lifted her up, wrapped her legs around my waist, and carried her down the hall to my bedroom, kicking the door shut behind me.

OUR LITTLE SURPRISE

Spencer Brooks was the most attractive man I'd ever laid eyes on. Not only was he my boss and father's best friend but he was also the man I had been sneaking around with for the entire summer.

That is why my world shattered the night my father caught us in bed together. Angry as hell, my father forbade us to be together, but Spencer promised me that everything would work out. In the coming days, my father demanded I quit my job. Only he didn't stop there. He also called Spencer's ex-wife, who threatened to take Spencer's daughter Nikki away from him, forcing Spencer to call us quits for good.

Heartbroken, I buried my feelings for the man I loved, and put in a transfer to another department to appease my father. Only to my surprise Spencer refused to sign it until after I helped him organize his company Christmas Party.

I could only do this if he promised to keep it professional, but soon I was noticing the soft touches and lingering glances. Then one night he delivered a kiss that brought all my feelings back to the surface. I try to fight it at first until I discover something that will either bring us together or tear us apart for good.

AINSLEY

IT WAS a chilly day for the beginning of October, and the first few flakes of snow danced down in front of the window, immediately melting away as they hit the ground. I sat in the living room with my chin resting on my arm, looking out the front window of the house, trying to decide what I was going to do tonight. Normally, on Fridays, Dad would head over to the local pub to play pool with the guys from work, and I would sneak next door to Spencer's, but he was still away on a business trip until Monday. Perhaps I would call Carly. We hadn't hung out in a while. It would be nice to catch up, I thought to myself, glancing at the clock. I was about to reach for the phone when I turned back to look out the front window in time to see a car pull into Spencer's driveway. I leaned forward to see if I could see who it was. I could feel my excitement building at the thought of him returning early. I tried to lean forward a little more to see but the car had pulled up further than my view would allow and I hit my head on the window. I laughed at myself and then felt my phone vibrate in my pocket.

I quickly removed my phone from my front pocket and looked down at the screen to see a message waiting for me from RomanticAlpha42. A soft smile came to my lips as my body filled with excitement. Perhaps he had come home early, I thought to myself, and then glanced down the hall to make sure Dad wasn't coming and opened the message and read the words "I'm home" on my screen, and I quickly responded.

BabyGirl89: Dad is just getting ready to leave. I will be over as soon as he leaves.

RomanticAlpha42: Not tonight, tonight I'm coming to you. Let me know when the coast is clear. I want to destroy you in your bedroom this time.

I COULD BARELY CONTAIN myself as I giggled with excitement and squeezed my legs tight together at the thought of Spencer between them after being gone for almost two weeks to set up the Denver office. We had spent an intense summer together, and this had been the first time we'd been apart for any amount of time. I shoved my phone back into my pocket when I heard my father clear his throat. "What are you so happy about?" he questioned.

"It's nothing," I said, shaking my head. "You look nice." I looked at my father. He wore dark dress pants, a shirt, and tie. It was odd to see my father in anything but jeans and a T-shirt, but it suited him, and besides, I needed to do whatever it took to take the focus off me.

"Thanks, I have a date tonight."

"Oh, I thought you were going to meet up with your work buddies at the bar."

"Not tonight."

"So who is the date with?"

"You don't know her. I met her through Spencer's company. That man was right. I don't know why I waited so long to join Finding Forever."

"Will you be out late?" I questioned as my father stepped in front of the mirror to straighten his tie. I watched him try to adjust it, and then he turned to me, a look of despair on his face at the fact his tie was still crooked.

"Who knows?" he said, laughing. "I will not rush it. I am going to adopt Spencer's rule. Whatever happens,

happens. So don't you wait up," Dad said, raising his eyebrows.

I couldn't help but giggle. I was happy for my father. After years of being single and focusing all his time on raising me after my mom left us, he was finally getting out there. It had taken Spencer a long time to convince my father to finally use his company.

Finding Forever was an elite matchmaking site. It wasn't one of those sign up and get laid sites as Spencer would call them. This one was meant to find you a forever relationship. He had spent years marketing the company, acquiring the right clients, and it had paid off. Even though my father said he didn't want a forever relationship, I knew deep down inside he did.

"Well, Dad, have a great time okay."

"I will. Oh and how are things going at work? I meant to ask you the other day, but it slipped my mind. Is Spencer still treating you okay?"

I felt a slight blush hit my cheeks at Dad's question. Spencer was treating me more than okay. I'd had a crush on that man for months, and after finding what I was sure was his handle on Finding Forever in a magazine ad, I'd created a fake profile and began messaging him. My friend Carly disapproved immediately, and I was convinced there was no way he would use his real handle on a magazine ad anyways. Soon, I found myself messaging with this person almost daily, and then one night while I was babysitting for him, he'd come home late and offered me a glass of wine. I'd been texting with RomanticAlpha42 most of the night, but when I'd accepted to stay for the drink, I sent him a quick text and Spencer's phone went off.

At first, I thought it was a coincidence, so I sent another one. However, when I heard his phone go off again, I panicked. I raced to leave, but he didn't give me a chance, and soon I was under him. We'd agreed to keep our relationship secret. After all, he was my dad's best friend.

I'd started working at Finding Forever. Spencer's executive assistant had transferred to a new location, and I had just graduated from college. It was a job I loved, and it gave us permission to fool around after hours, of course, with no interruption from my father, his ex-wife, or Nikki, his seven-year-old daughter.

I cleared my throat. "Things are going great," I answered, straightening the tie Dad was wearing.

Dad turned and looked in the mirror, impressed with my tie straightening skills. "Wow, where on earth did you learn to do that?" he asked, knowing full well I'd never held a serious relationship before.

Truth was I had come to learn to straighten ties almost immediately after Spencer and I had had an intense session of hot sex against his office wall.

I shrugged. "It's just easier when someone else does it," I said, turning away from my father.

"When is Spencer supposed to be back from that business trip?"

"Um, I believe he said Monday. At least that was what his schedule said. Why?"

"Good, I have to go out of town for work on Monday. I feel better knowing he is home next door to look over you when I am gone."

I felt a blush rise to my cheeks and hoped that my father hadn't seen it. He wouldn't feel better if he knew that Spencer and I were involved. He certainly wouldn't feel better if he knew the things Spencer and I had done together when he'd been gone.

"What time are you supposed to be meeting this woman?" I asked, feeling my phone vibrate in my pocket.

"I pick her up in ten minutes. I guess I should probably get going. She lives on the other side of town," he said, looking at his watch.

I handed Dad his jacket and practically shoved him out the door and watched as he ran down the front steps of the house. "Make sure you keep the doors locked, and if you're feeling ambitious, why don't you pull up some of the Christmas decorations from the basement," He called out as he climbed in the car.

"I might," I yelled. I waved just as he pulled out of

the driveway and watched until he was out of sight, then I took my phone and sent Spencer a message.

BabyGirl89: He's gone.

Spencer didn't respond. Instead, in a matter of minutes, he was standing in the entryway of the house, and I was pressed up against the wall in his embrace with his lips tightly pressed to mine.

"OH GOD, Ainsley, how I missed this," Spencer gritted out. My hand was wrapped around his cock, gently stroking him, as he ran his tongue through my wet center.

I let out a loud moan as he concentrated on the little bundle of nerves, first licking then gently sucking it into his mouth.

"Did you miss this?" he asked as he slid two fingers inside of me, curling them to hit that special spot inside me as he sucked my clit into his mouth again.

I arched my back up off the bed. I was ready to explode, but I knew if I said anything, Spencer would stop and wait for me to come back down.

"So much," I raggedly whispered, completely breathless.

"You ready for more?" he questioned, running his fingers lightly over the inside of my thighs, placing gentle kisses where his fingers had just traveled.

"Please," I begged as I arched my back off the mattress. "Give me more."

I heard his low, throaty chuckle, and then he knelt before me, gripped my ankles, and rested my legs on his shoulders, gripping my hips tightly as he slowly sunk himself into me. I cried out as he started to pump deep and slow inside of me.

He reached down between us, and with every pump, he ran his thumb over that small bundle, driving me crazy. I didn't say anything as I gripped his wrist, he already knew I was willing him to stop, begging him to stop, but he didn't listen.

"No way, baby girl," he whispered as my climax continued to grow until I couldn't hold back anymore. I screamed out his name as I tightened around him. He held me tight, his breathing became more and more ragged, he pumped harder, faster, and deeper inside of me until he had emptied himself inside of me and collapsed against me, breathing hard.

A little while later, I lay in Spencer's arms, my head against his strong chest with my eyes closed while he ran his fingers lightly along my arm, placing gentle kisses on the top of my shoulder. "I love you, Ainsley," Spencer whispered.

I swallowed hard at his confession. I'd been dying to hear him say those words. I had been dying to say them to him but figured he would think it was just me being a naive little girl. Instead, he had said it first, and yet as the words rolled off his lips, a funny feeling sat in the pit of my stomach.

It took me a moment, but I swallowed hard and then whispered, "I love you too."

He rolled me onto my back and kissed me hard, then he pulled me into his arms.

"I really should get home," he said, kissing my neck. "I have a pile of paperwork to get through plus I don't want to run into your father."

"Just stay a little while longer. I've missed laying in your arms," I pleaded, placing small kisses along his neck. I hadn't realized how much I had missed it until I felt them around me again.

"All right. I wanted to talk to you about something anyways."

I could see the troubled look on his face and I was worried that something was wrong. "What is it?"

"I think it's time we speak with your father, tell him the truth about what has been going on between us."

I swallowed hard. I'd been thinking about that as well and knew that if things between us continued to get serious then we'd have no choice. "Can we wait until after Christmas?"

Spencer shook his head. "I think we should tell him before. I'd really like to be able to have you spend nights with me without sneaking around behind your father's back."

"What about Brittany?"

"We'll tell her too. It probably won't go over well but I don't want to hide anymore. Nikki will be thrilled. She loves you. I love you."

I met Spencer's eyes and, even though I was unsure. "It will be fine. I promise," he whispered, placing his hand against my cheek and bringing his lips to mine in a deep, firm kiss.

I had no idea how or when we had drifted off, but when I opened my eyes, my room was dark. At first, I had thought Spencer's return had only been a dream, but when I went to move, I realized I was spooned in Spencer's arms.

I went to move but stopped. My body ached in places that fully reminded me of what had happened only a few hours before. Then his words came rushing back to me. He loved me. He wanted to tell my father and his ex-wife that we were together. Again, anticipation and nerves filled me, and I softly smiled to myself as I allowed the excitement of not having to sneak around fill me. I adjusted the covers so I could roll over and bury my face in his chest like I normally did when we'd spend the night together. Only instead of snuggling down, I froze. A dark figure standing just inside my bedroom door caught my eye, and the excitement I'd felt only seconds ago was replaced with alarm. I now remembered what had woken me—a noise, the click of my bedroom door when my father had opened it. Our eyes locked in the darkness. I could already see the look of shock, anger, and disappointment flooding his face.

I didn't know what to do as panic continued to fill me, and I froze. We'd been caught. We'd been doing this for months and we'd been so careful. Each of us always having an alibi every single time we'd been together, until now. Spencer had decided for the first time to come to me instead of me going to him and now we'd been caught.

"What in the actual fuck is going on here?" my father roared and turned on the bedroom light.

Spencer jumped, covering his eyes from the bright overhead light for a moment, and then he looked around the room, his eyes wide as he looked at my father.

"Daddy, please don't get angry," I pleaded. "Let me explain." I cried, pulling the covers up over my naked body.

My father looked at Spencer, and he shook his head. "I fucking trusted you with her, you son of a bitch."

"Jon, calm down. It's not what it looks like," Spencer said, trying to keep a level head.

My father let out this maniacal laughter I'd never heard before. "You can tell her that—she's a fucking child—but you sure as hell can't tell me that. This is exactly what it looks like. I'm giving you five minutes to get the fuck out of my house."

"Dad, I'm a grown woman. I'll do what I want!" I shouted.

"Ainsley, I don't want to hear it right now. Spencer, five fucking minutes, not a damn second longer. I don't want to see you around her again, you got it."

With tears streaming down my face, my father turned and slammed my bedroom door shut. I looked at Spencer, who threw the covers off himself, swearing under his breath, slid into his jeans. He came over to me, wrapping me tightly in his strong arms, pulling me against the warmth of his chest as I sobbed.

"This will blow over. When he isn't so mad, I'll talk to him, okay. Just like we talked about," he whispered, pressing his lips to mine. "I'll explain everything. It will be okay. Send me a message in the morning."

I nodded, trying hard to stifle the sobs, but it did little good as I watched him grab his shirt. He threw it over his head and ran his fingers through his messed-up hair. Then he turned back to me and kissed me one final time and opened my bedroom door and stepped out into the hall, closing it behind him. He hadn't been gone a minute when I heard elevated voices in the hallway. I climbed off my bed, threw my robe on, and opened the door to find my father and Spencer in an intense, heated conversation.

"You're not to see her anymore, you understand me. She isn't going to be babysitting for Nikki neither, and I want her to resign immediately from Finding Forever."

Spencer was about to say something, but I didn't give him the chance.

"No!" I screamed. "I will still babysit, and I'm not quitting my job."

"The fuck you will. You live under my roof. You'll do as I say. As for you, Spencer, our friendship is over. Now get the fuck out of here."

"I'm going with him," I said, taking a step forward, but my father stopped me, gripping my upper arms tightly.

"Get to bed," he gritted.

Tears welled in my eyes as my father pushed me back toward my bedroom. I tried to see around him, but he blocked my view from seeing Spencer turn and walked out the front door. I heard it click shut, and I stood in the hallway glaring at my father.

"When you return to work after your vacation, you resign, you hear me?" he said, looking into my eyes.

"Dad, you aren't being fair. Spencer and I—"

Dad held his hand up to my face to stop me from speaking. "Those are two words I don't ever want to hear used in the same sentence again. I'm so disappointed in you, Ainsley. In both of you. Now go to bed," he gritted as he walked by me, slamming his bedroom door shut.

I stood in the dark hallway wondering if I should just sneak out and go to Spencer. I felt empty inside, and I wanted to be comforted by him, but then I heard my dad banging around in his bedroom and thought twice. Spencer was right; it would blow over after he explained everything. I just needed to give him the chance.

AINSLEY

IT HAD BEEN two weeks since the mishap, and my father hadn't let me out of his sight. I looked over at the pile of boxes he had pulled up from the basement marked Christmas and let out a sigh as I looked down at my plate of breakfast my stomach feeling uneasy. In the past two weeks I had barely gotten out of bed or eaten anything since the night my father found us.

I had watched from my window as Spencer tried to talk to my father over the backyard fence as Dad was raking up the leaves, getting everything ready for winter. Even with my window open, I couldn't hear what was being said, but what I could see was the look on my father's face. A look I'd grown accustomed to over the last little while. He wasn't planning to listen to anything Spencer had to say.

I sat there swirling my fork through my already cold eggs, watching the screen of my phone for a message from Spencer, but my phone was silent and had been since eight last night. I knew that Spencer's ex-wife was coming to drop Nikki off for the weekend, so I figured that perhaps he was busy with that, or I hoped that was the reason why I hadn't heard from him.

I blew out a frustrated breath as Dad walked into the kitchen.

"I spoke to Brittany," he said as he reached for his lunch bag.

"You what?" I gritted, gripping my fork tight in my hand. "You had no right to talk to her."

Immediately, I wanted to pick up my phone and warn Spencer before she got there, but my dad stood there watching me, leaning against the counter sipping his coffee. Brittany was miserable at the best of times. I could just imagine what her reaction would be to this news.

"My ruling stands: no more babysitting, no more being around him when you are unsupervised. I have no idea how long the two of you have been sneaking around behind my back, but I am sure it's been a while."

"Why on earth would you have spoken to Brittany?" I questioned. "Besides, it's not like that."

"Really, what's it like then?"

I slammed my fork down on the table. I was tired of

listening to it. It had been utter hell at home since Dad had found us, and it got worse every single time Spencer tried to talk to him.

I'd snuck out of the house yesterday when Dad had gone to a work meeting and met Spencer for coffee. He assured me he had tried to talk to him, but every time he would bring up the subject of us with my father, he would immediately shut the conversation down.

"Dad, I can assure you this was all very consensual. He didn't force himself on me."

"Ainsley, please, I should have the man charged. He's taking advantage of you."

I shook my head. "No, Dad, he isn't. We are in love."

My father threw his lunch into his bag and let out a laugh. "Ainsley, your inexperience wouldn't allow you to see it. You're impressionable, and I can assure you that he is taking advantage of you. Besides, you wouldn't know what love is. You're just a kid. Now, I have to go to work."

"I'm an adult, Dad," I mumbled under my breath. "Why would you have spoken to Brittany?" I murmured, placing my face in my hands, my stomach rolling at the thought that she was going to ambush Spencer this morning without warning.

"Well, to be honest, I felt it was only fair that she knew what was going on behind closed doors when her daughter was involved."

Spencer and his ex-wife weren't on the best of terms. They had never been on the best of terms, and I could only imagine what her finding out this information may do. I glared at my father, "I hate you," I spat.

"Good, hate me. That's fine. One day when you realize what this really is, you will thank me."

"Dad, you're not being fair. Be angry at us, hate Spencer but you didn't have to say anything to Brittany."

"Oh, but I did. Her daughter spends weekends there and you spend nights there when you babysit. That means shit has been going on while she is there, and since you are an adult, as you put it, I hope you're prepared because she was angry."

I could feel the anger boiling over inside of me as I watched Dad grab his bag off the counter and walked out the back door. I looked down at my breakfast, my stomach turning, saliva flooding my mouth. I picked up my plate and carried it to the garbage, dumping the contents, and placed the plate in the sink when I heard the back door open. Dad walked back in and looked at me. I turned my back on him and looked out the back window.

"Ainsley, I forgot, make sure you prepare your resignation letter today. I want to see it before you hand to Spencer when you return to work on Monday. I know he will be expecting it."

I balled my fists tight, jumping as the back door

slammed. I stood there staring down at the mess of egg yolk all over my plate and buried my face in my hands, trying hard to fight back the tears. I pulled my phone from my pocket. I was about to message Spencer to see if we could meet for lunch, but there was already a message waiting for me telling me to call him as soon as I had a minute.

I looked out the back door to make sure my father was gone then quickly dialed his number. I'd hoped that he still had a few more hours alone. I needed him.

"Spencer Brooks," his sexy, deep voice came over the phone, instantly calming me.

"It's me," I said, doing my best to sound happy, even though every aspect of my life was in turmoil.

"One second," he said.

I waited, listening to the noise in the background, and knew he was in the office. "Sorry, had to shut the door."

"That's okay."

"Listen, I would prefer to talk to you in person, but since that isn't possible right now, this will have to do."

"I can meet you somewhere," I said. "Or I can come to the office."

"No, it's fine." His voice cracked, then he went quiet.

I knew something was wrong just by the sound of his voice. I took in a deep breath, "What is it?" I asked, alarm filling my chest.

"Ainsley, Brittany found out somehow what has been going on between us."

"Yeah, about that. Apparently, my father called and spoke with her," I bit out, worried at what he was going to say next. "He said he felt she should know what was going on between us. I don't know why my dad just can't stay out of it."

The phone was silent. I could barely even hear Spencer breathing on the other end. I was beginning to think he had hung up so I just said what came to my mind. "I tried to tell him everything was consensual and that we were in love—"

"She's threatened to take Nikki from me, Ainsley," Spencer interjected.

It felt as if all the air had been sucked out of the room, and if I thought I was going to be sick before I was really going to be sick now as the room started to spin. I knew how much Nikki meant to Spencer, and I knew that something like this would devastate him if she actually went through with it. "Can she do that? I mean…"

"Yes. If she deems my place to be unsafe place, and that I'm irresponsible, all she needs to do is call her lawyer. They will investigate and it will be over. Ainsley, I can't lose Nikki."

"I'm sorry, Spencer. I hate my father right now."

"I'm sorry, too, Ainsley." His voice shook, "I think it

might be best if for the time being we just go our separate ways until things cool off."

My hand immediately covered my mouth and tears spilled down my cheeks. I could barely breathe as Spencer continued talking, and the lump that sat in my throat hurt like hell. It was only a few more minutes before he had finished saying all he needed to say and then I heard him utter good-bye. I sunk to the kitchen floor, my feet unable to hold me, as my heart broke.

"How was your massage?" Carly asked as she took a sip of her cucumber water.

"Fine." I sat down in the lounge chair beside Carly, leaned back, closed my eyes, and let out a huge sigh. My entire body ached from all the stress I'd been dealing with over the last couple weeks.

"I know you think your life is over, but could you at least act as if you are enjoying yourself?" Carly said, looking over at me with a worried expression on her face.

"Please, just stop. You have no idea what I'm going through."

"I do. I have been involved with someone before you know."

"It's not the same. You really have no idea, Carly. I'm so mad at my dad right now. He has made my life hell."

"No, he didn't, you did that. I told you not to get involved with Spencer. I told you right from the start this whole ordeal would end with nothing but trouble, but you refused to listen."

I rolled my eyes. I was so tired of listening to her go on about this. I met her eyes, which gleamed nothing but 'I told you so.' "Please, for once, can you just be on my side, please."

Carly grabbed her robe and swung her legs over the side so she could sit up. "Look, I'm sorry. I feel bad for you, I really do. I just..."

"I know you just feel that I am getting what I deserve. You told me so, I know."

Carly's face fell at my words. I knew I wasn't being fair to her, but I was tired of my best friend not taking how I felt into consideration. I leaned my head back against the lounge chair and closed my eyes, trying to find something other than my troubles to talk about.

"What are you going to do about the job?"

I blew out a breath and looked out the sunroom windows at the lake. "I don't want to quit, but that is what my dad wants, and I am sure Brittany will be urging Spencer to let me go. So, my father will get his way in some regard. I will probably just put in a transfer. I do like working there, it's good money, and Christmas is right around the corner."

"Might be for the best. I'm glad to see that you are making the right decision in that regard."

"What is that supposed to mean?" I exclaimed, sitting up and looking at Carly, ready for a fight.

"Nothing. We should get changed and head down for lunch."

I watched Carly as she stood up, avoiding eye contact with me. I knew there was some meaning behind her comment. I just didn't know what it was in this moment. "I'll be along in a minute," I whispered as Carly got up and made her way toward the changing room.

Once Carly left the room, I leaned back on the lounge chair I was sitting on and tried to think everything through. I had been the one to start all of this. I had lit the fire, and now I was the one who was getting burned.

I picked up my cell phone and checked it for messages, praying there was one from Spencer telling me that he was sorry and had made a mistake, but there was nothing more from him. I took a minute and started composing a message to him, but halfway through, something stopped me and I deleted it. I had to let him go, I just needed to figure out how to do it.

____

I SAT across from my ex-wife. She sat there with a scowl on her face, her arms crossed over her chest as she glared at me. The tension in the room could have been cut with a knife. It seriously felt like our divorce proceedings all over again. I drummed my fingers on the table, more to annoy her than anything. She had come to pick Nikki up my weekend with her, and she looked even more miserable now than she did when she dropped her off.

"I swear, Spencer, she better not have been here this weekend. You know Nikki will tell me if she was so you're better off to spill it now."

"For fuck sakes, Brittany, how many times do I have to tell you, she wasn't here. Nikki and I went to see some Christmas lights, and then to the toy store so she could pick out some toys that she wants for Christmas."

"You're lying, just give it up already, I've already called my lawyer. He thinks I should pursue for full custody."

I chuckled. "Of course, he does." I muttered.

"What is that supposed to mean?"

I glared at her, leaning forward, "Should we go down the path of what really led to our divorce? Not to mention the shit that goes on in your home now?"

"What is that supposed to mean?"

"How quickly you forget." I looked down at my phone to see what date it was. Yep, exactly two weeks from today. "November 15th, I returned from a business trip from our Florida office. The house was dark. Figuring you were in bed, I ran up the stairs, checked in on Nikki, who was sound asleep, and then made my way down to our bedroom. I opened the door and heard the shower running. The door was partially open, and so I decide that I'd surprise you in the shower. Only the surprise was on me because, instead of finding you alone in there, I find you wrapped in the arms of another man as he is fucking you up against the shower wall," I said, elevating my voice.

Brittany looked at me shocked. She hadn't known I had walked in on her and witnessed that. She thought the coast had been clear because I had gotten dressed, left the house, and sat at the end of the street in my car until I had seen him leave.

"Keep your voice down," she bit out in a whisper. "How did you know about that?"

"For fuck sakes, Brit, I just told you, because I walked in and found the two of you. Instead of pulling him out of the shower and killing him, like I should have, I realized that was why you had been so withdrawn out of our relationship. You'd been seeing him behind my back for God knows how long. If you really want to draw this all out in court again, I'll make sure the judge knows not only about that, but about the other slew of men you bring home on a weekly basis."

"I don't," she said, crossing her arms.

"Really? Nikki sure seems to mention them. Paul, Sebastian, Cody, oh and my personal favorite, Axel. If you'd like, I can bring her down here and ask her about them."

Brittany let out a huff. "Nikki, honey, you almost ready to go," she yelled to our daughter.

"As always, run when things get tough."

"You're screwing your fucking babysitter," she said, turning her wild eyes on me. "The child you decided to put in charge of my daughter's well-being when you are away. At least the men I'm involved with are grown adults."

"I seriously doubt that and Ainsley is not a child."

Nikki came down the hall dragging her tiny pink suit-case behind her, carrying her favorite teddy bear under her arm. "Daddy, will Ainsley be watching me next time I'm here. I miss her. She always plays games with me too. I made her this," Nikki said, walking over to me and dropping a pink bracelet into the palm of my hand. "I think she will love it. She said she wanted one just like mine. I even made a card," Nikki said, handing me a pink piece of construction paper with a picture she had drawn on the front.

Brittany let out a loud huff and stood up. "Wonderful," she bit out under her breath.

"I'll make sure I give it to her."

"I'm sure you will," Brittany bit out.

I gave her a nasty look and turned my attention back to my daughter.

My chest felt empty at the thought of possibly never being able to hold Nikki in my arms again. I took the bracelet from her and placed a kiss on the top of Nikki's head then placed my hand on her back and walked her to the door where I helped put her little shoes on.

"Take your bag to the car, Nikki. I'll be out in a minute," Brittany said.

Nikki turned and looked up at me. "Daddy, when I come back can we get the Christmas tree. I want to pick it out, but maybe Ainsley can come with us. She loves hot chocolate with marshmallows, remember. I will save my allowance and buy her one," Nikki said, jumping up and down, waiting for me to say yes.

"I'll think about it, okay. Now do as your mom says and take your bag out to the car."

"Okay," she said with a pout as I bent to kiss the top of her head.

As soon as Nikki was out of earshot, Brittany turned back to me. "Look, I won't pursue full custody until after Christmas, but I swear to God, Spencer, if I find out that child is back in this house looking after our daughter, I will change my mind. It would be a sad Christmas for Nikki if she couldn't see you," she threatened and threw her purse over her shoulder and marched down the front steps of the house. I watched as she got Nikki into the car and then pulled out of the driveway.

The instant I shut the door, anger filled me and I went over to the phone and called my lawyer just to be on the safe side, leaving him a message to fill him in on what was going on. Then I grabbed a glass from the cupboard and poured myself a scotch, dropping two ice cubes into the golden liquid. I downed the first glass, relishing in the burn, then poured another glass and went to watch the news.

That night, as I lay in bed with my arms behind my head, my thoughts traveled to Ainsley. How I missed going to sleep with her lying in my arms. I thought about the call we'd had prior to Nikki arriving on the weekend. I had been wrong to tell her that I wanted to end things. I had strictly done it out of fear.

I reached over to my night table and grabbed my phone, opening our chat. I had typed out a full-on apology, and then something inside of me decided against sending it. I wasn't going to do this through a text. I'd wait and talk to her tomorrow morning the second she arrived at the office, and we would work everything out.

AINSLEY

THE LOBBY of Finding Forever looked amazing all decorated up for Christmas. I greeted a couple of girls who sat behind the reception desk and then walked over to the elevator. My nerves were uneasy. I had spent the entire weekend sulking, wishing that my father hadn't spoken to Brittany, and then wishing Spencer would message me, but when I didn't hear from him by the time I'd gone to bed, I had finally concluded that perhaps I really didn't know what was going on between us. As much as I didn't want to say everyone else was right, perhaps they were, and so I had gotten out of bed at one in the morning and filled out a transfer form.

The ride to the top floor didn't seem to take as long as it normally did, and when the doors opened, I stepped off the elevator, manila envelope in hand, and walked over to my desk. My stomach was in knots as I placed my coat on a hook in the corner of my space and shoved my purse into the bottom drawer of my desk. I saw that Spencer's door was already closed, which meant he had arrived early and was probably in a meeting. Again, doubt filled my mind, and I seriously thought of just shoving that envelope into the back of one of my desk drawers and forgetting about it. Instead, I sat down and turned on my computer and quickly checked his calendar to see if he was indeed in the middle of a meeting before going and knocking on his door. His calendar this morning was clear, which made my stomach flop yet again. I took a deep breath, grabbed the envelope off my desk, and knocked on his office door.

"Come in," I heard him say in that deep, business-like voice I'd grown used to.

I closed my eyes, composed myself, and opened the door. He was focused on something as he sat behind his desk looking as handsome as ever. His suit jacket hung on the back of his chair. The sleeves of his white dress shirt were rolled up, exposing his strong forearms. He wore no tie today, his shirt open at the neck, and immediately my thoughts went to kissing that soft spot where his neck met the top of his shoulder. I swallowed hard as I caught the scent of his cologne. He looked up from his paperwork, his eyes running over my body, and smiled.

"Good morning. Come in, shut the door. I have something I'd like to discuss with you."

I froze, unsure of what I should do. Instead, I didn't close the door I stepped forward. "I have something I would like to discuss with you. I'd like to go first," I said and held out the envelope for him to take. "Here."

Spencer looked at me, the smile he had on his face quickly vanishing. "What's this?" he questioned, taking it from me and opening it.

"I'm putting in a transfer." I swallowed hard, even though I felt this was wrong from the time I'd filled it out last night, but yet I somehow knew it was the right thing to do, especially after Spencer told me that Brittany could take Nikki from him. I didn't want the man to lose his little girl. I loved her as much as I loved him.

He sat there looking over the page, then he set it down on his desk and crossed his arms in front of him. "Are you not happy here?"

"No, I am. Dad wanted me to resign but I figured this was a better option. I just really need you to sign that, please. There is an opening in the finance department, and I would like to take that position."

Spencer looked down at the sheet again and then back up to me. "I didn't know you took any interest in finance."

I shrugged. I didn't take interest in finance and there was no way I was going to pretend that I did, but there were no other openings at this time. I looked to the floor and back up to him. "I'm, um, expanding my horizons."

Spencer sat back in his chair and chuckled, then shook his head. "You know, I appreciate people who aren't afraid to better themselves, but in this case, I'm sorry, I won't sign it."

My eyes flew open. "You won't sign it? What do you mean you won't sign it?"

"I mean, no. With everything coming up over the holidays, I am going to need you here. So, I am not signing this," he said, picking up my transfer sheet and setting it off to the far side of his desk.

"You can't do that. I mean, you have to sign it."

He chuckled. "Ainsley, I can do whatever I want. I own the company, remember? And I must do what is best for the interest of the company. We have our Christmas party in less than a month, and I am going to need your help to finish organizing it. If I were to sign this, I would need to hire and train a new assistant. You and I both know that will take months, and there would be no way that they could organize a function of this magnitude on such short notice."

"Spencer, that's not my problem. That is yours. Besides, you haven't even mentioned a Christmas party for your clients. Now, please sign the transfer."

"I haven't mentioned it to you because I was away for the last two weeks, but I was planning to talk to you today about it. Now if you'd care to get your notepad and pen we can start getting things down for this function."

I looked at Spencer, highly annoyed, first at the fact he wouldn't sign my transfer and now at the fact that he was assuming I would just bend over and organize this party. "I'm sorry, but I really don't think I am capable of organizing this function either. I have worked for this company for a few months, and besides, I have no experience in the event planning area, so I think you really should talk to the events department."

Spencer chuckled. "Well, you have no experience in finance either, yet you wish to transfer to that department."

I could feel my blood pressure rising as he sat there with a cocky grin on his face.

"I can learn," I gritted.

"Well then you can learn how to organize this event then. Colleen was working on it, but she is out of the office. She had surgery a week ago and will be off until January, maybe February. So, I'm left with no choice. We will work together to organize it, and you can learn."

I looked at Spencer and then glanced around his office, my eyes landing back on my transfer form that sat on his desk unsigned. This had totally blown up in my face. Not only did I do this so Spencer wouldn't lose Nikki, I had done it so that I wouldn't hear my father lecturing me on the fact he wanted me to resign. He would not be happy to know that instead I'd now be working in close quarters with Spencer. "I'll make you a deal."

"All right." He nodded. "What's the deal?"

"I'll help you organize this event and see you through the holidays on the condition that in the new year you sign my transfer form."

Spencer studied my face and nodded. "If that is what you really want."

I thought for a moment. It wasn't what I wanted at all. As I looked into his eyes, I knew that what I really wanted was to be back in his arms, but I knew that wasn't possible either. I looked down at the floor and then back up to Spencer. "It's what I want."

Spencer held out his large hand for me to take, but when I hesitated, he asked, "What is it?"

"It's just, if we are going to plan this party together, then it needs to be kept on a professional level."

Spencer looked at me, that cocky grin coming to his lips. "Are you suggesting that I don't know how to work with a woman on a professional level?"

His eyes danced with a look I knew all too well, and I had to bite my bottom lip to hide my smile. "I didn't say that. I just wanted to remind you."

Spencer looked at me and held out his hand again. I slipped mine into his and, as soon as we touched, a shock ran through my body. "Now, go get your notepad."

DAD WAS SITTING in his favorite chair watching TV when I got home. I dropped my purse by the back door and slipped my shoes off and then walked into the living room and flopped down into the chair.

"You're home late," he said, turning to me.

"I had a lot of work to do today."

"You put your resignation in?" he questioned, throwing a handful of nuts into his mouth and washing them down with a swig of beer.

I knew he was going to start this. I shook my head.

"Ainsley, we talked about this," he said, slamming his bottle down on the table.

"Relax, I put a transfer in. There is no need for me to quit a perfectly fine paying job, especially with Christmas around the corner."

"All right, when do you start in the new position?"

My stomach filled with nerves as he continued to pay attention to me instead of the fishing show he was watching. I wasn't sure what to tell him. I wasn't sure I wanted to tell him.

"Ainsley?"

"After Christmas," I murmured.

"That is over six weeks away. There is no way you are going to be working with this man that long. I fucking told him," Dad barked reaching for his cell phone.

"Dad. It's fine. He needs help to plan the annual Christmas party. The woman in charge of events is off on surgery, and a new person couldn't look after something like this. His hands were tied."

Dad looked at me skeptically. "Ainsley, you have no experience planning anything like that. I don't like this. He's doing this on purpose." I watched as he began to type.

"And I have no experience in the finance department either," I bit out. "Yet I put a transfer in."

Dad looked over the rim of his glasses at me. "Well you can learn," he said, going right back to whatever message he was planning on sending to Spencer.

"Yep, I can. I can also learn how to plan an event. Spencer promised to keep everything strictly professional, and after the holidays he told me he would sign my transfer."

Dad stopped typing. "You know I'll talk to him and make sure, so you better be telling me the truth."

"I am. I promise." I said and watched as he placed his phone down on the table and turned his attention back to the TV.

AINSLEY and I had worked diligently over the last two weeks getting all the details down for the Christmas party. I'd behaved myself as promised, working only in a professional manner, a far cry from what we were before, a far cry from where I'd hoped we be by now once again. I missed those moments where our hands touched and our eyes locked. I missed the secret looks we shared in front of other employees, I missed taking her on my desk when we worked late, but most of all, I missed those nights that I held her tenderly in my arms.

I'd searched my soul for a long time after Brittany had left me, always afraid to allow myself to get close to someone, afraid to fall in love with someone for fear of getting hurt. The first time I allowed it, I fell in deep, and now I'm forbidden to be with her, not only by my ex-wife but by her father, the second of which I can honestly say I understand.

I'd spent the last little bit doing more soul searching, and something felt different this morning as I watched her walk into the office. I don't know if it was the fact that I was tired of allowing someone else to dictate to me how I was supposed to feel or what. I'd spent the past twenty years of my life making others happy, while the last eight I'd been miserable, except for the past few months with Ainsley. That alone resonated so loudly with me, and I wasn't having it anymore.

I'd called Ainsley into my office more than usual today, pretending that I couldn't find something on a spreadsheet just so that I could feel her heat beside me. She looked amazing in the tight white sweater dress she wore. She stood beside me showing me what I had been looking for and then walked around to the other side of my desk and stood there.

I couldn't help but allow myself to look at her. She was amazingly sexy, and when my eyes met hers, I could tell from the look on her face that I had allowed my eyes to linger on her longer than was appropriate given our situation. Instead of saying anything, she looked at me and softly smiled, then turned and left my office. I knew in that moment that she still felt the same way about me as I did about her. Now I just needed to show her.

It was a little after seven, a storm raged on outside,

and I dimmed the overhead lights in my office and turned on the three smaller lamps that were scattered around. Then I poked my head out the door. Ainsley was sitting at her desk, phone to her ear, making notes, while discussing the menu for the party. I partially shut my door and went online and ordered food and wine from The Herbed Oyster for delivery. Then I quickly scribbled 'food is on the way' on a Post-it.

I casually walked over to her desk, dropping the note down on the pad of paper in front of her, and continued on my way to the washroom. When I glanced back, I saw her read the note and she raised her eyes to mine. I chuckled as I heard her ask the woman to repeat herself.

She was still deep in conversation when I returned, so I made my way into the office and sat down behind my desk, clearing everything out of the way. I had just finished when the delivery man knocked on my door.

"Sir, you ordered food?" he asked.

"Yes, please come in. You may set it right here," I said, pointing to the cleared space on my desk.

He did as I asked as I pulled the money from my wallet. Once he was gone, I quickly arranged the plate of oysters and poured two glasses of Chablis.

"How about you just email me the menu and I will look it over and confirm with you tomorrow," I heard Ainsley say. "That way if I need to make any changes I can."

I laid out a couple other dishes I had ordered, and then I stepped out into the hall just in time to see Ainsley gathering up the notes she had made, placing them in the event folder.

"The menu should be finalized tomorrow morning, and as soon as you've approved it, I'll confirm and book the caterer. Oh and she said she won't need final guest numbers until a week prior, which is good because two days prior to her due date is when we had set the RSVP cut-off date."

I didn't respond. Instead, I leaned up against the wall and looked over at her. She was adorable as she stood there all business like struggling to get the folder into her bag.

She looked up, probably expecting me not to be there, since I had not responded, and locked eyes with me. "What? What is it?" she asked.

"I ordered in a little late-night snack. Why don't you come join me?"

She looked around at her desk and then nervously down at her watch. "Um. I really should be getting home. It's getting late."

"Ainsley, it's a little after seven thirty. This is nothing more than a simple bite to eat between friends. A little thank you for all the work you've been doing. Nothing more," I said, disappointed that she hadn't jumped at the chance like she used to.

She looked around at the quiet office and nodded. "You're right. I am a little hungry actually." She put the folder down on her desk and went to slip her shoes on.

"There's no need to put shoes on. It's after hours, you can be comfortable," I said, nodding to the heels she was about to slip on.

She stopped and looked down at her shoes, her brow furrowed, and then she walked into my office. I closed the door behind us, giving us privacy from the cleaning crew that would be arriving any moment. I walked over and picked up the two glasses of wine, handing her one.

"To another successful day of planning," I said, raising my glass to hers.

She hesitated at first, and then she took the glass from my hand and took a sip. Setting the wine glass down, she eyed the plate of fresh oysters that sat on my desk. "What's that?"

"Oysters on the half shell. Tell me you've had them before."

She bit her bottom lip and looked up at me, shaking her head. "No. Never. How do you eat them?"

I walked over to where she stood and picked up one of the lemon slices, squirting it over one of the oysters. Then I gently loosened it with one of the cocktail forks and turned to her. "Close your eyes."

"Spencer…"

"Close your eyes," I repeated.

She looked at me but then did as she was told. I gently placed my hand on her lower back, her body tensing as it responded to my touch . Immediately, I felt a surge of excitement run through my body as my hand rested there.

"I'm going to bring the shell up to your mouth. I want you to part your lips and tilt your head slightly back. Allow the oyster to slide into your mouth, chew twice, and swallow."

She nodded. I brought the shell to her soft, full lips and tilted it to allow the oyster to slide off. I was lost as I watched the expression on her face as the oyster slid off the shell and into her mouth. I felt my cock harden as her tongue jutted out as she licked her lips then slowly opened her eyes.

Her eyes met mine, and for a moment, we were lost in each other's stare. Instead of leaning in and kissing her like I wanted, I smiled. "How was that?"

"Different," she said in a low, sultry voice.

"Want another?"

She studied my gaze then nodded. I repeated everything, only this time, I couldn't hold back. When she opened her eyes and gave me that heady gaze, I leaned in and took her mouth with mine. Immediately, she brought her arms up and rested them on my shoulders as her lips moved with mine. When I heard a soft moan escape her throat, I pulled her tightly into me, allowing her to feel how hard I was for her. I could feel her body start to let go, but then she placed her hands on my chest, breaking the kiss.

"I can't...we can't..." she said, breathless, looking up at me with watery eyes. "What about Nikki."

I didn't have a chance to say anything because she was already gone, having bolted from my office. I clenched my hands into fists and leaned onto my desk. Everything was a mess, and as I stood there trying to figure out how to explain to her that I didn't want us to be over, I heard the loud ding of the elevator. My heart sank as I stepped out into the hall just in time to see the elevator doors slide shut. She was gone.

I SPENT Saturday morning clearing the driveway from the snow that had fallen the night before. I'd secretly hoped to see Ainsley, as she normally went out early on Saturday mornings for her yoga class, but she was nowhere to be found this morning. I wanted to talk to her, to apologize for last night. I'd left her messages, but she still hadn't read any of them.

I was putting the snowblower back in the garage when I heard my name. I turned to see Jon standing in my driveway. I was expecting Ainsley had talked to him about last night and he was here to blast me but was surprised when he smiled instead. "Hey, you feel like getting out for a beer tonight?" he questioned.

I wasn't sure where this was coming from. The man had not spoken to me in a couple of months, ever since he had caught us in bed.

"Sure. Where you want to go?"

"Just over to Darcy's. It's close. We don't have to worry about driving," he said.

"Sounds good."

"All right, meet you over there at five?" he asked.

"Great, in time for the game."

"Yep. See you then."

I'd hoped that his invitation meant that he was ready to forgive me and that it would give me an opportunity to explain to him how I truly felt about his daughter. I'd spent the afternoon running over what I wanted to say to him in my mind, and when I was sure I finally had every-thing down, I got ready. I made my way over to Darcy's and was surprised when I walked into the little neighbor-hood pub to see Jon already there, milking down a beer and digging into a plate of nachos.

"Hey," I said, sliding into the booth across from Jon.

"Hey, thought we'd watch the game?" Jon said. "You know, like old times."

"Yeah, sounds good."

I ordered a beer and then sat there watching the game, debating on when I should bring up the subject.

"What's new?" Jon asked, trying to break the awkward silence between us.

I shook my head. "Nothing. I really want to take a minute and talk to you about something," I bit out.

"About what?"

"I want to talk to you about Ain—"

Jon held up his hand, stopping me from saying anything more. "Spencer, I think out of respect for whatever friendship we might have left that we should just leave all that in the past. Let's just move forward and pretend that nothing happened okay. Ainsley is off-limits to you now, you know that, and once the new year hits, you will sign her transfer and allow her to move on with her life and job."

When he was finished, he looked right into my eyes. I could tell just from the glare that he was serious, then he turned his attention back to the TV, while I sat there holding my beer. All I wanted was to be able to express just how empty I felt without her in my life. Explain to him how much I loved her, but even if I did, I knew now that Jon would never approve of me dating his daughter, and that no matter how I felt about her, his opinion would probably never change.

AINSLEY

Monday morning had arrived, and I knew that I could no longer hide out in my bedroom. The weekend had gone by in a blur, not because I'd been busy, but because I had spent the entire weekend in bed, thinking about that kiss. I had even missed my Saturday-morning yoga class. When I'd arrived home Friday night, I walked by my father, mumbling that I felt like I was coming down with the flu just so he wouldn't see the tears that had fallen on the way home.

I'd worried all the way into the office, white-knuckling it through traffic that I would have to face Spencer after running out on him on Friday night. Instead, his office door sat closed from the time I'd arrived. He was knee deep in phone meetings with some of his CEOs, and I couldn't have been happier.

I'd felt the weight lift off me as I left for lunch, and I now sat alone at a table in my favorite restaurant with a hot bowl of cheese ravioli in front of me and garlic bread smothered in cheese.

I scrolled through my phone at the messages that had come in over the weekend—three from Spencer and about fifteen from Carly. I hadn't spoken to her all weekend and decided I should probably return her messages. I dialed her number and smiled when I heard her pick up the phone.

"You're alive." She giggled.

"Yes, how are you?"

"Fine. Where the hell you been all weekend? I thought we were going to hang out."

I shoved a piece of ravioli in my mouth. "Sorry, I was sick."

The phone was quiet. "Are you all right?" Carly asked, concern lining her voice.

"Yeah. I've been working long hours, and Friday was more than I could handle. I guess it all just caught up with me."

"What did?"

"Spencer, all the feelings I still have."

"Ainsley."

"I know what you are going to say. I need to get over him, but I've wanted him for so long. You have no clue how I feel about him, and now not to be able to have him is just unbearable." My voice cracked and my throat burned as I held back tears.

"How many times do I need to tell you to let him go," Carly said, getting annoyed. "I told you he was too old for you in the first place and that you'd end up getting hurt. Besides, I thought you were putting in a transfer or a resignation."

"I did. He refused to sign the transfer."

"What? Why? How can he do that?"

"Because he can. He is the boss, remember. Besides, he can't train someone new at this time of year, and with the Christmas party needing to be organized, he would rather have someone experienced. A new person would just be totally overwhelmed."

"Ainsley, he has an events division. You aren't an event planner."

"Yes, however, the girl is off. She just had surgery, so he is helping me plan the event."

"Ainsley, can't you see what he is doing?"

I knew exactly what he was doing. He was doing exactly what I wanted him to do. I didn't want to work in another division of his company. I wanted to be as close to him as I could, only with everyone pushing against us, I couldn't let on that that was what I wanted. I certainly couldn't tell Carly about that kiss on Friday night and how it stirred emotions in me that I had hoped were dead.

"He's looking out for his company. I told him I would stay and help only if he promised to sign the transfer in the new year."

"Uh huh, and what did he say?"

"He agreed."

The phone was silent for a moment. "You know, Ainsley, I think for your own good, you need to come away with me next weekend. There is someone I think you should meet, guaranteed to get Spencer off your mind. He's tall, handsome, funny, and most importantly…your age."

This was just like Carly, trying to persuade me to date someone else. She sounded just like my father. All I wanted was for one person to understand how I felt.

"What if I don't want to get my mind off of Spencer?"

"Ainsley, did something happen between you? What's got you all wrapped up in him again?" Carly questioned. "Last time I talked to you, I was sure you agreed it was over."

I debated not telling her, but she was my best friend, and the only one I could share this with. I let out a heavy sigh, playing Friday night over in my mind, my body filling with that tingling feeling I'd felt the moment he'd placed his hand on my lower back.

"He, um, he kissed me."

"Ainsley, are you serious."

"Yes, and, Carly, it was just as wonderful as I remembered."

"What happened?"

"At first, I kissed him back, but then I ran. All the feelings hit, and as much as I feel for him, I don't him to lose Nikki, and I don't want my father pissed off at me for the rest of my life."

"Your father loves you. He isn't going to be pissed off at you for the rest of your life."

"Carly, you have no idea how hard these past couple of months have been between us. He looks at me through disappointed eyes. He's finally speaking to me again the way he used to. If he were to find out, he would be livid all over again."

"Exactly how much time have you been spending at the office?" Carly asked.

"Almost every night of the week until eight or nine. There is a lot of planning to do for this event. I want to do a good job and make sure I don't mess up anything or miss something."

"I'm sure there is. Are you there working alone or are you there with him?"

"Spencer works all the time. Some nights he's there long after I leave, others he leaves when I do."

"I see, and over the last few weeks, how many times has he tried something?"

I rolled my eyes. "Only this once."

"I don't believe it. There has been no touching, no trying to make a pass at you, nothing."

I thought back to a few times I'd dodged him. An innocent touch on the arm, a lingering look, or a hand resting on my lower back as I walked through a door. That had been all, and I'd evaded them all, except for Friday night. It had been a moment of weakness on my part. I'd spent the better part of my day in my own head wishing that things were back to normal. I'd wanted him to pin me against the wall like he'd done before, to kiss me until I was utterly breathless, panting and begging for him to touch me more. Only when he had taken that step, I got scared. Scared at how I felt as his lips danced over mine. I'd run out of his office like a scared little girl, instead of allowing myself to succumb to those feelings.

"No, there has been nothing. He promised me he would be professional," I lied.

"I'm sorry, Ainsley, but I don't believe you," Carly said matter of fact.

I was about to roll my eyes when I looked up to see Spencer standing in front of me, a dozen red roses in his hand with a balloon that said "I'm sorry" floating in the air.

"Are you there?" Carly blurted into my ear, pulling me away from the man standing in front of me.

"Yes, sorry. Look, I have to run. It's time to get back

to the office. I have a meeting with the caterer in twenty minutes, and I need to set up the board room."

"Okay, but you better call me later on."

"I will."

I hung up the phone and looked at Spencer who held the flowers out for me to take. I reached out, gripping the bouquet, and brought them to my nose.

"In case you're wondering, they are because of Friday night. I'm sorry. I crossed a line. I hope you'll forgive me."

SPENCER

THE SECOND SNOWSTORM of the season raged outside, and I sat by the fire in my living room going over all the details for the event that Ainsley had put together. I looked over the spreadsheets, my mind running back to earlier today when she'd come into my office happy as ever that she'd struck a better deal with the hotel than she had originally. She was so happy and proud of herself, and I'd done only what I would naturally do: I hugged her and leaned in for a kiss. Only instead of expecting her to allow me to, she shoved me away and left my office in a huff. I had blown my apology to her in under two hours.

I shook my head, bringing me back to the present, and began looking over the invitation list. Some names were highlighted in green, others red, some yellow and orange. I had no idea what all that meant, even though Ainsley had gone over it with me three times today. I ran my hand over my face and picked up my phone and dialed Ainsley's number. After four rings, I knew she wasn't going to answer, so I went to old faithful in case she was with her father.

ROMANTICALPHA42: Are you busy?

Instantly, the three little dots danced on my screen.

BABYGIRL89: Perhaps. Why do you think I didn't answer my phone.

I smiled and quickly typed out another message.

ROMANTICALPHA42: Would you be able to pop by. I'm having issues with this spreadsheet for the invites.

BABYGIRL89: What kind of issues?

ROMANTICALPHA42: Guess you could say I'm just lost without you.

I knew there was a double meaning to that last text,

and I'd hoped she'd picked up on it, but she didn't respond.

ROMANTICALPHA42: Think you could do me a favor and stop by?

I sat there waiting for a response for five minutes before I threw my phone down on the couch and blew out a breath. I threw my head back and slouched down on the couch, squeezing the bridge of my nose. I picked up my phone and looked at our texts. Still nothing. I was about to get up and drown my sorrows in a glass of scotch when I heard a knock on the door.

I jumped up, and walked over to the door, pulling it open. I was shocked to see Ainsley standing there, shivering, her arms crossed over her chest trying to keep herself warm.

"Sorry, had to wait for Dad to leave."

I glanced out at the dark road and pulled her inside. I watched as she slipped her shoes off and turned to look at me. "What help did you need?" she asked.

"Come with me," I said, allowing her to go first. "I'm working in the living room."

She walked in and stopped at the end of the coffee table and waited until I sat down, then she moved over beside me, close enough that her thigh touched mine.

I pointed to the screen, to the different colored names on the spreadsheet. Then she chuckled.

"I told you about this today. Red is a no, green is yes, orange and yellow are maybe and maybe with guest."

"Oh, that's right," I said, trying to play it up, but Ainsley wasn't having it.

"Spencer, I know you don't forget that easily. I also know that this was the same system your old assistant used because I was the one who found her notes. So what am I doing here."

I blew out a breath and looked down at the floor. Aside from the fact that I had barely heard a word she had said this afternoon because I couldn't stop imagining her under me, I really only had one more shot at trying to win her back.

"Ainsley, I'm done with everyone else making my decisions for me. I'm done with letting Brittany run my life for fear of her taking Nikki from me. I'm done with your father putting his foot down when he knows next to nothing about how I feel about you. I'm in love with you. No one needs to know or believe that but you, and it kills me when, every time I try to express that to you, you push me away, when I know from your body's responses that you feel the same way."

I turned and looked at her. Her eyes said everything, and I leaned forward and slowly brought my lips to hers. I braced myself for her to shove me away, but instead she surprised me by placing her hands on my neck and kissing me back.

As the kiss deepened, she hoisted herself up and straddled my lap, kissing me hard. Instantly, my cock hardened, and she ground herself down on me, a soft moan escaping her lips as I ran my hands down the side of her body, my thumbs running over her already hardened nipples.

"I want you," I murmured between kisses. "So bad."

"Then take me," she whispered back. "Please take me."

I secured my arm under her and stood up, carrying her down to my bedroom. I kicked the door shut and placed her gently down on the bed. She pulled her shirt off over her head, while I opened the button on her jeans. I was surprised to find she was wearing my favorite pair of black-and-pink panties, ones I'd gotten her for her birthday, and I leaned down and kissed her just above the waistband. Gripping the waist of her jeans, I inched them down her body, kissing her as I went.

By the time I'd made my way back up her body, she was panting, her eyes heady with want. I knelt before her and pulled my shirt off over my head then flicked the button open on my own jeans. She couldn't wait, and before I could object, she'd already pulled my cock from my pants and had started to stroke me.

I gripped her one ankle, biting gently into the calf of

her leg before I ran my thumb over the crotch of her panties. They were already soaked, and I pressed just hard enough that she would feel me touching her through the silky fabric. She dropped back on the bed, letting go of my cock. I grabbed her other leg and slid her panties off, spreading her legs.

I could feel my own orgasm building as I ran my cock through her slick heat and pressed at her opening, sliding in slowly. She let out a soft moan, and I started to move inside of her as I held her close. She gripped my back, and wrapped her legs tightly around my waste. As bad as I wanted to reach this first release, I slowed our love making down and allowed myself to get lost in her, something I'd almost forgotten how to do.

When I felt her fingers dig into my back and her start to tighten around me I knew she was close. I wrapped my arms around her even tighter as she started to moan.

When she yelled out my name one final time, I felt myself let go and I poured myself into her.

AINSLEY

As THE DAYS passed and Christmas crept closer, I started to regret handing in my transfer form. I'd regretted making that deal with Spencer. Things between us were back to normal. Over the last two weeks, I had come home late every night. Spencer and I had been busy making up for lost time while I continued lying to my father telling him that it was either work keeping me at the office late at night or I was busy with Carly.

I lay in bed looking up at the grey sky and snow-covered trees. It was a week before Christmas and the day of the party and I glanced at the clock. It was only nine. I didn't have to be at the hotel until at least three to go over and make sure everything was ready.

"Ainsley, are you getting up for breakfast?" Dad called from the hall.

"Be out in a few minutes," I called as my stomach turned at the thought of food.

"Good, because your eggs are getting cold."

I swallowed hard, trying to stop myself from being sick, but it did little good, and I bolted from the bed and into the bathroom just in time to be sick. I took a cloth and ran cool water over it, soaking it and then placing it on the back of my neck, when I heard a knock on the door.

"Ainsley, are you okay in there?"

"Yeah, Dad. I'm fine," I said, getting up off the floor and opening the door. "It's just nerves. I was feeling pretty off when I got home last night. All this planning for one day, I don't know how on earth these event planners do it."

"Ainsley, you're flushed," he said, bringing his hand up to my forehead. "You don't feel like you have a fever." He looked concerned as he reached into the medicine cabinet for the thermometer.

"I'm fine, seriously," I said, pushing past him and into my room.

"You've been overdoing it. I'll be happy once your transfer is completed. That way you will get your proper rest."

"Yeah, but just you wait and see the party. You are going to be so proud of me." I smiled.

"I'm sure I will be. Get dressed. I'll be in the kitchen,"

he said, taking another concerned look at me before turning to leave.

I threw on my favorite pair of jeans and sweatshirt and put my hair up into a high ponytail. Then I made my way to the kitchen for breakfast.

I'D BEEN fine the rest of the day until they served dinner. I'd ordered the roast beef and as soon as the plate had been placed in front of me, my stomach turned. Spencer looked at me, concern lining his face as I excused myself from the table numerous times throughout the meal, barely touching any of my food. This last time had hit when they placed my favorite dessert, creme brule, in front of me. I'd taken one bite and couldn't even swallow. With my mouth full, I'd gotten up and excused myself from the table. Now, I sat on the floor huddled in front of the toilet in the washroom just off the ballroom, feeling like I could be sick again at any moment when I heard the door open.

"Ainsley, it's Kate. Are you all right, dear?"

"Yeah, I'm okay. I must be coming down with the flu," I answered. "Too many late nights working on this event."

"Oh dear. Spencer just wanted me to pop in and make sure you were all right. Do you need anything?" Kate was an older lady, the assistant to one of Spencer's executives. She sat at the desk next to me, and she knew how many late nights I'd been working. "Do you want some water? Ginger Ale, anything?"

"Maybe some motion sickness medication if you have it?"

"I do." I heard her unzip her clutch and slip two tablets under the stall door along with a little cup of water. "You know I always have those in my purse."

I giggled. Her purse was like a drugstore. "Thank you. I'll be out shortly. Let Spencer know I am fine."

"All right, dear."

I swallowed the two tablets she had given me, and, once the sick feeling passed, I stood up and opened the door. I stood in front of the mirror smoothing the material of the red dress I'd purchased just for tonight. Then I reapplied my lipstick and started on my way back to the party.

The plates had been cleared, music was playing, and people were up dancing. I glanced over to where Spencer stood. He looked amazing. He wore a perfectly fitted, perfectly pressed black suit, and he smiled as he stood there speaking with a couple of clients. I watched as he worked the room, moving from client to client, greeting them, talking to them, and then moving to the next. He was just about to approach another couple when he saw me. Instead of striking up a conversation with them, he greeted them and excused himself, letting them know he would be right back. I watched as he made his way over to me.

"Are you sure you're okay?" he asked, placing his hand on my lower back.

"Yes. I've just overdone it. Kate gave me a couple of her motion sickness tablets, so I should be okay now."

"You're sure?" He looked at me, concern still lining his face. "I can take you home."

"That's not necessary. Let's go and mingle, shall we," I said, smiling up at him and placing my arm through his.

We'd spoken to a few couples, and then we turned and headed for the dance floor for the first slow song of the evening.

"Care to dance?" he whispered in my ear.

"Love to. Probably wise to do so now before my father arrives. He said he would be here after work."

He gathered me in his arms. I rested my head on his chest and we danced together. Once the song was over, we turned to leave the dance floor to continue mingling when we both stopped in our tracks. My father had seen the entire dance. He stood there, glaring at us both. I'd been caught in the lie once again.

Spencer didn't even try to hide the fact that we were

together. Instead, he took hold of my hand and he led me off the dance floor in the direction of my father.

"What are you doing?" I whispered as I felt the nauseous feeling strike again.

"I told you, I'm done hiding," he whispered back, looking directly at my father as he approached us, a look on his face I'd never seen before.

"Spencer, can I have a word with you," he said in a low tone.

Spencer nodded at my father and then looked at me, letting me know not to panic as he left my side and began to follow my father over to a quiet corner of the room.

"No, I want to speak to the pair of you."

AINSLEY HELD my hand tightly as we walked across the room following her father. I just prayed he wasn't going to have some sort of meltdown at the fact he'd caught me with his daughter again. I couldn't afford to have all of my clients witness this. I was surprised when he continued his way out of the room and into the hall, and I felt a weight lift off my shoulders at the fact that the drama wasn't actually going to happen in front of my clients.

Ainsley's hand started to shake as I allowed her to exit before me. Then she turned and looked at me, worry in her eyes. Jon had already walked across the hall and stood in front of one of the tables, watching us while he waited for us to join him.

I grabbed Ainsley's hand and stopped her from going

ahead any farther. I pulled her into me and whispered in her ear, "If you'd prefer I talk to him on my own, that is fine."

She nodded. "I think that is best. I just can't bear to hear what he has to say."

I nodded and leaned in and placed a long kiss on her cheek and she turned to go back into the party when Jon cleared his throat. "Before you leave, Ainsley, give me a chance to speak to both of you. It's something you both should hear."

Ainsley turned and looked to me, completely unsure of what she should do.

"I've got you," I whispered to her as she hesitated. She looked to her father and back to me and then stepped up beside me and wrapped her arm around mine. Together we walked over to where Jon stood, Ainsley gripping my hand.

Jon looked at both of us, then down to where our hands were clasped together. I was prepared to be blasted and placed my arm around Ainsley's back, letting her know I had her.

"I think it's time that I apologize to the both of you," he said, looking to us.

I nodded, but Ainsley stood there, an unsure look on her face.

"I was wrong, Ainsley," Her Dad said looking to both of us. "Spencer, I was watching you guys tonight on the dancefloor. I can tell you care a great deal for my daughter."

"I do."

"Ainsley, I sometimes forget that you are a grown woman and not the five-year-old little girl you once were. I forget that you are capable of making your own choices, and even if I don't approve of them, they are still your choices and they should be respected. If they are wrong, well, they are your mistakes to live with."

"Spencer isn't wrong for me, Daddy. I'm in love with him," Ainsley said.

I gripped her tighter in my arm, pulling her against me.

"After watching you both tonight, I realize that now."

"Your daughter is in good hands, Jon."

"I know. I've seen how the two of you look at one another. I was a fool. I hope you both can forgive me."

I looked over at Ainsley and smiled, then held out my hand for her dad to shake. Then her Dad turned to Ainsley and held his arms open. She stepped forward and they hugged.

"You did a phenomenal job on this party. I'm so proud of you."

"Thanks. Does this mean I don't have to quit my job?" Ainsley asked him, and I chuckled to myself.

"That's up to Spencer," Jon said.

Ainsley turned and looked over her shoulder at me,

and I shrugged. "I've already submitted your transfer," I kidded.

"You did what?" she asked, looking at me shocked.

"I submitted it already…to my shredding bin."

Ainsley smiled at me and started to laugh, and then I heard my name inside the ballroom.

"That's my cue," I said, glancing at my watch. "You guys need to come inside. It's time for me to give my speech."

I took off in the opposite direction of Jon and Ainsley and made my way through the door that led to the back of the stage and walked out just in time to take the microphone. I looked out over the large crowd and finally spotted Ainsley standing off to the side with her dad.

"I want to thank each and every one of you for coming to this amazing Christmas party. As many of you know, I have spent the better part of last few years building this company from the ground up. What you don't know is why I started Finding Forever. You see, my older brother lost his wife after twenty-two years of marriage. After a few years, he started dating again. Friends tried to fix him up, he tried numerous online sites, and after watching these relationships fail over and over, I decided that there was something lacking with each of them. That is how Finding Forever was born, an elite site meant to match you to your forever partner using the power of psychology instead of an 'at first glance' approach.

"I am happy to say that, after all these years, we still hold a ninety-eight percent match rate. Which brings me to announce that even I decided to use my own company. This past summer I was fortunate enough to meet a young woman who awakened my soul."

I paused to take a drink and looked over to the side where Ainsley stood, her eyes wide as she waited for what was next. "You will know the young woman as Ainsley Matthews, my executive assistant and the woman in charge of putting this amazing party together. Ainsley, would you come up here for a moment please."

I looked down to where she stood, shaking her head, holding her hands over her mouth in shock, while her father walked her over to the stairs. Kate stood at the bottom of the stairs to help her up, and soon she was standing at my side.

IT WAS after one when I pulled my car into my driveway. I glanced over at the passenger's seat to see Ainsley sound asleep. I cut the engine and placed my hand on her knee, shaking her gently.

"We're home," I whispered and watched her sleepy blue eyes open.

"What? Oh, I didn't mean to drift off," she said, gathering her items in a bit of a panic.

"Sweetie, relax," I said, leaning over and taking her purse from her hands. I climbed out of the car and walked around and opened her door, helping her out of the car. We walked slowly up the slippery walkway, and I slid my key in the lock. This was the first night that Ainsley would be spending the night with me, under my roof with her father's blessing.

I hung my suit jacket on the banister and guided Ainsley up the steps. I flipped the light on, lighting the twelve-foot tree that stood in the corner of living room. "Why don't you take a seat. I'll get us a glass of wine," I said, placing a kiss on her cheek.

"I think I'm going to change first."

"Sure, there are T-shirts in the top drawer in my room."

Ten minutes later, I sat in the living room, glass of wine in hand with soft Christmas music playing on the radio. Ainsley walked into the living room, looking sexy as hell in one of my T-shirts, her hair falling softly on her shoulders.

She sat down on the couch beside me, reaching for the glass of wine I'd poured for her, and took a sip. She closed her eyes as she swallowed and relaxed into the couch, placing her feet across my lap.

I set my glass down, grabbing her foot, rubbing it gently in all the spots I knew she loved. A soft moan escaped her lips as I traveled up her calf. She looked at me, her eyes half asleep. I raised her leg and placed a kiss on her ankle, watching her response as I kissed my way up her calf. When I hit her knee, I reached for her wine glass, taking it from her hand, and placed it on the table beside mine.

"What...what are..."

I said nothing. I stood, slid one arm under her leg, the other behind her back, and lifted her off the couch and carried her down to the bedroom.

AINSLEY

I WAS BREATHING hard when I woke up. I looked over to Spencer, who was uncovered to the waist, sound asleep. I wasn't sure what it was I had been dreaming about but I kicked the covers off and swung my legs around. I sat there for a moment in the darkness when my stomach started to turn. I covered my mouth, got up, and bolted to the bathroom.

Placing a cool cloth on the back of my neck, I rinsed my mouth with water and made my way to the living room where I curled up on the couch with my cell phone and called Carly. I could only imagine how irritated she would be for calling her so early, but I didn't care. I needed someone.

"Hey, sorry, I know it's early," I whispered into the phone.

"Ainsley, early? It's not even six. What is it? What's wrong?"

"I'm just not feeling well. I spent most of last night sick and again this morning."

"Is it nerves or the flu?"

"I don't know."

"Look, why don't you come over. We can go for breakfast, you can tell me all about the party."

I looked around the living room. I was sure Spencer would sleep in. "All right, I'll be there shortly."

I quickly ran home and slipped into my jeans and sweatshirt, climbed into my car, and headed to Carly's.

An hour later, we sat in the local diner waiting for our breakfast to be delivered.

"So, my father gave us his blessing," I said, looking at Carly for her reaction.

"You mean he is okay with you and Spencer?" she asked.

I nodded. "Yes. I am so happy, Carly, I can't even begin to tell you."

I could already tell from the look on Carly's face that she didn't approve of what my father had done, but she smiled anyways. "I'm happy to hear that. Are you feeling better now?"

I nodded, and then the server arrived holding our plates. "Pancakes and bacon for you," she said, sliding a plate in front of Carly, "and for you, eggs, bacon and toast. Eggs over easy just the way you asked," she said, smiling, and then turned to walk away.

"This looks amazing," Carly said, digging into the steaming pile of pancakes. "I've been dying to come here for breakfast again."

I looked down at my plate, took one look at the eggs, and felt my stomach start to turn. I bolted from the table without a word and ran to the washroom. When I finally returned to the table, Carly sat there looking at me with a curious look on her face.

"So, yesterday you said you got sick at the party."

I nodded.

"What were you doing?"

"They brought out my dinner, and just like this morning, I had to run."

"I see," she said, nodding and looking at me with curiosity.

"What?" I questioned.

"I think we need to make a stop on the way home."

I looked at her, wondering where she wanted to stop. "Where?"

"The drugstore."

An hour later, we were back in Carly's room with her door locked. I looked over at my friend who stood there holding the bright-pink box out for me to take.

"No way, you are crazy. I'm telling you it's the flu," I said with my arms crossed.

"How many times have you had unprotected sex with him?" Carly urged.

I waved my hand, dismissing the idea, deep down inside praying that she didn't know what she was talking about. "It's the flu."

"Yes, okay, sure. It might be, but it's better to be safe than sorry. So get in there and take this," she said, waving the box in front of me.

I looked at my friend and shook my head. I knew she wasn't going to give up, so I took the box from her hand and slowly made my way into her bathroom. It was the longest three minutes I think I had ever lived as I stood in the bathroom looking down at that little white stick. I blinked hard as I saw the first little line appear, followed by a faint second line that got a little darker the longer I waited. I closed my eyes and let out a breath, looking back down at the little white stick, making sure that what I had seen was really there as my stomach started to turn for a completely different reason.

"Are you coming out or what?" I heard from the other side of the door. "It's been like five minutes."

I picked up the stick and turned to the door. I closed my eyes as I grabbed the handle and pulled the door open. Carly took one look at me and already knew what I was about to tell her.

"What are you going to do?" she asked, more panicked than I seemed.

"Um, well, I guess I need to tell Spencer," I said, shrugging.

"Today? Aren't you going to let it sink in or perhaps have it confirmed by a doctor first?" Carly questioned, following me around her room while I slipped into my coat.

I shook my head, picked up my purse, and slid the pregnancy test inside. "I'll call you later?" I said, turning to her.

She wrapped her arms around me, pulling me in for a hug, and then walked me to the door.

SPENCER

I SLOWLY OPENED my eyes and rolled over, reaching to the other side of the bed for Ainsley, but the bed was cold and empty. I sat up and looked around the room, listening hard to see if I could hear her in the kitchen, but the house was silent. I kicked the covers off me, picking my boxers up off the floor and slid them on.

I walked down the hall to the living room. The tree was on, soft Christmas music played. Ainsley was sound asleep, curled up on the couch, covered by a blanket. I smiled and walked over, sitting down beside her, placing my hand on her cheek.

"Morning, beautiful," I said in a low voice.

She took in a deep breath and then opened her eyes, looking up at me. She smiled gently, stretching her arms over her head. "Morning."

"Is everything all right?" I questioned. It wasn't like her to sleep in the living room when she spent the night with me. Normally, I would awaken to her curled into my side.

"Yes," she whispered. "Everything is fine."

"Good. It's just normally you don't sleep out here," I said, looking around the room. "Did you have a bad dream."

She shook her head and smiled. "No."

"Well, then, come back to bed and let me ravish you for a couple of hours," I said as I started to pull the covers off her only to be disappointed to find that she was already dressed.

"Can we talk for a minute?" she asked, her hand resting on my wrist.

I took one look at the expression on her face and became rather concerned that something was wrong. I was instantly worried that she had changed her mind about us and started to prepare myself for the worst. "Sure."

She reached down beside the couch and picked up her purse. Opening it slowly, she reached inside and then looked at me. "I don't even know where to begin," she said, closing her eyes and taking in a breath.

"Well, you just say it," I said, smiling at her. "Our relationship will always be better if we are open with one another from the start."

She nodded and placed a pregnancy test in my hand. I looked down at it and then up to her, my eyes moving back down to those two little pink lines. I knew exactly what those meant, thinking back to when Brittany had told me about Nikki. I felt a twinge of excitement run through me.

"Okay," I said, trying hard not to show how I really felt because I wasn't sure how she was going to react.

"Okay, is that all you can say?"

I nodded. "What's going through your mind?" I questioned.

"Um, I'm scared."

"Why?"

I watched as she lay back against the couch. "Because I don't have any idea how you feel about this. You are much older than I. I have no idea if you want to be a father again."

"Well, one thing I can tell you is that Nikki is going to be so excited to find out she could have a little brother or sister, and honestly I feel the same way."

"You're excited that you could have a little brother or sister?"

I couldn't help but laugh. "No, silly."

"Then what?"

I looked at her, at the panic that lined her face, leaned down and kissed her softly. "I'm a little shocked, but ecstatic all at the same time. Ainsley, I'm in love with you. Nothing could change that."

"Really?"

"Really. Now I think that we need to head on down to my bedroom and spend some time celebrating, then we should make an appointment with your doctor. Then I will take the pleasure of telling your father."

"Oh God, do we have to tell him?" she asked, looking even more worried than she had moments before.

"Yes, we have to tell him. We have to tell Brittany too. Then after that, we are going to go shopping."

"Shopping?"

"Yes, we will need some baby things. A crib, change table, diapers, and clothes. However, one thing I know for a fact that we are going to need is already under the tree over there," I said, nodding to the tree.

I watched as she frowned and turned to look over at the tree. There was a pile of gifts under the tree that I'd had Ainsley personally wrap for Nikki at the office one night because Nikki had been staying with me and had been on a kick to find what Santa had gotten her.

I stood up and walked over to the tree, pulling a box out from under it. Then I walked back over, sat down, and pulled at the paper.

"I was going to give you this Christmas morning, but now is as good a time as any."

She lay there propped up on her elbow watching as I opened the package, dropping the gold paper on the table.

"Close your eyes."

She did as I asked, and I opened the box, holding it in my hand. "Go ahead, open them."

Her eyes met mine and then fell to my hand where inside that box sat an engagement ring. I couldn't help but chuckle as shock lined her face. I could tell she had no clue that this was coming, and so I took the ring I'd purchased two months earlier from the box, grabbed her hand, and slowly slid the ring onto her finger.

"Ainsley, I've known for a long time how I've felt about you. I also know what it's like not to have you, and I can say that I would rather have you at my side forever than not have you at all. Ainsley, will you be my forever?"

I watched as a tear slipped from her eye and ran down her cheek. She quickly wiped it away and looked at me, her eyes full of tears, and nodded. She wrapped her arms tightly around me. "Yes. Yes," she whispered.

She looked into my eyes. "Now we need to plan the wedding and tell my father," she said, looking a little worried.

I smiled and shook my head. "One thing at a time. I promise we will tell your father together, and we will hire someone to do all the wedding arrangements. However, first, we need to go and celebrate."

"What?"

I said nothing more. I stood up, slipped my arms under her body, picking her up off the couch, and kissed her as I carried her on down the hall. I could not wait to start this new chapter in my life with my soon to be wife.

OUR LITTLE WEDDING

Ainsley Matthews was my everything. Not only was she twenty years younger than me, she was the woman I fell in love with and was soon going to be the mother of my child.

The second she told me about the baby, I had a ring on her finger. I didn't want to risk losing her. We'd gotten engaged and soon started planning our wedding. Engaged, we began planning our wedding.

The night of our engagement party I heard her best friend exclaim, 'wrinkled old balls' and suddenly doubts crept up in my mind. Was this how Ainsley felt? Was the age difference really too much? Then we found everyone thought I had only put a ring on her finger because of the baby. Suddenly it felt as if everything were against us, friends, family, my ex, hell, even the venues and caterers we'd called couldn't commit to the dates we wanted.

Stress piled on and soon I found myself at Ainsley's side in the emergency room and everything came crashing down.

From USA Today Bestselling Author S.L. Sterling comes the final chapter in this steamy age gap romance.

AINSLEY

"Anyone want coffee?" I questioned.

I stood in front of the sink, washing the last of the dinner dishes.

"Love some," my father called out.

"Yes, please," Spencer answered.

After I wiped down the counters, I flipped the switch on the coffeemaker and emptied the dishwater from the sink. We'd spent New Year's Day with my father. Jane, his new girlfriend, was working at the hospital, and I felt bad that he'd be alone. It was easier now that Dad had given Spencer and me his blessing to date. Things had seemed to improve between the three of us since the holiday party Spencer had held for his clients.

I worked diligently to put the dishes away, while my

father and Spencer retired into the living room. They'd thrown on a replay of the most recent hockey game and now sat shouting at the TV. I giggled, listening to them banter back and forth as I pulled three plates out of the cupboard and cut three pieces of cake for dessert, and then I waited for the coffee to finish perking while silently humming a song to myself.

I heard laughter coming from the other room, and I smiled. It was nice to see them getting along again. It was also nice not to have to sneak around anymore. Once that happened, not only did my relationship improve with my father, but so did theirs. They were back to speaking again and going out for wings and beer on game nights.

However, while that was good for now, my dad still didn't have any idea about the baby or our engagement. We'd decided not to tell him everything at once. Spencer had told me he wanted to ask my father's permission to marry me, but we agreed not to tell him about the baby until later. Besides, it was too early to say anything. My family doctor figured I was only maybe four weeks along and we didn't want him to think we were having some shotgun wedding because I was pregnant.

I'd just pulled mugs down from the cupboard when I felt Spencer wrap his arms around me from behind and pull me against him. "Need any help?" he questioned, kissing the side of my neck.

"I think I got it," I said, placing my hand on his muscular forearm. "You haven't said anything to him yet have you?" I questioned while closing my eyes as he kissed my neck again.

"I promised you I'd wait until you are in the living room with me." Spencer placed a kiss on my shoulder and chuckled. "Don't you trust me?"

I smiled and said, "I trust you," while spinning in his arms and kissing him.

He wrapped his arms around me, kissing me a little harder, his tongue parting my lips and meeting mine, while his hands cupped my ass. The second our lips parted, I leaned my head against his chest, breathing hard. I could already feel his hard cock pressing into me.

"You better calm that down." I giggled.

"I could take you right here, right now." He whispered and let out a chuckle while adjusting himself. "Anything I can help you with?"

"Could you take the cake in?"

"I can," he said, grabbing my ass and kissing me one more time before picking up the three plates.

I poured two cups of coffee and filled my mug with hot water from the kettle, plopping in a tea bag. Then I put the three mugs on the small tray and carried them into the living room.

"This looks fantastic," my father said, taking a bite of

the double fudge chocolate cake I'd made. "I've been missing your baking around here."

I smiled. "Dad, anytime you want anything, just ask me. I'm more than happy to make you something."

I'd basically moved out and in with Spencer the second Dad had said we could date. I kept some of my things at the house here, and occasionally to please my father, I came back home for a night. Those nights were few because it was easier to be with Spencer since the morning sickness had struck me hard.

"I'm so glad you are feeling better. That flu you had really hit you bad," Dad said.

I looked at Spencer out of the corner of my eye. His eyes met mine for a split second. "Yeah, it was a bad one," Spencer bit out.

"Looks like you lost a lot of weight, too," Dad replied, giving me a once over.

"You think I've lost weight?" I questioned, looking down at myself. "I don't think I have." I shrugged, trying to play it off.

"No, neither do I," Spencer said.

"Well, I do, but don't worry, you'll put it back on in no time," Dad said. "You always lost weight when you got the flu."

I glanced again at Spencer, who sat there watching me. Then he sat forward. "So, Jon, how are things with Jane?"

"Good, very good. We are looking at planning a trip in the coming weeks."

"Great. That is exciting. Things must be going well then between you two."

"Yes, so well, in fact, that I put my Finding Forever profile on pause. I hope that is okay."

Spencer nodded. "Of course. That is why we have that feature."

"I'm glad you guys are getting along so well. She seems nice. Maybe someone that I could bond with," I said, hoping that maybe one day she might be like a mother to me.

"She really likes you, Ainsley. It would be nice if you guys got to know one another a little better," Dad said.

The room grew quiet. My body seemed to be filled with tension as I took a small bite of my cake. My stomach turned. I just wished Spencer would get on with this and ask him already.

"What about you two?" my father asked. "Things all right?"

I could tell my father cared but really didn't want to know any details. It had been hard on him to start when he'd found us in bed together. It had been hard on all of us, and that had almost ripped Spencer and me apart from one another for good.

"Things are going better than expected," Spencer said. "That's why we wanted to talk to you about something." Spencer set his plate down and placed his hand on my knee, giving me a gentle squeeze.

"Oh," my father said, taking the last bite of his cake and washing it down with coffee. Then he looked up at us, then down to where Spencer's hand now rested on my inner thigh. My nerves were so bad that I had to set my plate down to stop shaking. "Well, what is it?"

I blew out a breath as Spencer took over the conversation. "As you know, I'm really in love with your daughter, and she is with me."

My father looked at the pair of us, not saying a word. I feared this was going to be another blowup, and I bit my bottom lip and wrapped my arm through Spencer's, while my father sat there watching my every move.

"I've given things considerable thought and, well, I'd like to ask you for permission to marry her."

I'd lowered my eyes as Spencer had spoken. I'd was afraid to look and see my father's reaction because I feared it was going to be the same as the night he'd caught us. I wouldn't be able to take that, and I prayed that wasn't what was coming. The only sound in the room was from the game on TV. I hated the silence and I wanted someone to say something. I shyly glanced up to see my father staring at us both.

"Married?" My father cleared his throat.

"Yes, sir," Spencer answered, his voice calm and even, never once faltering.

"Ainsley, what do you think about this?"

Spencer and I hadn't gone over what would happen if he asked me anything. All Spencer had said was not to worry, that he'd handle it because he knew how nervous I was.

When I didn't answer him, my father cleared his throat again. "Ainsley, I asked you a question."

"Daddy, we want your permission. I've said it before. I'm in love with Spencer. I'm happy. I want to spend the rest of my life with him."

My father grew quiet, sitting there looking at us. Then, without another word, he got up and wandered down the hall to his bedroom. I looked over at Spencer, who sat there looking at me with the same perplexed look on his face.

He'd been gone for a few minutes, and I was about to say something to Spencer when my father returned to the living room and looked at us both. "I knew this day would come, eventually. Given the brief history with the pair of you, I already know you won't take no for an answer, so I'll give you my blessing."

I couldn't believe what my father had said, but I wrapped my arms around Spencer and hugged him tight.

"Spencer, just make sure you take care of my baby girl."

Spencer let me go and looked up at my father. "Jon,

you know I will." He stood up and shook my father's hand.

Relief flooded me as I stood up and hugged my father tightly. "Thank you, Dad." I whispered in his ear. Then the three of us sat back down, but not before I pulled the ring Spencer had surprised me with from my purse so I could show the only person in my life who had always been there for me, until now.

AINSLEY

I STOOD in the bedroom looking at my reflection in the mirror, turning to the right and then the left, and again looking forward. "I don't know about this dress. It just doesn't seem to hang right," I cried. "I knew I should have gotten the one I was looking at the other night, but it was so expensive."

"Don't worry, you look fabulous," Carly answered, not paying attention to anything I'd said as she lay across our bed, flipping through one of our favourite magazines.

"I don't know." I smoothed the fabric of the dress down my body. "This one just doesn't hang right."

Carly closed the magazine and rolled onto her back. "Ainsley, it's just the engagement party. What difference does it make? You've worn that dress plenty of times before, and you weren't picky about the way it hung."

I shrugged. "Well, it matters to me now." I slid the dress off and put my jeans and T-shirt back on. "I just want everything to be perfect." I sat down on the edge of the bed beside Carly just as Nikki walked into the bedroom.

"I know, but seriously, it's only a small gathering of a few people."

"Yeah, only a few people." I giggled, thinking about all the invitations I'd sent out.

"Ainsley, can I have dessert now?"

"Sure, bug, let's go," I said, putting my hand on her head and leading her out of mine and Spencer's room. Carly let out a sigh and got up, following behind us.

"What kind of ice cream do you want? Chocolate, vanilla, or strawberry?"

Nikki put her forefinger to her lips. "Mmmm, chocolate and strawberry," she said, her eyes lighting up.

I shook my head and placed my hand on my hip. "No, one or the other."

"Mmmm…" Nikki thought hard for a moment and then yelled, "Chocolate with syrup and sprinkles!"

I laughed as I turned and pulled a bowl down from the cupboard, while Nikki climbed up on a stool beside Carly and watched as I plopped a scoop of ice cream into her bowl.

"Anyway, back to what we were talking about earlier.

Now I'm being serious, and I want a serious answer. Picture your life for me for just a moment?"

"I am picturing it. I'm happy, Carly," I said, drizzling chocolate syrup onto the ice cream in Nikki's bowl, then covering it with pink and white sprinkles.

"I don't mean now. Yes, sure, you're happy now. You have all the warm and fuzzy feelings of being in a rather new relationship. I mean, think about your future."

I put the lid back on the ice cream container and shoved it in the freezer. "I am thinking about the future! We have Nikki and two other babies. This one, and perhaps a little boy, who looks just like Spencer."

"A brother and a sister!" Nikki exclaimed, taking the bowl from me. "I thought you said there was only one baby in there? Two can't possibly fit in there?" she said, pointing to my flat stomach.

Carly looked at Nikki and mouthed to me, "She knows?"

"Nikki, eat your ice cream," I said, knowing full well we shouldn't be talking about any of this in front of her.

"She only knows because she heard Spencer and I talking about it and asked. Spencer doesn't believe in not telling her. So, we sat her down and told her that one day she would have a little brother or sister," I whispered to Carly.

"I see. Well, regardless, two others? You are nuts. And I'm talking distant future. He's all hot now, but what do you think he is going to look like in, say, twenty years?" she said, keeping her voice low.

"Can I go into the living room and colour?" Nikki asked, grinning at me.

"Sure, just don't spill, okay? Keep everything at your little table."

"I will." She grinned, shoving a spoonful of ice cream in her mouth. "Bye, Carly."

"Bye." We both watched as she carefully carried the bowl into the living room with two hands, leaving the two of us in the kitchen. "Now seriously? What about twenty years from now? What do you think it will be like then?"

"God! What are any of us going to look like in twenty years?" I cried.

"I'm being serious! You'll only be forty, but he'll be sixty," she said, scrunching her nose up in disgust.

"So am I being serious. Now please, I am marrying Spencer. I'm happy, I'm excited, and it would be nice for my best friend to be excited for me as well."

"You say that now."

"She says what now?" Carly jumped at the sound of Spencer's voice as he poked his head around the corner.

"Nothing," I immediately said, looking at Carly letting her know the conversation was ending.

He stepped into the kitchen carrying a suit bag. He

made his way over to me, put his arm around me, and kissed the side of my neck.

"Hey," I said, meeting his lips. "See that you picked up your suit from the cleaner. I meant to do that right after I left the office today, but Carly called, and I forgot." I shrugged.

"Don't worry about it, but no, this isn't my suit. I made a stop after work. This is for you." He held up the suit bag and lowered the zipper. It shocked me to see the champagne-coloured dress I wished I'd bought when I'd tried it on at a little boutique outside of town last weekend. I'd wanted it for our engagement party, but after seeing the price, I had decided against it.

"What is this?" I questioned. "Tell me you didn't," I cried with excitement as I removed the bag from the hanger.

"I did." He grinned. "You looked…mmm…well, it's not suitable to say how you looked in it the other day in front of a guest," he said, leaning in a biting my earlobe.

"Oh God, save me," Carly said, sticking her finger down her throat and pretending to gag.

"Not in front of little eyes," I whispered as Nikki stood before us, holding her empty bowl.

I smiled as I took the dress from Spencer, while he took the bowl from Nikki, wiping her mouth with a paper towel before he picked her up and threw her in the air. "How's my baby girl?"

Nikki let out a squeal, followed by a laugh as Spencer held her up over his head. "Put me down, Daddy," she squealed.

Spencer put her down and watched as she ran off into the other room. He walked over to the table and sorted through the pile of mail I'd left there.

"Oh, and we got a couple more RSVPs in the mail today for the engagement party," I said, showing Carly the dress.

"Was one of them from my brother, Max?"

I shook my head. "No, have not heard from him yet. I can call him tomorrow if you'd like? Today was the last day to respond."

"I'll take care of Max. I've got to call him tonight about work," he said, leaning in and kissing me before he made his way down the hall to his office.

I smiled as I looked at Carly, excitement filling me as I looked at the dress. "Come, let's try this one on."

"I sure hope this dress hangs better." Carly giggled, following behind me.

SPENCER

"SPENCER BROOKS IS GETTING REMARRIED. Never thought I'd live to see the day," my older brother, Mike, said as Ainsley and I approached him and his wife, Trina.

"Hey, Trina, Mike. Enjoying yourselves?"

"Yes, everything is wonderful. The food is fantastic, and these little appetizers are amazing," Trina said, holding up one of my favourites, Cranberry Pecan Goat Cheese Truffles. "You did a fantastic job organizing everything, Ainsley. And this dress… is just gorgeous on you."

Trina and Mike had met through Finding Forever. They'd been the first successful match that Spencer's company had, and Mike had been the reason Spencer had started the company.

"Thanks." Ainsley smiled and leaned into my side as

I looked around the room. Everyone seemed to have a good time, but a huge part of me felt tense. As I skimmed the room, I noticed Carly staring over at us as she talked to her date. Whatever she said caused him and another one of Ainsley's other friends to turn our way and watch us as well, whispering to one another.

I was about to turn back to the conversation with my brother when I noticed Jon and Jane standing off to the side. They both held a glass of wine, talking amongst themselves, neither looking thrilled. Carly moved over to them and whispered something. Both Jon and Jane laughed, then they both looked over in our direction with an odd expression.

I felt as if I were becoming paranoid, as I never usually cared about what people thought, but after hearing Carly talking to Ainsley about our age difference the other day, and trying to give her reasons that we shouldn't get married, I worried she was now having second thoughts and had said something to someone, which was why we were getting all the looks. I searched my mind, trying to remember if she'd given me any sign of that, but she hadn't.

I glanced over toward where I'd last seen Nikki playing with some other children, but she wasn't there. Panic filled me for a moment as I searched the crowd until I spotted her with Brittany, pulling on the bottom of her dress to get her attention. Brittany ignored her because she was glaring at us from across the room. I knew the look on her face well, and it clearly wasn't one of happiness, although that would be a look I wouldn't recognize anymore, anyway. I hadn't wanted her here, but she'd insisted on bringing Nikki instead of just allowing us to have her for the night.

"Ainsley, how's things going for you at Spencer's office?" Mike asked.

I felt Ainsley grip my side a little tighter, and I turned my attention back to the conversation. "Things are going well. I'm enjoying my position very much."

"Good. My brother is treating you well then? I've heard he can be a hard man to work for."

"Mike, stop it," Trina said, jabbing his side.

"She knows I'm kidding. Don't you?" Mike said, winking.

Ainsley smiled and rested her head on my shoulder as the four of us laughed. I glanced around the room one more time, looking for our younger brother. "Mike, have you seen Max yet?" I questioned.

My brother shook his head. "Not yet. I didn't even hear from him to know if he was coming or not. I called, but there was no answer. It's just like Max, wrapped up in his own affairs all the time. Been that way his entire life."

I chuckled. "Yep, neither did we. Guess that is the

thanks I get for giving him the Denver branch of Finding Forever to run." I shrugged.

Handing over the Denver branch to my brother had been a hard decision for me. After all, I'd built this company, with no help from anyone. I'd originally planned to spend half my time in Denver and the other half here, until I'd found out about the pregnancy. I wasn't comfortable leaving Ainsley alone now, after we spent a few nights talking about it, and even though she told me that whatever I decided, she'd support, I knew I didn't want to be far from here. I looked at other options. There were many, but I knew Max needed some help. I just didn't want to end up regretting the decision.

"Give him a chance. Perhaps something came up last minute at work?"

"That would be hard to believe. The soft launch is next week. Right now, it's basically employee training week. If something has come up already, we may be in trouble." I swallowed hard. I wasn't that much of a control freak, but Max also didn't have the best track record, and giving him some control over this made me nervous.

"So, how are the plans coming for the wedding?" Trina questioned. "Do we have a venue yet?"

I wrapped my arm around Ainsley tighter, waiting for her to answer.

"Good. We are still waiting to hear from the venues,

and I am currently trying to set things up with a couple of caterers and, of course, bakers for the cake. This week is a big week though. I am going shopping for a wedding dress," Ainsley whispered, like it was a secret.

"Very exciting. If you'd like, I will send you a list of stores to check out."

"Oh, please," Ainsley said, smiling up at me. "It would help me a lot."

"I will. Why don't you call me this weekend and I'll give you a list."

"Thank you, I will do that. I am looking for a certain dress, and I'm hoping one store here will carry the designer I am looking for."

"Send me the designer and I will see what I can find out."

"All right, Ainsley, we should get moving. We have many more people to talk to before the night is over. Can we catch up with you in a little while?" I asked.

"Sure thing, and if I see Max, I'll let him know you are looking for him."

Mike shook my hand, while Ainsley hugged Trina. Then we quickly switched before making our way to the next couple.

AINSLEY WAS LOUNGING on the couch in one of my T-shirts when I came into the living room carrying a glass of water for her and a scotch on the rocks for me. I was looking forward to relaxing with her. We finally had the house to ourselves for the weekend.

"Here you go."

"Thank you. God, I really wish I could have a glass of wine," She muttered, resting her head on a pillow.

"Everything okay?" I questioned, sitting down beside her and pulling her bare foot into my lap, giving her a gentle massage.

She let out a breath and closed her eyes, relaxing farther into the couch. "I don't know. Tonight just didn't feel as fun as I thought it would. It seemed like everyone was staring and whispering. To be honest, all I felt was tension."

"I know what you mean. At one point, I thought it was just my imagination, but I got that feeling as well. Also, I am certain, at one point, I heard Carly whisper to one of your mutual friends something about 'wrinkled old balls,'" I said, taking a sip of my scotch and placing the glass back down.

She giggled. "I'm sorry. She's still so hung up on the age difference. It's not a secret that she has never really approved of us. To be honest, I think she was more shocked when I found out I was pregnant than I was."

We both grew quiet as I continued rubbing her foot, digging into all the places I knew she loved. My mind was still reeling from the ball comment, and I hoped Ainsley didn't feel that way. The more I tried to put it out of my mind, the more it kept gnawing at me. "Ainsley?"

"Hmmm?" She opened her sleepy eyes and looked at me.

"Do you think that?" I questioned.

"Think what?"

"That my balls are old and wrinkled?" I asked, trying my best to keep a straight face.

Ainsley was serious for a moment, and then she burst into laughter. "I'm sorry… I can't answer that."

I laughed as well, but not because it was funny; it was more because I was relieved to see her expression change. "Sorry, I couldn't help that. After hearing you and her talk the other night, I was worried that perhaps she was convincing you to leave, to find someone younger."

"It's okay. Never worry, I will always love your balls."

"I'm glad." I chuckled.

"Seriously though, Spencer, a younger man couldn't

even hold a candle to you. I see how these guys treat Carly, and to be honest, I think I'd lose my mind. It's all games with them, and when she's told me about the sex, well…"

"What does she say?"

"That none of them last and that most of them are more concerned with getting themselves off and not worrying about her."

"Ah, yes, well, that comes with age and maturity. As for lasting, well, there are times I can barely hold it together with you."

"Oh." Her cheeks flushed, "It was nice to see Mike and Trina there. They seemed to really be happy for us." She said, changing the subject.

"Yes, Mike was thrilled when I told him, albeit a little surprised, but only because he never thought I'd marry again after Brittany."

"Can't say I blame you there. Did you see the way she was glaring at us tonight?"

"How could I not? I also couldn't help but notice how she was ignoring Nikki as well. I really didn't want her to go home with her tonight, but it is her turn to have her. Besides, I think we could both use some alone time."

"I know. At one point, Nikki came to me to take her to the bathroom. I was worried Brittany might follow us into the bathroom and bitch me out, but when we came back out, I found her flirting with Paul, head of tech support. I don't even thing she noticed Nikki had come to me."

"If that ever happens again, you need to come and get me right away. She will not ignore the needs of my daughter to satisfy her own. I've been fighting her on that for years."

Ainsley nodded and then rested her head back against the pillow as I continued rubbing her foot, then switching to the other one. "You might want to warn poor Paul, too."

"Noted."

"Can I talk to you about something?" Ainsley whispered, placing her hand on my forearm.

"Of course. What is it?"

Ainsley blew out a breath before beginning. "The other day, while I was in putting Nikki's clothes away, I realized we don't have a separate bedroom for the baby. So, Nikki will have to share her room when she is here."

"You know, I was thinking the same thing myself. I was planning to bring this up to you later in the week. What would you say to finding a place of our own?"

"What do you mean?" Ainsley questioned. "This one is our own."

"No, this place isn't one we chose together. This is the house I chose after my divorce. I needed a place to live, and I needed to have room for Nikki so I could bring her here on my weekends. We are clearly going to outgrow this place, and I thought it might be nice to find a place that we can build together."

Ainsley nodded. "Where would we look?"

"Well, on my way home the other night, I drove through a neighborhood close to here, just a few blocks over. The houses are bigger, which means we'd have another bedroom or two. Plus, if we plan it right from the start, perhaps I could also fit an office in. That way I can work from home if need be and help you when the baby comes."

I watched as she thought for a moment. "Were there any houses for sale?"

"There were a couple that I saw. I can make an appointment with an agent to see them. See if we like any of them. There is no harm in looking."

I watched her eyes light up while the idea I'd planted floated through her mind. I wanted her to have everything she wanted, things I knew were important to her. Over the last few weeks, she asked me if it was okay if she made some subtle changes around the house. I kept telling her she didn't need my permission, but she still came to me. I knew she'd never come out and say she wanted a place she could make her own, but I knew it was on her mind.

"Don't be afraid to tell me how you feel, Ainsley."

She shrugged. "It might be nice to have someplace we can call our own. I know that eventually I won't think of this as just your place, though. It's just going to take me some time."

"I'll call the agent this week and set something up." I smiled, picking up my drink and taking a sip. Ainsley smiled and then closed her eyes while I continued rubbing her feet, and she sank farther into the couch cushions as she relaxed. I grabbed the remote and turned the radio on, soft jazz music floating through the air.

I loved these quiet times with her. There was something about being with her that brought out a fire in my soul. She had made me feel alive when, most of these past few years, I felt dead inside.

AINSLEY

"Nikki's dinner is in the fridge on her favourite plate. Hopefully, that will make it easier for you to get her to eat tonight. All you need to do is take it out and heat it in the microwave. Reheat it for about three minutes. She will try to tell you she can eat in the living room, but she needs to eat at the table. Spencer thinks she is getting away with too much at Brittany's, so he is implementing stricter rules for when she is here. She's been horrible since she returned."

"What about drinks?"

"She can have a juice box or a glass of milk, whichever she wants. Don't let her con you into giving her pop. It gets her crazy hyper, and lately she has been sneaky about that, too."

"Okay, plate, no pop, and at the table. I think I got it," Carly said, hopping up onto the counter.

"Oh, and I got out some construction paper and some new markers. She wanted to do some arts and crafts tonight. I believe she wanted to make Spencer a birthday card. She needs to do that at the table as well, since we found a minor cut on the couch the other day that we had to have repaired."

Carly nodded and then took a sip of the pop I'd gotten for her. "No problem. I'll help her with that. Maybe I'll even make Spencer one." She winked.

I laughed, imagining what Carly would put inside the card. I shook my head as I reached up into the cupboard and grabbed a box of crackers, put five on the plate, and then grabbed the cheese from the fridge and began making Nikki a snack before we left. I had just added a handful of grapes when Carly cleared her throat.

"Don't you find this a little weird?"

"Find what weird?" I asked.

"I dunno, this. You used to be the babysitter, and now here he is, hiring a babysitter."

I looked at Carly, who wore a smug smile on her face. "I am a former babysitter. Currently, I am a personal assistant."

"Ooh, I forgot. You've moved up in the world." Carly giggled.

"Don't make fun of me. You know one day you too

could end up not babysitting and spending time in corporate America." I laughed.

"I don't think so. I'll be living the wild life, working with young kids in a school somewhere, not in corporate America under my boss's desk!"

"You bitch!" My mouth dropped open, and we both laughed. I shoved Carly's shoulder just as Nikki walked into the kitchen and placed a few sheets of construction paper on the table.

"Carly, if you give me two desserts, I'll tell my dad nice things about you." Then she turned and looked at me with a smile.

I looked back at her, trying not to laugh, and was about to say something when Carly interjected.

"If I give you two desserts, you'll be sick, and unfortunately I don't do puke, so…"

Nikki hung her head, and then, almost as if Carly had said nothing, she looked up at me with hope in her eyes. "Will you and Daddy be back in time for dessert?"

"Mmmm, I'm not too sure. We might be, but to be on the safe side, you should have dessert when Carly gives it to you."

"But Mom lets me have two," Nikki cried.

I glanced at Carly and shook my head. This was totally abnormal behaviour for Nikki, and I was glad when I heard Spencer's voice from the hallway.

"Well then, maybe you shouldn't have any," he said,

coming around the corner dressed in jeans and a sweater. The scent of his cologne combined with the sound of domination in his voice made my knees weak. "Ready to go?"

I nodded.

"Carly, please. Can I have two desserts?" Nikki questioned as she climbed up on the kitchen chair.

Spencer looked at me and smiled. "What did Ainsley tell Carly?" Spencer questioned.

"She said maybe."

Spencer looked over at me and then back to Nikki. "No, I don't think she did. Now you behave yourself for Carly, and if there is mention of two desserts again, I will tell Carly you can't have any. We've got to get going," Spencer said, placing a kiss on the top of Nikki's head.

"Awww, Daddy," Nikki cried.

"Call us if you need anything," I whispered to Carly, then I hugged her. "Thank you for doing this."

"No problem. Have fun house hunting!" Carly called before sitting down beside Nikki, distracting her from us leaving while helping her cut the paper.

We had seen two houses already, and now were just pulling into the driveway of the third. Immediately, I could see us living in this one. The front of the house was beautifully landscaped, and I was already in love with the wrap-around porch. Spencer cut the engine, and we climbed out of the car just as our agent pulled in behind us.

"All right, so this one has four bedrooms, 2.5 baths, and a fully landscaped backyard complete with a pool and hot tub," Nick said, walking with us up to the front door and unlocking it. "It's also currently empty, so that means there is way more flexibility on the move-in date," he said as he opened the door.

We stepped inside, and immediately I fell in love. The entire house had been renovated, and they had turned one bedroom into an office, complete with built-in shelves and a desk. We walked through the entire house, then went into the backyard, which was beautiful.

"Nick, could you leave us alone for a few minutes? Give us a chance to speak in private?" Spencer questioned, shoving his phone back into his pocket.

"Sure, of course. I'll be in the kitchen," Nick responded.

The back door closed, and Spencer and I stood alone in the backyard. I hadn't been able to read Spencer's thoughts at all as we'd walked through each of the homes. It would have been easier had I been able to. At least I would have known not to get my hopes up.

"Well?" he questioned, coming over to me. "Thoughts?"

Immediately, my stomach knotted. I didn't know if he liked any of them, and I certainly didn't want to be the one who decided. This was supposed to be a joint decision. This house, though, was perfect.

"Did you like any of them?" I asked.

"I did. I'd like you to share your thoughts with me. I want to know what you think!"

Spencer had done all the work. He'd contacted Nick, he'd booked the appointments, he'd chosen the houses to look at. I had no clue how much any of them even were, or what we could afford, but each of them would have fit my father's house and Spencer's current house inside of them at least four times. I let out a sigh and shifted my weight from one foot to the other.

"Do we need to keep looking?" he questioned.

I'd been quiet the entire afternoon, doing my best to hide my excitement in any of the houses we'd been in. "I don't know."

"You don't know?" Spencer questioned. "From the look on your face walking through this place, I was sure you'd have attacked me by now and told me to get this one." Spencer shrugged. "I guess I'll tell Nick to keep searching." He turned to head back inside.

"How did you know I loved this one?" I questioned, just as Spencer placed his hand on the doorknob.

Spencer walked over to me and pulled me into his arms. "There have only been a handful of times I've seen that look on your face. You know, the one you have when you are completely in love with something… or someone," he said, bringing his hand to my cheek before he leaned in and met my lips with his. "The one that is on your face right this minute, actually," he whispered, nipping at my lower lip.

"Oh, I didn't know I had a look." I could feel the heat rise to my cheeks.

"It's the same look you get when I kiss my way down your body…" he murmured, running his fingers down my side to where my shirt met the waist of my jeans, his fingers grazing my bare skin.

I closed my eyes. "Stop it," I whispered, grabbing his hand as a shiver of excitement ran through my body. "Concentrate." I giggled.

"Oh, I am concentrating," he whispered in my ear, the feel of his breath sending chills through me. "Shall we put an offer in?"

I pulled out of his arms and looked around the backyard. The house was perfect, and it would accommodate our family nicely. "How much is it?" I questioned.

"That is not something you need to worry about. All I need to know is a yes or a no."

I nodded my head and smiled, excitement building inside of me. "Put an offer in," I said, leaning in and meeting his lips.

"Okay, I'll go talk to Nick. Call Carly and make sure everything is going okay with Nikki. Let her know that once we finish here that we are going out to celebrate."

WE STOOD at the hostess desk at The Porterhouse restaurant, waiting to be seated. Spencer had worked with Nick to come up with an offer on the house, and once they had finished, Nick told us we would hear from him soon.

"Was Nikki behaving when you called?" Spencer questioned as we waited.

"Yes, Carly said she only asked for double dessert three more times." I giggled.

"That child. I'm going to have to talk to Brittany about her behaviour. However, I remember when she pulled that on you the first couple of times you watched her."

"Yeah, only I fell for it because someone didn't warn me. This is different though. Her attitude toward everything is bad." I shrugged.

Spencer pulled me to his side. "I'll talk to Nikki and Brittany. However, what can I say? Kids will be kids." He chuckled.

"Right this way, Mr. Brooks," the hostess said, grabbing two menus before leading the way to the table.

We'd been seated for about ten minutes when we heard a familiar voice greet us at the table. Spencer's eyes met mine, and we both looked up at the same time to see his ex-wife, Brittany, holding an order pad.

"Well, well, if it isn't my two most favourite people in the entire world, my ex-husband and the slutty babysitter." She sneered.

I swallowed hard and looked at Spencer, who sat there looking at her with a straight face. I'd seen this exact face before, at the office the other day when he had a meeting with an employee who had broken company rules. It hadn't ended pretty, and I suspected this little interaction wouldn't end well either.

"Brittany, I'll care for you not to allow personal issues to interfere with your job," he said, clearing his throat.

"Who the fuck are you? My boss?" she whispered. "I'll care for you not to allow personal issues to interfere with your job," she mimicked.

Immediately, I saw where Nikki's behaviour was coming from, and I glanced to Spencer to see if he recognized it too. Spencer looked at me out of the corner of his eye.

"We'll both have the fillet, baked potato with a side of mushrooms for myself, and asparagus for Ainsley. And two waters," he said, closing the menu and grabbing mine, handing them both to Brittany.

She glared at him. "Still ordering for the woman, I see. Does she not have a mouth?"

I lowered my eyes to the table when I felt her steely stare on me.

"Oh wait, of course she does, otherwise you'd never would have fucked her."

I could still feel her stare. I wanted to hide; her words mortified me.

"Brittany," Spencer said through his clenched jaw.

With a smirk on her face, she marched off and across the restaurant.

"Oh God, Spencer, I can't do this. Can we please just leave?"

Spencer shook his head. "You can do this. You're stronger than her. She is trying to get me to cause a scene in here. I didn't know she worked here. She probably got a job here because she knows this is where I do most of my lunch meetings with the executives. I was late one day when I dropped Nikki off and I mentioned it to her. Since she knows that, she also knows this would be the worst place for me to lose my patience."

"I know. I just can't do this." I could feel the tears burning behind my eyes. "I can't have her say things like that about me."

He reached across the table and took my hand in his. He was about to say something when two glasses of water were dropped onto the table in front of us, and I glanced up to see Brittany once again glaring at me.

"Where is our daughter, Spencer?" she said, placing her hands on her hips.

"At home… with a sitter." Spencer met my eyes, reassuring me with a look.

"Oh, how convenient. You know you really have a thing for babysitters, don't you? Let me ask you, are you screwing her as well?"

I glanced over at Spencer. His jaw was tight, and I could see the vein in the side of his neck throbbing. The look on his face was one of pure anger. I'd never seen him like this. I gripped his hand a little tighter to remind him of where we were when someone called out to Brittany. She whipped around and took off over to another table.

"Are you okay?" I questioned, as I noticed he'd followed her movements.

"She is just doing this to get at me. I won't lie, it's working."

"Perhaps you should speak to the manager," I

suggested, not wanting Spencer to take matters into his own hands and lose his temper.

"Oh, I plan on that," Spencer said, gripping my hand tighter as he stopped a server walking by the table, asking to speak with the manager.

"I'm just going to use the washroom," I mumbled as I stood up.

"It's over there," Spencer said, nodding in the washroom's direction.

"I'll be right back."

I'd taken a few moments to gather myself before I opened the door to the stall and approached the sink. I ran my hands under the warm water and lathered the soap as I looked at myself in the mirror. I could see the tension and worry on my face. I let out a breath and grabbed a paper towel to dry my hands. I pulled my mascara from my purse and was about to apply it when the door to the washroom opened. My heart started to pound when I saw Brittany walk in.

She said nothing. I frowned as I watched her bend down and look under the stalls. Then she turned to me. Her eyes ran the length of my body before they met mine.

"You think Spencer is marrying you because he loves you, don't you?"

I stood there, my heart racing as she waited for my response. When I said nothing, she let out a small laugh.

"I thought the same thing when I was pregnant with Nikki. Boy, was I wrong. Don't get too comfortable, because when the next best thing comes along, Spencer will be gone."

"That's not true," I said, my voice cracking.

"It's not? Let me guess, he isn't interested in anyone else. He only wants you to be happy and secure."

I blinked hard. I could feel the tears burning behind my eyes as her words hit me. Words Spencer himself had said to me time and time again.

"You'll find out. Trust me."

I wanted to fire back at her. I wanted to ask her if she didn't want me to have him, then why did she cheat on him? I stood there, courage growing inside me and just as I was about to, the door opened, and a woman came walking in. She stopped in her tracks and looked at both of us clearly sensing the tension between us. I looked at the woman, and that was when I dashed out the door. I made my way over to the table where Spencer stood speaking with, I assumed, the manager. I slid into my seat and wiped my eyes.

"What is it?" Spencer demanded. The gentlemen he was speaking with turned and looked at me.

"It's nothing," I whispered, wiping my eyes again without looking at Spencer.

"She approached you, didn't she?" he questioned. "In the bathroom." Anger lined Spencer's face.

I looked up to meet Spencer's eyes, only to see that he and the man he'd been speaking to were now looking over toward the washrooms, just in time to see Brittany step out onto the floor. She made brief eye contact with them before she cleared an empty table.

"I'll take care of it, Spencer," the man said, shaking his hand. "Again, I am sorry about this. Please enjoy your meal tonight. It's on the house."

Within seconds, the manager had pulled Brittany from the floor. Spencer looked at me, worry lining his face. "I'm sorry about this," he said. "Now, what did she say to you?"

It took me only a few seconds before a tear escaped my eyes. I knew deep in my heart that what she said wasn't true. I knew their past; I knew why they'd divorced, but what I didn't know was why Brittany was doing this. I decided not to tell Spencer what she'd said. I just wished this was going to be the last time I ever laid eyes on Brittany.

SPENCER

I was exhausted as I sat at my desk going over reports the next morning. It had been a long and somewhat stressful night for the pair of us after we'd returned from dinner. I'd put Nikki to bed, while Ainsley had crawled into the soaker tub and had a hot bath. Afterward, we'd sat up late, talking about what had happened with Brittany at the restaurant. Ainsley had burst into tears many times as I tried to get her to talk to me about what Brittany said in the washroom, but she refused to tell me. Instead, I could only imagine all the cruel things she'd said, and even though she assured me she knew what Brittany told her wasn't true, I was still upset that I wasn't able to defend myself. She finally curled up in my arms and fell asleep, but I stayed awake for hours, staring at the ceiling.

I heard a soft knock on my office door. I looked up to see Ainsley holding a steaming cup of coffee, a soft smile on her face.

"You are a godsend," I said, throwing down the report I'd been going over as she set the mug down on the warming plate she'd gotten me last week, after I'd complained that I kept drinking cold coffee.

She said nothing. Instead, she nodded and turned, heading toward the door.

"Ainsley? Is everything okay?" I questioned.

"Yep." She smiled, but I knew it wasn't a real one. She appeared to be far more upset than she was when we'd left for the office this morning and that concerned me.

"Ainsley, shut my door and come over here."

She stopped. I watched as she clenched her fists at her side and then shut the door and approached my desk. "What?" she demanded, crossing her arms in front of her chest, completely closing me off.

I pushed my chair away from my desk and studied her. "Come over here," I said, nodding to the space between me and the desk.

She let out a sigh and reluctantly walked over to me, wedging herself between me and my desk. She leaned against it and looked down at me. "What is it?"

"I think I'm the one who should ask you that."

She let out a deep sigh. "There were messages for me

this morning… from Brittany," she said through clenched teeth, her eyes glistening with tears.

"I see. Why didn't you forward them to me?" I asked, doing my best to remain calm. I'd had it with that woman.

"Just better to delete them." She shrugged. "No need for the both of us to hear her cruel words." She looked away so I could no longer see her eyes.

I shook my head and placed my hands on her hips. "No, you should have sent them to me."

"Did you know she got fired last night?" she questioned. "She left that in one message and how she blames me for it."

I nodded. "I knew. She deserved it."

"I know, but in her message, she is blaming me."

"That is ridiculous. She deserved it, and you know it."

Ainsley slowly nodded her head and wiped her eyes.

"Ainsley, I want to know what else is bothering you."

I studied her face. Her eyes watered, and soon they filled with tears and she broke down. She brought her hands up to her face and sobbed into them. I placed my hands on her hips and rested my head on her abdomen. I closed my eyes and felt her fingers run through my hair.

"All of this just hurts so much," she cried.

"All of what? Brittany? Don't give her that kind of power."

I watched as she wiped the tears from her eyes. "Everything, Spencer. The venues won't call us back. My best friend keeps asking me to think about what it will be like to be married to you in twenty years, and your ex-wife hates me. I still don't have a dress. It's just…" She let out a huge sob.

"Brittany hates me too. Honestly, I think she hates herself as well as everyone else." I chuckled as I pulled her onto my lap and leaned back in my chair, pulling her into my chest.

"It just seems like she is…dare I say it… jealous."

"Ha, she can be jealous. Remember, it was I who found another man between her legs. She has no right to be jealous or to say a damn word about us."

"I know."

"You know what I think?"

"What's that?"

"That most of this is all just baby hormones. Take a breath…" I said in a calm voice as I ran my fingers through her hair and looked her in the eyes.

"No, it's not." She sniffled.

"Oh, I think it is. You aren't this sensitive, that much I know. Perhaps it would be a good idea for you to take a day off. I think you need to be by yourself to relax. It's been a lot, yes, but it's not as bad as you're thinking," I said in a low voice.

"It's not?"

I shook my head. "No, we've only had a call into a couple of venues for a week. I'm not worried. Everything is going to work out fine. I promise. As for the calls from Brittany, I will block her number from your extension. I will direct all her calls to me and me only. As for Carly, well, she'll learn when she meets someone."

Ainsley met my eyes, leaned in, and kissed me softly on the lips, while running her fingers through my hair. "Thank you," she whispered.

"You're welcome." I kissed her mouth hard as she sat on my lap. I hated seeing tears on her face. Our lips parted and I met her eyes, "I love you." I whispered.

"I love you too." Her hands rested on my shoulders, as I kissed her again.

I allowed my hands to travel up underneath her skirt, I was expecting to feel the silkiness of her panties, but they weren't there.

"Okay," she said, laughing as she grabbed my arm and pushed my hand away. "You need to behave." She giggled, sliding off my lap and adjusting her skirt.

"Are you not wearing any panties?" I questioned, my cock instantly growing hard at the thought. I remembered the last time that had happened. I'd ended up with her on the top of desk, legs spread, while I devoured her pussy until she screamed my name.

The light blush on her cheeks said it all, and my cock ached as she turned around, her perfect ass in my face as she adjusted and smoothed her skirt. She wasn't getting away from me. Instead, I grabbed her hips and stood up behind her, pulling her body against me.

"Spencer," She whispered, her voice cracking.

"Put your hands on my desk," I commanded in a hushed but firm tone. I didn't move while I waited for her to do what I said.

"Spencer, everyone is here. We can't do this now.,"

I leaned over her, bringing my lips to her ear. The smell of her, combined with the fact that I knew she wasn't wearing anything under that skirt, went straight to my cock. "Put your hands on my desk," I growled.

Her cheeks darkened as she did as I asked. I walked around to the door and turned the little lock I'd had installed after she'd started working here and turned back to see her standing there with her eyes closed. I smiled to myself and walked back around behind her. She sucked in a breath as I ran my hands up her sides, around to the front and held her full breasts in my hand, running my thumbs over her already hardened nipples.

"Remember what happened the last time you weren't wearing anything under your skirt?" I whispered.

"I do." She let out a breath as she pushed her chest into my hands. She was already breathing hard and I'd barely touched her. I kept one breast in my hand and reached down and pulled at her skirt, lifting it up over her ass. I ran my hand over her bare skin and reached around in front, my fingers finding that small bundle of nerves. She let out a soft moan as I kissed the back of her neck.

"Do you do this to me on purpose?" I questioned as I pressed up against her so she could feel my arousal.

"No." Her voice trembled as I continued gently rubbing her.

She was about to move her hands, but I shook my head. "Keep your hands there," I whispered. My cock strained against the fabric of my suit pants. I opened the zipper, allowing for some relief before continuing.

"Bend forward," I whispered, "and keep quiet."

She lowered herself down on the desk a little, and I gripped my cock, pulling it from my boxers and lining myself up with her opening. I slid myself into her and we both let out a moan. I could feel her tightening around me already as I thrust myself deeply into her again and again.

I reached around her, stroking that little bundle of nerves as I continued pumping into her. She grabbed my other hand, interlocking her fingers with mine. "Keep quiet," I whispered as I sucked her earlobe between my lips.

"Spencer."

"Shhh baby, just feel me, know how much I love you." I whispered, nipping at her neck.

"I'm gonna come," she cried a little louder than she should be.

"Shhh…" I pumped into her harder, working my hand faster between her legs. Her hand gripped mine tighter. I could feel her beginning to tighten and pulse around my cock, her once muted cries now audible as she let herself go. I took her mouth with mine, silencing her, as I pumped into her the last few times before I let go.

Both of us breathing hard, I held her in my arms as we both came down. Then I slipped myself from her and pulled her skirt down over her ass. She turned around and looked up at me, a satisfied yet tired look on her face. I zipped up my pants and then leaned onto my desk as I kissed her lips.

"You better fix your shirt and your hair," I whispered, nipping at her lower lip. "Don't want anyone to see how beautiful you are after I just fucked you." I winked.

Her cheeks went a deep pink again. "And you better tuck your shirt in," she answered back.

We both took a minute, adjusted our clothing so we looked suitable again. "So, you're taking the day off correct?" I questioned as I reached for my wallet that sat on the corner of my desk and flipped it open, pulling out my credit card.

"Ainsley?"

"Hmmm?" She looked up at me, then down at my hand.

"You're taking the rest of the day off. Go do some wedding things. Get your dress, have a massage. Enjoy your day."

She looked at me. "I thought you said we would do the dress thing together."

I shook my head. "It's bad luck, remember?"

"But I have work things to complete before I do any of that today," she argued, pushing my hand away.

"Yes, I know you do. However, most of those things can be done later tonight, from home. I want you to take the day." I walked around my desk and over to her. I slid the card into her hand and leaned in, taking her lips with mine. "Go, before you get me all worked up again. There is nothing more that I want to do than eat that sweet pussy for hours, but I need to concentrate," I said, gripping her ass and kissing her lips one more time.

She slipped the card from my hand and looked up at me. "Thank you," she whispered.

"I'll see you at home tonight. Drive careful."

AINSLEY

"AINSLEY AND CARLY." The barista called as she placed our coffee down on the counter.

I stopped talking as we both stepped forward and picked them up.

"Thank you," I called, waving to the girl as we made our way out the door and over to the only bridal shop in this shopping area. We stepped inside to be greeted by a sea of white dresses.

"This is a little overwhelming," I said, looking around, wondering where the hell to start.

"Do you have any idea what it is you're looking for?" Carly asked as we removed our shoes as the sign inside the door asked.

"I have a couple of ideas of what I want," I said, removing my jacket and hanging it up on the coat rack.

"I found the perfect dress in a magazine. Trina told me they may have it here or at another store."

"Well, let's see if we can find it, shall we?" Carly said, taking a few steps into the shop.

"Oh, girls, no coffee on the floor." I turned in time to see a panicked woman who worked at the shop rushing toward us. "Welcome, ladies. Sorry, there is no coffee on the floor. Now, what can I help you with today?"

I let out a sigh and looked at Carly, who smiled smugly at me, then slipped my cup from my hand and took a seat on the couch just inside the door. "I'll just sit here. Go browse. See what she can help you with today."

I looked back at Carly and stifled a laugh as the woman pulled me toward a rack of dresses and began showing them to me one by one. By the time I got to the third rack, I was annoyed. This woman's attitude was the pits, and she was showing me everything I told her I didn't want. When I glanced over at Carly, I saw boredom lining her face as she flipped through her phone.

"Do you not like any of these, either?" the woman asked.

I shook my head. "No but thank you. I think I am just going to go somewhere else."

The woman gave me an irritated smile as I left her standing there and made my way back over to Carly, who stood up with an excited look on her face.

"Tired of Miss Stuck-up?" She giggled, handing me my coffee. "No coffee on the floor," Carly mimicked.

I laughed. "Yes, let's go somewhere else."

Within minutes, we were back in the car and headed to a shop that Trina had suggested. This time, we left our drinks in the car and headed inside to find a very relaxed atmosphere. A couple of groups of girls were there shopping as well, laughing and giggling at the dresses as they pulled them off the racks. I smiled at Carly, and together we made our way into the store. The first rack of dresses we came to I pulled out one dress and held it up. It was almost what I was looking for.

"Have you even set a date yet?" Carly asked as she pulled a dress off a rack and looked at it.

"No, not yet. We are still waiting to hear from the venues we contacted. We need to know what dates they have first. I think we sent requests to six places, and since it's such short notice, we kind of have to play by their rules."

"Okay then, let me rephrase my question. When are you trying to get married?"

I pulled out a dress and quickly changed my mind, then looked over at my best friend. "You know… in the next six weeks. For obvious reasons," I said, placing my hand on my belly.

Carly shoved the dress she'd been looking at back into the pile and turned to me with a frown on her face.

"You mean in the next six weeks, so the pregnancy isn't obvious? Is that your idea or his?"

I immediately stopped looking at the dresses and turned to my best friend. "Why did you ask me like that?" I questioned.

"Like what?"

"If it were his idea or mine? You know, Spencer is a good man, despite what you and some others might think. I know you've had challenges with us, and I know you aren't his biggest fan, but I love him."

"I didn't mean it in any way, Ainsley. I guess I just meant it was a good reason. Was it your idea or his?" she said, changing the tone of her voice before turning back to the dresses in front of her. "Now, what do you think of this one?" she said, pulling out the next dress.

I just about screamed because it was the exact dress I'd bookmarked off the site. "Oh my God, that's it!" I cried, looking at the gorgeous white dress.

"What is it?"

"That's the dress!" I said, taking it from her and looking around for someone to allow me access to the changing room.

Half an hour later, I stood at the counter with Carly by my side as they completed the order for the dress. Lucky for me, they had one close to my size in stock, which made alterations much cheaper and easier. I paid for the dress and then we made our way to the car.

"When does the dress come in again?"

"Should be here by Friday," I sang. The feeling of removing one weight off my shoulders felt amazing.

"That's good."

"Yes, it will be perfect, since we do not know where the wedding is going to be held. That dress will work perfectly both at an inside and outside venue. I cannot wait for Spencer to see it!"

"Ainsley, you can't show Spencer!"

"Why not?"

"What do you mean? It's bad luck, like super bad luck. On second thought, you should wear it home. I'll wait for you here. Just take the one they have inside."

"Ugh, you aren't helping. Let's go." I giggled.

We'd just hopped on the freeway and began driving as Carly cracked open the bag of chips she purchased from the store before we left. "Want any?" she questioned.

"No, I'm good, thanks," I said, concentrating on the road in front of me. There was no way I could stuff my face with chips now that I needed to make sure I could fit into that wedding dress once the alterations were done.

"Oh, we should also work on the baby shower invites," Carly suggested.

"I wasn't planning on having a baby shower." I shrugged. "Besides, it's super early."

"There is no way on this planet that this baby will not

get a shower from her Aunt Carly. I mean, just because I don't agree with your relationship decisions doesn't mean that a baby needs to be punished." She giggled. "We'll just invite a few people from school and our parents, of course."

"Okay." I sighed. "Whatever you say. When did you want to have that?"

"Oh, after the wedding, which was why I wanted to know the date, silly. I already bought the cards. I just need to let people know when to RSVP by."

"I don't know, let's do it in July. Pick a date."

"All right! July 15th. It's a Saturday," Carly answered as she checked the calendar on her phone. "I already sent you an invitation. It should go directly into your calendar."

"Perfect. Can't wait." I sighed, "When are you planning to send out the invites?" I questioned.

"Soon. I mean it will be in the middle of summer, so I'd like to give people the opportunity to go. You know, summer holidays and all."

"Whatever, do me one little favour please." I knew there was no way to stop her. Her mind was made up, the invites were going because she'd already decided that she was throwing me a shower.

"What is that?"

"Do not invite my father and Joan until after Spencer and I speak to them."

"I thought you guys spoke already. You said your father was down about getting married."

"Yes, we did. About the wedding, that is all," I muttered.

Carly stopped eating, and out of the corner of my eye, I knew she was staring at me. "You mean you didn't tell him everything?"

I shook my head. "No, we figured we'd drop that bomb after the wedding. Besides, it's so early. We really shouldn't be telling anyone."

"Ainsley, why?" Carly cried. "Why are you being this way? It's your father."

"I'm being that way because it's too early. I haven't even had my appointment with this OB/GYN my doctor is referring me to. So please, do as I ask." I could feel myself on the verge of tears as I looked at my best friend.

"Okay, okay," Carly said, shoving her hand back into the bag of chips.

SPENCER

One week later

IT WAS ALREADY after six when I made my way across the parking lot to my car. I shoved my laptop bag and the pile of reports I still needed to go over in the back seat and climbed in, starting the engine. I was about to back out of the spot when my phone vibrated. I pulled it from my breast pocket to see that my brother Max had texted. Instead of responding, I dialed his number and waited while his voice came over the line.

"You got my email?" Max questioned.

"I did. Haven't looked at the attachment yet. I'm just on my way home."

"Gotcha. Well, first I'd like to say that I'm sorry I couldn't make it to the engagement thing. You know how it is."

I let out a breath. "No, Max, I don't know how it is."

"Well, you know, things just sort of crept up." He chuckled.

I frowned. "Things sort of crept up?" I repeated. "Let me guess, a woman?"

I knew my brother well—too well, to be honest.

"Yeah, and the situation, it was, shall we say, unavoidable? Besides, it was only an engagement party. It's not like it was an enormous deal, like the wedding."

This was Max. However, it was a big deal. It was a big deal to both Ainsley and me. I cleared my throat and thought a moment before speaking. "Max, you know, the least you could do is show a little support. Especially since I just handed you an enormous opportunity, basically on a silver platter. I gave you the reins to oversee the Denver office, when it should have gone to one of my senior executives working right under me. I pride myself on promoting and hiring from within first. Instead, I somehow took pity on my brother, who's fucked up more than the average person, only to have him spit in my face."

"Come on, Spencer, I didn't spit in your face." Max huffed.

"Whatever, Max. You didn't even send back the

RSVP." I didn't really have the energy to deal with this phone call right now. I was tired and hungry and still had a few hours of work to complete before the meeting tomorrow morning. "Listen, I'll call you in the morning. Be prepared to go over all your opening numbers tomorrow on the call."

"Tomorrow?" Max questioned.

I was silent for a moment as I stopped at the traffic light. I ran my hand over my face. "Yes, Max, tomorrow's meeting. Nine, does it sound familiar?"

"Yeah, yep, I'll talk to you then."

I hung up the phone and turned up the radio just as my phone rang again.

"Hey, Spencer!" Nick's voice came over the line.

"Hey, Nick! Any news?"

"They accepted the offer. We set the closing date as you asked. I also have a few appointments lined up to show your place. Honestly, it should sell fast. I've had lots of interest so far."

"Perfect, thanks, Nick. Whatever needs to be signed, just fax it to my home office. Also, can you send me the dates you need to show our place? I want to make sure we have everything in place."

"Can do. Talk to you soon."

I hopped on the highway, turned the radio up, and made my way home. Twenty minutes later, I pulled into our driveway, gathered my items from the back seat, and headed to the door. I'd just slid my key in the lock and opened the door to be greeted by Carly walking behind Nikki.

"Daddy!" Nikki cried.

"Shhh… Ainsley is sleeping, remember?" Carly whispered. "Take your crayons and colouring book into the kitchen."

Nikki looked at me and then hung her head and stomped into the kitchen. "Why is Ainsley asleep?" I asked, dropping my stuff inside the door, and heading up the stairs, glancing in the living room to see Ainsley sound asleep under a blanket on the couch.

"She just passed out on the couch. We were sitting talking about the baby shower. I was telling her I'd mailed out all the invitations, and when I looked over, she was out." Carly shrugged.

"Is she all right?" I asked, taking another look at Ainsley. "Baby shower?" I questioned when I realized what she'd said.

"Yes, baby shower. I planned one for her."

"I see," I said, looking at Ainsley. "Don't you think it's a little early to be inviting people to a baby shower?"

"God, you sound just like Ainsley." Carly shrugged.

"Yes, we haven't even seen the OB/GYN yet, and besides, we aren't even married yet!"

"Yes, but we aren't having the baby shower until July, and I wanted to make sure people save the date."

I rolled my eyes. "Who did you invite?"

"Don't worry. I will tell you who I didn't invite, and that is Ainsley's father and Jane."

"For the love of God." I breathed under my breath, praying that she was only joking with me now. "I'm concerned," I said.

"Why?"

"It's not like her to sleep in the middle of the day. Was she feeling okay?"

"She was feeling fine when we returned today. However, if you wake her, I will hurt you. Got it, Big Guy? She probably just needs some rest."

"Yeah, I got it, but is she okay?" I questioned again, worried that perhaps something happened today to make her not feel well. I knew that her and Ainsley were going to the bridal shop again for sizing and to pick out a bridesmaid dress for Carly. Maybe it was all the baby shower talk, or that Carly had apparently sent out invites. Then there was the thought that perhaps she had run into Brittany again.

"My God, what do you mean is she okay? You knocked her up! She may be twenty, but it seems your baby is sucking the life out of my best friend. Also, be forewarned, you may have ruined that body forever!"

I rolled my eyes and let out a sigh. "Yes, I knocked her up, fine. However, women give birth every day, Carly. Her body will not be ruined."

Carly shrugged. "All I'm saying is I hope you aren't too attached to it."

"For the love of God, Carly. You do realize that I am in love with the person, not the body. The body is just a bonus. It's not a requirement."

"Huh?"

I looked at the shock on Carly's face and smiled inwardly at myself. "Exactly what I said. The body is a bonus, not a requirement. I'm in love with Ainsley."

Carly was quiet for a moment as she stared at me. "God… make me want to puke."

I smirked to myself as she turned her back to me and slipped her feet into her shoes. "I'm going home now, before you begin growing on me. Can't have that happening or the next thing I know I'll be rooting for the pair of you."

Just then, Nikki appeared in the kitchen doorway and attached herself to my leg. "That's probably a good plan," I said.

"Just don't you wake her up. I'll keep you guys updated as to the RSVPs for the baby shower."

"Great." I chuckled to myself as she pulled the door open. "Good night, Carly. See you soon." As much as she annoyed me, she was growing on me. However, I was concerned with the slew of phone calls Ainsley may get once her friends began getting invites to a baby shower.

When the door clicked shut, I turned to Nikki. "She is crazy," I said, crossing my eyes and sticking out my tongue. Nikki burst into a fit of giggles.

"What do you say you help me with dinner? We have a surprise for Ainsley," I whispered.

"We do? What is it?" she whispered, her eyes growing wide.

"It's a surprise for you too. Now come into the kitchen and we will quietly get things ready. Plus, you can help me put this up," I said, producing a package containing a banner.

Nikki jumped up and down and then turned and ran into the kitchen while I followed behind her.

AINSLEY

I WOKE up to the sound of music and Spencer's voice in the kitchen, then the aroma of garlic bread hit my nose, making my stomach growl. I looked at my phone to see it was almost eight. I must have fallen asleep, I thought to myself as I kicked the blanket off me. I got up off the couch, stretched, and made my way into the kitchen. Nikki was sitting on the counter, helping Spencer. "Okay, sprinkle the cheese into the pot," he said.

I smiled, watching the two of them. Nikki let out a little laugh as she sprinkled cheese into the pot.

"Sorry, I must have drifted off," I said.

Spencer turned and smiled in my direction, while Nikki added in another handful of cheese into the pot he was stirring. "All right, miss, that is enough cheese." He chuckled, putting the pot to the back of the stove and grabbing Nikki, placing her down on the floor.

"Don't look behind you, Ainsley." Nikki giggled, covering her mouth with her hands.

"Why not? What's behind me?" I questioned.

Spencer walked over and pulled me into his arms, kissing my cheek. "A surprise," he whispered.

"Can she see now, Daddy?" Nikki cried. "Please."

Spencer looked from me down to Nikki and let out a sigh. "Well, I guess," he said, turning me around.

I looked up to see a banner on the wall that read 'Congratulations on your New Home!"

I couldn't help but stare at the words on the sign. Thoughts of us owning our own place, the one we chose together, brought tears to my eyes. I was so excited. I could feel Spencer watching me, and I quickly wiped away the tear that sat at the corner of my eye before it slid down my cheek.

"You happy?" Spencer questioned.

I nodded my head. "Yes, very much so. I'm very excited," I said, throwing my arms around his neck and hugging him.

"As am I. Now we should eat," he said, meeting my lips. "I'm sure you're starved."

I nodded, wrapping my arm around Nikki as she hugged my leg. I'd just gotten her settled in her chair when I remembered I still had Spencer's credit card in my purse from a week ago. I reached for my bag that sat on the counter and opened my wallet, taking the card out.

"Before I forget," I said, holding the card out for him to take. "I should have given this back to you last week. I totally forgot."

He shook his head, his hands full. "Keep it. Honestly, you are going to need it for the wedding, especially if I am in a meeting. Plus, we now have a house to furnish." He winked. "I'll see about ordering you a spousal card as well. But for now, use it at your leisure."

I softly smiled and slid the card back into my wallet, then took the salad from Spencer and put it on the table while he brought over the pasta and garlic bread.

"How did the dress fitting go?" Spencer questioned as he began plating dinner.

"Good, just a few minor alterations." I smiled. "I go back for another one in a couple of weeks. I can't wait for you to see it."

"I want to see it too!" Nikki said.

"Of course you'll see it, probably before Daddy." I winked. "Especially since you are going to need a flower girl dress," I said, tickling her tummy.

She let out a loud giggle. "Really?"

"Yes, really." I winked.

"Carly told me she is planning a baby shower."

"Yes, she sort of took that upon herself. I tried to tell her it was too early, but she insisted on sending out the invites."

"Yes, she seemed proud of herself as well. Has anyone messaged you yet?"

"No. I'm afraid of that starting though." I shrugged. "It's too early to tell people."

"Agreed."

"Invites are out, though, so I'm not sure what I am supposed to do." I shrugged, pinching the bridge of my nose to try and stop the headache that was coming. "Guess I'll just cross that bridge when I come to it."

We all sat down to eat. The conversation during dinner was about the house. Nikki was excited that she was going to have a bigger room, and when she found out that there was a pool in the backyard, all she wanted to do was get into her suit and go swimming, which caused Spencer and I both to laugh.

Once dinner was over, I gave Nikki a bath and got her tucked into bed while Spencer went over some reports, then I too got into my pajamas. I took a few minutes and cleaned up the kitchen while I made a cup of tea and then settled into the living room, resting my head as my favourite jazz album played over the stereo. My dad would be returning from his trip with Jane tonight. I was excited to see him in the morning.

I looked down at my hands while sitting on the couch and noticed my fingers were swollen. I pulled at my engagement ring, finally feeling it slip from my finger, and set it on the side table. Spencer and I had talked about when to tell him about the baby. We'd agreed to do it before the wedding, and we figured that once they returned from their trip, and we'd seen the OB/GYN, we'd tell them. That way, Jane could help with Carly's baby shower.

Spencer came upstairs and glanced in the living room at me. "I'm just gonna grab a coffee. I fear it's going to be a late night for me," he sighed. "I still have a lot of things to go over."

"I'd offer to help, but I'm exhausted, so I'll probably crawl into bed soon," I replied, getting up and following him into the kitchen where I ran my swollen hands under water and dried them. "I hate going to bed alone," I said, wrapping my arms around his waist and pressing my body into his back. My hands traveled down to his hips, and I was just about to run my hand over the bulge I already knew was growing when the doorbell rang.

"I'll get it," I said, releasing my hold on him.

"Just check who it is first," he cautioned.

"I will." I walked to the door and glanced out the side window to see my father standing there. I pulled the door open and opened my arms, expecting a hug. Instead, he pushed past me and stormed into the house, shutting the door behind him.

"Where is he?" he demanded. "I think I might kill him this time."

The crazed look on his face scared me. "Dad, what is it? What's wrong?" I questioned, my heart beating hard in my chest. I looked down at his hand to see a torn, open envelope.

My stomach churned at the thought of what that envelope contained, and I silently hoped it wasn't the invitation to the baby shower.

"Ainsley, what is it?" Spencer demanded, coming out of the kitchen, alarm in his voice.

"I really hope this is some kind of sick joke." My father's voice boomed throughout the entryway as he threw down the envelope he'd been carrying. I instantly recognized it as the envelope that had contained the baby shower invitation.

Carly had promised me she wouldn't give Dad his until later. Why would she have done this I wondered and then it hit, I'd sent her with some mail we'd had for him, and maybe it was accidentally put in his mailbox along with the other envelopes.

"Jon, just come in and we will talk this through," Spencer said, trying to calm my father down.

"How dare you? Is this what this wedding is about?" my father demanded.

"Jon, please, let's just talk about this like grown adults," Spencer repeated, keeping his voice at a level tone.

My dad glared at Spencer and then looked at me, disappointment flooding his face. Then he climbed up the stairs and followed Spencer into the kitchen. I'd just stepped into the kitchen while Spencer was getting ready to pour a coffee for my father when I remembered I hadn't ripped down the banner Spencer and Nikki had made. I did my best to grab my father's attention, but he'd already seen the banner, his face growing serious and angry.

"What the hell is that?" he questioned, looking toward the banner.

Immediately, I looked at Spencer, and I covered my mouth to keep the sobs from starting. Spencer gently shook his head, telling me not to say anything as he approached the table.

"Jon, we need to talk," he said.

"No shit, we need to talk. I agreed to you guys dating, and now marriage. However, I feel like you both have blindsided me once again. Now a baby and then this?" he said, pointing to the colourful banner that only a couple of hours ago had brought me joy.

"Daddy, please…"

"Don't Daddy me," my father said, turning his glaring eyes on me.

"Spencer is a good man." I cried.

Spencer reached for me and pulled me in behind him, protecting me from a man I'd known my entire life.

"He wants to marry you for all the wrong reasons, Ainsley. He knows I'd kill him if he impregnated you and then left you to raise that baby all on your own. Isn't that right, Spencer?" my father screamed.

"That is true, Jon. You would kill me. However, that isn't what this is. I'm in love with her. Yes, she is pregnant, and yes, we are getting married, but I planned to ask her to marry me before I even knew about the baby. We bought a house, one we can call our own, but not one of these things has anything to do with one another."

"How would I know that? There seems to be no truth to any of this!" my father shouted. "You know, this is all just going way too fast. Young lady, you need to move back home this minute. I will not allow you to ruin your life. Now go get your things."

My throat got tight, and tears streamed down my face. I was finding it hard to breathe and began panicking at the thought of losing Spencer and Nikki again. I grabbed hold of Spencer's arm as I fought to control the panic I was feeling. Dizziness was setting in.

"Stop it, Ainsley. I will not allow you to move away with this man. I should have stuck to my decision last year. I should have forced you to quit your job. I'm guessing the flu was really morning sickness! I knew I should have immediately made you see the doctor. I never dreamed…"

"Jon, please… just calm down," Spencer commanded as he wrapped his arm around me, trying to get me to calm down. "Ainsley, breathe, baby," he said in a low voice.

Only I couldn't. My chest was so tight I couldn't inhale. The thought of losing Spencer, Nikki, or my father was too much for me to handle as tears streamed freely down my face. Spencer wrapped his arms around me, holding me as I sobbed.

"You know, when I told you to find a younger woman to help you get over Brittany, I honestly never thought it would be my daughter you'd turn to. Sneaking around behind my back. I tried hard to be rational and allow you two to date. I even swallowed my fears of what your intentions were with the proposal, but to find all this out now, I have nothing left to say. I want you home!"

"I was going to talk to you. You shouldn't even have gotten one of those invites until after we spoke."

"When were you planning on talking to me, after the fucking wedding?" my father yelled and stepped forward, taking hold of my upper arm.

Immediately, Spencer grabbed his arm, forcing him to remove his hand from me and stepped in front of me. "Jon, I'm warning you. Don't touch her. Now, I never meant for this to happen this way. I never meant to fall in love with your daughter, but I have zero fucking regrets. Now I will not tell you again. You either calm down and talk to us or you leave our home. This isn't good for Ainsley or the baby."

As the words left Spencer's lips, my heart began racing. At first, I thought maybe my father hadn't heard him, but he stopped moving and stood there, staring at us.

"Tell me I didn't actually hear what I think you said," my father said in a low, controlled voice.

"No, you heard me correctly." Spencer stood there, his back straight, his eyes glued to my father's. He wasn't backing down, not this time. I turned my back away from the two of them, afraid of what was coming next. I left the kitchen, stepping into the living room and up against the wall as the room I'd just left fell completely silent.

I tried to breathe, tried to calm down, but the room spun. Still, there were no words spoken between the two of them. The kitchen was completely silent. I wanted them to yell at one another, to get it over with so we could sit down and talk things through after, like rational adults. Instead, the silence was overwhelming, until I heard my father speak.

"Fine, kick me out. She can stay here tonight, but I want her home in the fucking morning. Got it." The front door opened and then closed. Then, suddenly, Spencer appeared beside me.

"He left?" I questioned, looking at Spencer with tear filled eyes.

Spencer nodded his head. "He did."

Tears poured. "Just like that, he left?"

Spencer grabbed me, pulling me into him, doing his best to comfort me. "It's okay, Ainsley, shhh. I promise things will be fine. I'll speak to him tomorrow."

"I'm not going there." I sobbed. "I'm not leaving us."

"You don't have to." Spencer's arms tightened around me, and I cried harder. I was afraid that with all this backlash that Spencer would soon tire of being the one to hold us together and that he too would give up on us. After all, he didn't need this type of drama in his life.

"Come, we are getting you into bed," he whispered, grabbing the remote for the stereo and silencing the music I'd been enjoying before all the craziness had erupted. He turned out all the lights, then quickly locked the front door and walked with me into the bedroom.

I pulled back the blankets and crawled into bed as tears still ran down my cheeks. My body was exhausted, and as soon as my head hit the pillow, I let out a yawn. He turned his bedside lamp on and then shut off the overhead light, coming around to his side of the bed. He stripped down and slipped under the covers, his warm body sliding behind me, providing me with comfort, while I shivered.

He pulled me into him, my head resting on his shoulder, and wrapped his arm around me. Not another word spoken between us. He just held me tightly against him. I never wanted to leave his arms. I closed my eyes and took comfort in the security and warmth he provided, finally drifting off into a restless sleep.

SPENCER

IT HAD BEEN four days since the confrontation with Ainsley's father.

Ainsley had asked me repeatedly when I planned to speak to Jon. I could see the stress piled not only on her face, but in her actions and body language. However, I took it upon myself to decide it was just best to let things calm down before I tried to speak with him. I wanted things to be as stressless for Ainsley as possible, and I figured letting him calm down first would help the situation and make him more receptive to hearing me out.

Even though I knew this, I was still worried about her. She hadn't been feeling well the last few days, and I was concerned for not only her wellbeing but that of the baby too. I feared if Jon wasn't receptive to talking this through, our situation would become worse, and that would only upset Ainsley more, which was the last thing I wanted.

I got up from my chair and walked over to my printer when my office door opened and Ainsley appeared. "I made myself a tea, thought I'd bring you a coffee," she said, placing the mug down on my desk. She didn't make any eye contact with me, instead, she walked over to the window, looking thoughtfully at the city beyond and saying nothing.

I frowned. "How are you feeling?"

She looked at me over her shoulder. I tried to hide the worry from my face, but I knew she could see it. She turned and went back to silently looking out the window.

"Ainsley, how are you feeling?" I repeated.

"Okay," she answered, then she began quietly humming a song to herself as she looked back out the window. I guessed she was only trying to wash away my fears, but I also knew by the look on her face, and this odd behavior that she wasn't telling me the truth.

"You're sure?" I questioned.

She nodded. "I sent through the reports from Max," she said, picking up a sliver of paper off the floor. "Did you get them?"

I nodded. "I did. I'll be going over them shortly. When do you have your next visit with the doctor?"

"My family doctor booked me in with an OB/GYN. I'm just waiting for the appointment date." She walked over to me and placed her hand on my chest and looked me in the eye. "Please, Spencer, I'm okay. I'll order you some lunch. What would you like?"

"Just order from the same place you are ordering from for yourself." She didn't respond. She just walked over and looked out the window again. "Ainsley, did you hear me?"

"No, I'm sorry."

"I told you to order me whatever you were having. Now I know you heard me." I frowned.

"Oh, sorry, I'm not eating today. I'm not really all that hungry," she muttered.

As it was, Ainsley ate like a bird. Her family doctor had told her she needed to make sure she was getting enough at the very first appointment when they'd gone over her diet. There was no way she wasn't eating. She'd barely touched dinner last night, and I was sure she'd thrown her breakfast in the garbage this morning, after I'd told her I may need to make a trip to Denver.

I cleared my throat. "Don't order me anything. We are going out for lunch," I said, putting an end to what I feared would become an argument. "Be ready for one, right after my meeting." I glanced at my calendar, making sure I had nothing booked until at least three.

"Fine," Ainsley huffed. She made her way to the

door and stepped out into the hallway, pulling the door closed behind her.

My meeting made my head ache. I'd gone over all the documents with Max over the phone again and to say they did not impress me was an understatement. I was glad I'd decided to take Ainsley for lunch; I needed to get out of this office to clear my head.

I glanced at my watch and grabbed my suit jacket off the back of my chair. I stepped out into the hallway and saw that Ainsley had stepped away from her desk. I was about to text her when she came walking around the corner, holding her stomach.

"You feeling okay?"

"Yep, of course. Just a little upset stomach is all."

"It's because you haven't eaten. Let's go."

"I've eaten, Spencer," Ainsley bit back.

It was out of character for her to snap back at me. I ignored it. "Ainsley, half an egg does not count as eating." I walked over and grabbed her coat from the rack in the corner and helped her into it, and then I grabbed her hand and guided her to the elevator where we both stood in silence, waiting.

Once at the restaurant, Ainsley sat with the menu open in front of her, trying to decide what it was she wanted to eat. I'd decided ten minutes earlier, and I glanced at my watch as she continued to go back and forth between the three dishes.

"Okay, I think I've got it," she said, closing the menu.

Immediately, I signaled for the server. Once we'd ordered, I sat back in my chair and looked at Ainsley.

"How did the meeting with Max go?" she questioned.

I knew she was trying to avoid me asking her anything, which was fine for now.

I cleared my throat. "Well, I am not pleased. I am going to need to make a trip out there for a few days. Max has never overseen something this large before, and to save a disaster, I'd rather take control and set things right at the beginning, as opposed to waiting."

Ainsley nodded her head and muttered, "That's understandable," then looked away from me. "I know how hard you've worked to get Denver up and running."

"Would you be willing to stay with Nikki at the house for a few days while I go?"

When she didn't immediately respond, I leaned forward. "Ainsley? What is it? Talk to me, please."

Her chest heaved as she took in a full breath. Avoiding my eyes, she shrugged. "Are you sure you're not running away from things here… from me?" Her voice cracked as she choked out the last two words.

"From you? Why would I be running from you?"

"Oh, I don't know, because of everything that has been going on in our lives as of late. I am sure you're growing tired of everything with my dad, the wedding,

Brittany, the new baby, the new house, and probably a million other things I forgot to add to that list. I don't doubt that you'd be looking for space," she said as she counted items on her fingers. "Oh, and don't forget the baby shower invites."

I frowned. "No, Ainsley, this isn't about needing space. This is about business. While all of those things are going on, and yes, it can be stressful, you need to keep yourself focused on the end goal. That goal is us and our family."

"I know. It just feels like all we are doing is treading through rough waters, and it's been that way since all this started. It's literally killing me that the two most important people in my life are showing me zero support."

"Your father will come around. That I can promise you. I assume Carly would be the other one."

Ainsley nodded. "Yes."

"She is throwing you a baby shower. Doesn't that count as showing you support?"

"Sure, but it's a baby shower I asked her to wait for. Other than that, her entire focus has been coming up with reasons I should just find someone else."

"Well, all I can say is that she will understand much better when she meets someone."

"I never looked at it that way. She hasn't ever been in a relationship. She has no idea how I feel about you."

"Exactly. When it's true love, nothing should stand in

the way of it. No matter what anyone says. Deep down, I know Carly is there for you. She puts on a good game, but you mean a lot to her. I can see that, otherwise she wouldn't be there every time you need her. I also know you mean the world to your father, so please never think for a moment he'd disown you. I know how that man feels about you. If he didn't care, he wouldn't fly off the handle every time. He's just having a hard time accepting what is happening, but eventually he is going to have to accept it. He will come around."

Ainsley nodded. I watched as her eyes fell to her hands. I cleared my throat. "Look at me." I waited until she lifted her head and her eyes met mine. "I meant what I said the other night. I regret nothing about us. You need to know that. But you also need to ask yourself the question, is this what you really want?"

"What do you mean?"

"Do you really want us?" I replied, praying, and hoping she said yes, because I didn't know what I would do if she said no. I'd grown to love her more than anyone I'd ever been with. She meant the world to me, and I had vowed to myself that I would fight to keep her, no matter what, because my world would shatter the day she ever walked out of my life.

"I do, but I also want everyone else to be happy for us, too."

"Well, love, that is impossible. There will always be

someone who doesn't approve of every relationship, especially ours. What matters is that you and I are happy. That is it. That's all that matters."

Her eyes met mine, and she sat there for a minute saying nothing, then she softly smiled. "I want this. I want us so badly. Those few weeks we were apart were hell for me. I never want to feel that way again."

"I feel the same way. Without you was hell. So how about we focus on us and put a lot of this noise behind us? Everything will work out," I said, taking her hand in mine.

"Thank you for being here. I love you."

"I love you, Ainsley. I'll always be here for you, for whatever you need. Now let's get back on track and focus on my question…"

"Of course, I'll stay with Nikki."

"Good. I thought you could work from home and possibly take her shopping for some things for the new house. She was showing me some new bedding she'd like. I told her to put it on her Christmas list, but I don't see any reason to make her wait."

"Yes, I could also begin packing, too."

I shook my head. "No, I am hiring a company to do that. They will begin after I am back. Now what you can do is call those venues we contacted and find out what ones are available."

"I can do that," she said with a smile.

"Good, and after lunch, can you also book my flight?"

"Yes, of course. I'll do it as soon as we get back to the office."

"Perfect. Now let's enjoy this beautiful day and our lunch."

AINSLEY

Spencer was leaving for Denver. I'd gotten him an early-morning flight and booked his hotel for three nights. Nikki and I drove Spencer to the airport, and we sat in the car watching as he headed to the front doors with his luggage.

"Bye, Daddy!" Nikki yelled from the backseat window.

Spencer turned around and waved at us. "See you soon," he called.

We watched until he'd gone through the doors, then I hit the button to roll up the windows and turned on some music. I hadn't told Nikki that she wasn't going to school today. Instead, I figured I'd surprise her when I pulled into the mall parking lot.

"Ainsley, am I going to be late for school?" Nikki asked from the backseat.

"No, babe, you're not. We are on our way right now," I said, glancing in the driver's side mirror to make sure the lane was clear before I pulled away from the curb.

"Ainsley, did Daddy tell you I want a pink blanket for my new room?"

"He did. He even showed me the picture you showed him. It's really pretty."

"Do you think you could get it for me? Then I could be like my friend Haley, who lives across the street. She has one just like it, and I just love it so much."

I did my best to keep a straight face. "Well, what did your dad say? Did you ask him?"

"He told me to put it on my Christmas list, but I know that if you got it for me, he wouldn't be angry."

I smiled. "Well, I don't know. I think maybe I should talk to him about it first," I said and glanced in the rearview mirror just in time to see her pout.

"Okay," she said, letting out a huff and crossing her arms in front of her chest.

I did my best not to laugh at her actions as I drove down the freeway and pulled off at the exit for the mall, coming to a stop at the lights before turning into the large parking lot. I drove around, finally finding a spot, and shut the car off.

"Where are we?" Nikki asked, looking out the back window. "This doesn't look like school."

"It's not. We are at the mall. You and I are spending the day together. We are going to get some things for your room at the new house," I said, climbing out of the car and opening the back door.

"Yay! Can we get my blanket, please, Ainsley? I promise I will be a good girl."

"Well, I wanted it to be a surprise, but yes, we can," I said, kissing her forehead as I helped her out of the back of the car.

Nikki pulled on my arm as we headed into the mall, excited to get her blanket. I wasted no time. We made our way into the bedding store and right over to the kids' section. Within minutes, she'd found the same one her friend had, and she also found three others she liked. Now we stood before four sets of bedding, two of them pink, and two light purple.

I watched as Nikki walked around each bag, looking at each one repeatedly. I glanced at my watch. We'd been standing here for the past twenty-five minutes.

"I just don't know, Ainsley. I love this one…" she said, hugging the bag that contained the original blanket, "but I like the others too."

"Well, sweets, you need to decide. You really seemed to have your heart set on the first one. I say we go with it, and perhaps we could also get you a new sheet set, only get that in purple. That way, you have a little of both colours," I said, reaching up and pulling a set of purple sheets down from the shelf.

"Ohhh, I like that idea!"

"All right then. You take these sheets, and I will carry the bedding," I said, winking at her, while I put the three other comforters back on the shelf.

I grabbed her hand, and we began walking toward the cashier when Nikki spotted a pink pillow. "Can I get this too?" she asked, letting go of my hand as we walked by to grab the heart-shaped pillow.

I took one look at her face. Her eyes said it all as she held the pillow to her chest. "Okay, fine." I winked again.

We headed to the cashier where I paid for the bedding, then we took it all out to the car before continuing through the mall. Nikki walked beside me, talking a mile a minute about how excited she was to use her new bedding, and I had to remind her many times that she had to wait until we moved.

We walked the mall the rest of the morning, stopping at some of Nikki's favourite stores. She showed me all the things she was going to put on her birthday list. She wanted me to make sure I knew what each item was because, according to her, Spencer had gotten the items wrong last year. I couldn't help but laugh at her seriousness as I took a picture of a few toys she said she just had to have.

After lunch, we made our way back to the car. I now had a long list of items Nikki wanted for her birthday, and for Christmas. I pulled out of the parking lot and turned left, heading toward the bookstore.

"Can we get one of those special drinks at the bookstore?" Nikki asked as we made our way inside.

"What special drink would that be?" I asked, knowing full well she wanted a vanilla frappe.

"You know, one of those whipped-up drinks you bring home when you come here."

"Ohhh, one of those. I think we can." I giggled, pulling her close to me.

We stood in line, and when it was our turn, I stepped up to the counter and waited to place our order. Nikki pulled on my arm, wanting to show me something, and that was when I heard her voice.

"What can I get for you?"

I didn't want to turn around. I wanted to grab Nikki and run, only it was too late. She'd already seen us.

"Well, well, well, if it isn't the babysitter." Brittany stood behind the counter staring at me, and then she noticed Nikki. "Why the hell isn't Nikki in school?"

"Don't worry, her father knows. Actually, allowing her out of school for the day was his idea. Now, we'd like two vanilla Frappuccinos please."

She punched a couple of keys on the register with attitude and then looked at me. "Loading my child up on sugar, huh? Not a wonder why she always acts like a little brat when she's home."

"I highly doubt that I'm the problem."

"Oh, my dear, how naïve are you? You are the only problem that I see here. If you honestly think that by you ordering I am just going to drop the subject, you're more naïve than I thought."

Ignoring her, I pulled Spencer's card out of my wallet and handed it to her without thinking. I didn't understand what her problem was. All I knew was that I wanted this confrontation to end and for us to be away from her.

She looked down at the card and then up at me and chuckled to herself, shaking her head. "Living the high life, are you? You're living with him, fucking him, and also getting a paycheck from him. Why do you need his credit card, too?"

I felt my cheeks heat at her words.

"Oh wait, I know why. I mean, he was a mediocre fuck. He can only make up for it by padding your chequebook."

I was about to lean over the counter and tell Brittany to fuck herself when I heard Nikki call out to her. "Mommy, oh Mommy, just wait till you see what Ainsley got me."

Brittany looked at me and rolled her eyes.

"She got me a pretty pink blanket for our new house!" Nikki cried with excitement.

Brittany completely ignored her and continued to glare at me.

"Nikki, not now," I whispered as Brittany looked down at her. Once her eyes were off me, I closed my eyes and took in a breath. I just wanted out of here because I knew from here on things would not go over well.

"Is that so? Did you put it in on this card too? Perhaps I should call him and let him know I found his credit card, that some tramp stole it," she whispered as she leaned over the counter.

I glared at her. "Brittany, you really should calm down before you get fired from yet another job."

Brittany glared back at me and yelled out for two vanilla Frappuccinos. She ran Spencer's credit card through the machine and handed it back to me. Then, in a huff, she disappeared behind the counter, saying nothing to Nikki, who looked up at me with tears in her eyes.

"Did I do something wrong, Ainsley?" Nikki asked me, a tear slipping down her cheek.

"No, sweetie, you did nothing wrong. It appears your mother is having a bad day."

I occupied Nikki while we waited for our drinks, and I prayed Brittany didn't return to the counter. Once I heard my name called, we took our drinks and made our way into the bookstore, where we headed into the children's section to pick out a couple of new books for Nikki, when all I really wanted to do was go back home.

IT WAS ALMOST nine thirty by the time I crawled into bed. I'd put Nikki to bed at seven and read to her until she drifted off to sleep, then I sat down and caught up on work emails before taking a hot bath.

I then crawled into bed and snuggled down under the covers and turned on the TV. I searched until I found a show I'd been watching and then grabbed my phone to text Spencer. It was a pleasant surprise to find a message waiting for me instead.

RomanticAlpha42: I'm at the hotel. Call me.

I dialled his number and waited for him to pick up. "Hey, sweetie."

"Hey, how did things go today?" his tired voice asked.

"Okay. We picked out her bedding for her room."

"Good. Was she happy?"

"She was so excited. I wish you could have seen her

face. I also have a wish list of items for her birthday and for Christmas."

"I see." Spencer chuckled. "Everything else go okay?"

"Yeah, I ordered pizza for dinner. After spending the day shopping and getting her bathed and ready for school tomorrow, I was exhausted."

"That's good. I am sure she enjoyed that."

"Yes, she did." I bit my bottom lip. I swallowed hard. I knew I had to tell Spencer about running into Brittany. What I didn't want was her calling him and lying about things at the bookstore today. For all I knew, she would turn the whole incident around on me.

"What else did you do?"

"We went to the bookstore." I grew quiet for a moment and took in a breath, "Oh, and we ran into Brittany today."

"What? Where?"

"At the bookstore. Well, actually, at the coffee shop. Nikki wanted a Frappuccino, so we went into the coffee house there. Brittany apparently works there now."

"And…"

"Oh, and she was her usual charming self."

"Did she take a tone with you?"

"She was worse there to me than she was the night at the restaurant. However, it's not me I'm worried about. It's how she treated Nikki."

"What the hell did she do?"

"Ignored her. Completely ignored her. I'm wondering if the acting out isn't from that."

Spencer was quiet for a few moments. "Perhaps I'll make a call to my lawyer, you know, and add more to the custody case. She always wanted to fight me on this. What else did she say?"

"Well, it made her angry Nikki wasn't in school. Then, without thinking, I gave her your credit card to pay for the drinks. She said she was going to call you."

"Did you tell her to go ahead?" he questioned.

"No, Spencer, I just wanted to be done with her."

"Are you sure you're okay on your own there? I hate you being alone."

"Spencer, please, don't worry about me. Nikki is fine, I am fine. Also, remember, my father, who still isn't speaking to me, is right next door. I know he would let nothing happen to us. I know he knows you're away because I saw him watching Nikki and I through his front window when we were getting out of the car. He also kept coming to his kitchen window when we were in the backyard after dinner."

"I know. It's not the point. I should have brought you guys. It's not too late. You can book a flight, and I will have you picked up at the airport."

"Seriously, Spencer, we are fine. Carly is going to

come over and spend the night tomorrow. If Brittany wants to stop by, she can deal with Carly." I giggled.

The line went quiet for a moment, then I heard Spencer clear his throat. "Perhaps alone may be better. Is she still all for team breakup?"

"Probably. Who knows with her? Last I spoke to her, she told me she needed to limit the time she spent when you were around because you were growing on her. I don't even know what that means."

Spencer laughed. "I see. Perhaps I'll be in her good books one day after all."

"Did you speak to Max yet?"

"No, he doesn't even know I'm in town. I wanted to get settled in. The flight was late, so I decided I'd pop into the office tomorrow morning instead. I'll know more about what is going on after that meeting. I think I am going to treat him to dinner, just two brothers."

"That's good," I said, yawning.

"You in bed already?" Spencer questioned.

"Yeah, what about you?"

"No. I'm still working. I went over a lot of stuff on the flight, but I wanted to prepare a plan for Max. You know, goals. So that is what I'll be working on tonight."

"Yes, you had mentioned that you were going to work on that."

The line grew quiet, neither of us saying anything. As I lay there listening to him breathe, I wished Spencer were here beside me, holding me instead of being so far away.

"What are you thinking?" he asked, his voice low.

I didn't want to make him feel worse than he already did. I knew he didn't enjoy being away from us, and this time he was worried about us being alone, but I couldn't help wanting to be with him.

"Just a little lonely. Wishing you were here is all."

"Are you sure you don't want to come to Denver?" he asked.

This was why I didn't want to say anything. I sighed. "Yes, I am sure, there is no need for us to come to Denver."

"Okay. I'll be home before you know it. Why don't you get some sleep and I will talk to you in the morning?"

"Okay, good night. I love you."

"Love you too."

I hung up the phone and lay in bed staring at the TV and thinking of Spencer. I felt like I'd upset him by telling him what had happened. He wasn't acting like himself. Normally, by now, we'd have been hot and heavy into dirty talk, when instead he seemed to just want to get off the phone.

I arranged the covers partially over my naked body in such a way that would leave him wanting a little more and snapped a picture, which I sent straight to Spencer with the words 'wish you were here' attached to the message and hit send. It had barely been a minute when my phone vibrated, and I looked at the screen to see a crying emoji face. I couldn't help but laugh out loud.

RomanticAlpha42: Just wait till I get my hands on you.

BabyGirl89: Cannot wait ;)

SPENCER

I GLANCED AT MY WATCH; it was already after seven and I was starving. I looked down at the menu, going over my options, while I waited for Max to arrive. It had been his suggestion to come here and, as usual, he was late.

It had been good to see my brother again. Over the years, we'd drifted apart, I'd married Brittany, and we'd had Nikki, while Max had gone off to find himself. Then I was in the middle of a horrible divorce. Mike and I would only hear from him occasionally, until he'd returned to the States.

This afternoon, I'd sat down with my brother to go over my plans for the Denver office, and over the course of two hours, I'd learned that Max had lied to me about everything. He'd lied about most of his experiences, and I also found out that he'd been fired from his last two jobs.

I knew he was worried that I'd be firing him from this one, and I really should have, but when I realized how desperate he was to get this job, it changed my mind.

He'd only been back in the States for sixteen months when he'd woken one morning, no job, on the verge of getting evicted from his apartment, and heard a knock on his door. He'd opened it to find his ex-girlfriend, who'd walked out one morning, standing in front of him holding a baby. His baby. So yes, he'd been desperate.

I'd let out a breath. "Why is it you never told me all this to start?"

"I don't know. I needed something to get myself up in the morning. Everything fell apart when Pam left me. You know how that is, but when she showed up with the baby and dumped him on my lap, I was desperate. Are you going to fire me?"

I looked down at the reports I'd brought from the office back home and shook my head. "No, I will not fire you, Max. In all honesty, I did not know what I was doing when I started this company either. Most of it was trial and error, until I found most of my core team. I can train you, regardless of how angry I am. I still want you to be a part of this. I want to build a legacy."

Max chuckled. "A legacy, really. That is a really interesting way to put it."

No matter how angry I was, I still felt for him.

However, we went over all the plans I had written for him, along with all the goals, and I planned to work with him to get him where he needed to be instead of taking the easy way out.

"Sorry I'm late," Max said, sliding into the booth across from me.

"That's okay. I hope you know what you want, because I am ready to chew my arm off." I chuckled.

Max reached for the menu and opened it, , closing it two minutes later while I signaled for the server.

"So, since you know all about my issues, tell me, how are things with you? How did the engagement thing go?" Max questioned.

"Went well. I still say it would have been nice for you to have been there, to meet Ainsley."

"Well, given the circumstances…"

"I know." The baby was the entire reason we hadn't heard from him. Instead of calling us, he'd kept all of that to himself, until today.

"I don't really get why you're rushing to get married to this chick. I mean, twenty years' difference in age is huge. What if she is just after your money?" Max questioned.

"She isn't after my money," I replied.

"Do you know that for a fact? Did you ask her to sign a prenup?"

I rolled my eyes. "No, Max, no prenup. We are in love."

"Yeah, in love, that is what I said about Pam, until she walked out on me and then walked back into my life with a baby. Just wait until she tells you she is pregnant." Max chuckled.

I grew quiet. "Well, Max, I don't need to wait for that." I sat back putting my hands behind my head.

"Are you fucking with me?"

"No, I'm not. Ainsley is pregnant."

"You got the sitter pregnant?" Max questioned, leaning forward, interested in whatever gossip he may find out.

"Careful, that is my soon-to-be wife you are speaking of," I gritted.

Max sat back. "True. Tell me, what could you possibly see in her long-term? Have you even thought about your future?"

"My future is all I think about, Max. Providing a home for Nikki and Ainsley and now the baby, maintaining the growth of the company."

"That may be, but have you thought about how you have absolutely nothing in common? I mean, in twenty years she'll be changing your diapers, for fuck sakes. She's gonna want to party, and you're going to want to go to bed at nine."

"Why don't you tell me how you really feel, Max?"

"Fuck, I am. It's the truth, Spencer."

I frowned. "I just told you to be careful. I've given you a job, and only a few hours ago you were begging me to keep it. This is an opportunity for you to make a fresh start, to leave your past behind."

"I'm grateful, Spencer, really I am. I just…"

I put my hand up to stop him. The last thing Ainsley and I needed was yet another person who disapproved of our relationship. Max was my younger brother, and we'd only just reconnected a few months ago. He had no right to judge us. He was also my employee, and this type of talk needed to be stopped immediately.

"You will respect my decisions, Max. I'm in love with Ainsley. We are getting married, yes she is having my baby, and Nikki adores her. Honestly, had you of been around the last year or so or had shown up to our engagement party, you would probably feel the same way about her."

"I will do my best to keep my opinions to myself. And look… Nikki will have someone to grow up with."

I looked at my brother, unsure if that was a hit directed at Ainsley's age or if he was talking about the new baby.

"I really hope you are referring to the new baby," I gritted.

"Of course, that is what I meant. I am sure Ainsley is

very mature for her age, 'cause lord knows she has to be because you don't have an immature bone in yours."

AINSLEY

"ALL RIGHT, YOU, CRAWL IN," I said, pulling the covers back so Nikki could climb into bed.

Nikki looked up at me, then grabbed two more stuffed animals from a pile in the corner. She carried them over to the bed and crawled in.

"You don't normally sleep with those," I said, taking notice that she left her favourite teddy bear on the floor by the door.

"Oh, can you get me Teddy?" Nikki cried, reaching her little arms out for the bear.

We'd gone through this every night since Spencer had been gone. I walked over and grabbed the bear and brought it to the edge of the bed, tucking her under the covers with all three of the stuffed animals. I kissed her on the forehead and was about to turn out the lights when

Nikki sat up.

"Aren't you going to read me a story?"

I glanced at the clock to see it was almost eight thirty. Which meant it was already an hour past Nikki's bedtime. If she didn't get to sleep soon, she would be impossible to get up in the morning. "Not tonight, sweets. It's already past your bedtime. Now, you need to lie down and close your eyes and get some sleep," I said, pulling the covers up over her a little more.

"Just one," Nikki begged.

"No, sweetie, you need your rest. You have school in the morning."

"But I'm not tired."

"I beg to differ," I said, sitting down on the edge of her bed.

"Please, Ainsley."

"Nikki, what did your father say?" I questioned.

"Please, Ainsley, just one."

I bent down and kissed her forehead and then shook my head. "No, now go to sleep," I said, shutting her bedside light off. I walked over to her bedroom door and pulled it partway shut. "Good night."

"Night," she huffed.

I turned the small light on in the bathroom just outside Nikki's door and headed to the living room where Carly was searching through Netflix for a movie.

"I made popcorn. What do you feel like watching?" she questioned.

I took a handful and shoved the kernels in my mouth. "Something romantic," I said, flopping on the couch. "What about you?"

"True crime. I'm in the mood for blood and guts."

"Ugh, true crime? No wonder you're still single." I giggled.

"Romance!" Carly said, sticking her tongue out at me. "That is why you're pregnant. I'm comfortable and confident with my choices."

"As am I." We looked at one another and laughed.

Carly continued scrolling through choices. "Well, we will see how comfortable and confident you are in twenty years."

I rolled my eyes. I didn't want to hear it. I pulled the blanket off the back of the couch and threw it over my pajama-clad legs and took a sip of my coke.

"How about this?" Carly said, shoving the computer toward me to read the synopsis.

"Fine, that's fine. At least it isn't true crime. Drama will have to do."

"Since when are you against dramas?" Carly questioned as she started the movie.

I shrugged and rested my head on the back of the couch. "Since there is now enough drama in my life to satisfy an entire movie plot."

"Why?" she asked, pausing the movie. "What's gone on now?"

I had kept things quiet from Carly, since I knew how she felt about Spencer and me. I also didn't want to trouble her with my adult issues. However, I knew I needed to talk about things with someone other than Spencer. I let out a sigh and looked at my best friend.

"We will start by saying I really don't want to hear you say I told you so, but things haven't been so great. My father came home from his trip and found an invitation in his mailbox to the baby shower."

Carly's eyes widened. "Oh my God, Ainsley, I wondered where that one went."

"What do you mean?" I questioned.

"Well, remember you asked me to drop the mail off that you had gotten. I took it and shoved it all in the mailbox, and then…wait a minute." Carly got up and took off toward the front door. I heard it open, and after a few minutes she returned, her face as white as a ghost.

"What is it?"

"It was my fault. I took the mail over, and when I got back in my car, I just took the top envelope off the pile of invites and shoved it in my glove box. Which was where I'd put your father's, so I didn't mail it. I never even looked at the name. I just took the pile to the post office and mailed them. I just looked now, and it was Jenna's invite in my glove box, not your dad's. I bet I grabbed it when I put the mail in the mailbox," Carly said, covering her mouth. "I'm so sorry, Ainsley. Please forgive me."

Carly stood there in near tears, staring at me. I knew no matter how much she disapproved of our relationship, she would never do something like this on purpose. "I forgive you."

She took a moment and wiped her eyes. "So, what happened?" Carly asked, sitting back down beside me.

"He came over here and got angry. Then he saw the banner that Spencer and Nikki had made for the night we got the house. He blew up. Demanded I come home."

Carly looked at me, almost shocked that my father had found out about the baby and the house in such a short period. "You mean he found everything out that night?"

"Yep, in about ten minutes. Ten minutes, he learned we were having a baby and that we were moving. He demanded that I return home, which I didn't, and now he won't speak to me."

"It's your dad. I am sure he will come around."

I shrugged. "I hope so. However, that isn't all of it. Brittany hasn't exactly been wonderful either. She was the server at the restaurant we had gone to the night you stayed and watched Nikki. She attacked me and Spencer and ended up losing her job. I ran into her yesterday at the coffee shop inside the bookstore, and she attacked me again there as well."

"What the hell is with that woman?"

"I don't know."

"Do you think she wants him back?" Carly questioned.

"I don't think so. I mean, she cheated on Spencer, so I am just thinking she either really hates the pair of us or she hates herself for what she let go."

"Maybe, perhaps, she wants him back. You know, she realizes what it is she lost."

I shrugged. "Perhaps."

"The fact that she cheated on him doesn't really mean anything. Perhaps they were going through a dry spell. I mean, he is old."

"Ugh, please. Don't start with the age thing again, please."

"I'm only saying I read an article in *Cosmo* about men in their forties, and that sometimes they have a hard time, you know, getting it up," Carly said.

I rolled my eyes. "Don't worry, Carly, there isn't any dry spell. He has no problems. In fact, he loves to—"

Carly held her hands over her ears and closed her eyes. "I don't want to know. Now what else?"

"The venues still haven't called us back. I spent all morning calling them and no one would take my calls. Plus, we close on the house in about three weeks. Possibly two now, and this place isn't even on the market yet."

"Whoa, relax. I'm sure Spencer has everything under control."

"I know. I am trying to calm myself down. It's just I look around and every which way I turn, it's one disaster after another," I said, a tear slipping down my cheek.

"Okay. We are coming up with a plan of attack. Tomorrow, after we take Nikki to school, you and I are going to go to the places you've called. We are going to find you a location for your wedding," Carly said, taking hold of my hands in hers. "I want to see my best friend smile again."

"Thank you." I sniffled. "It means the world to me."

"Of course. I'll also lay off on the Spencer attacks. He really isn't that bad of a guy. Now let's relax and watch this movie."

SPENCER

The cab pulled into our driveway, and I paid the driver as he pulled my bags out of the trunk. I'd never been so happy to return home. The trip to Denver was great. Not only had it given me a chance to help Max with the Denver division, but it had given us the chance to spend some time together.

I waited for the cab to pull out of the driveway before turning and looking up at the house. Most lights were off, except for the ones in the front windows. I was excited to see Ainsley and had hoped she was still awake. I'd done the best I could to get home at a decent hour, but with the weather delay, that hadn't been possible.

I walked up to the door and slid my key in the lock, opening the front door. Soft music filled the house. I smiled. Ainsley normally had music playing when she was working in the evening. I knew she hadn't been in the office much while I'd been gone, so I figured she was probably playing catchup. I put my bags down and climbed the stairs and poked my head into the kitchen to find her standing at the counter plating food.

"Hey, sexy," I whispered as I stepped up behind her and wrapped my arms around her.

She rested her head on my shoulder, a smile coming to her lips. "Well, this isn't how you were supposed to find out about dinner. I must have timed your drive back wrong," she said, placing the pot back on the stove before turning in my arms. "I missed you," she said in a low voice as her arms rested on my shoulders and she met my lips, her body fitting perfectly against mine.

"I missed you too," I whispered, pulling her tighter against me before kissing her again. "What's all this?" I questioned, reaching over her shoulder and grabbing a carrot off one plate.

"This is dinner. I hope you're hungry."

"I'm starving, actually. They didn't offer food on the flight back because of the weather. The turbulence was brutal. Can I help you with anything?"

"Nope. I have it all taken care of. Why don't you take a minute, get comfortable and then go have a seat in the dining room and I will bring in dinner."

"I can do that." I placed a kiss on the side of her neck and listened as she giggled.

"Did you want me to make you a drink?" she questioned.

I shook my head. "No, I got it. I'll just pour myself a scotch," I said, pressing my lips to hers one more time.

I grabbed a rock glass from the cabinet and placed three cubes of ice into it and headed into the dining room, where I poured myself a glass and took a seat in my usual spot.

"Here we are," she said, setting a plate in front of me." I looked down at the carrots, asparagus, and chicken.

"This looks amazing."

"Thanks. I wanted to make you something special for tonight," she said, sitting down in her usual spot beside me.

I smiled. "Thank you. Everything go okay while I was gone?" I questioned. I'd been worried about leaving her to begin with, and once I knew she had run into Brittany, it had made it worse. It still bothered me that I hadn't just taken them both with me instead. I also knew that Ainsley could lie to me over the phone, however face-to-face, I could read her like a book. I knew when she was sad, upset, worried, and frustrated, her eyes gave everything away.

"Yeah, everything went fine. Of course, Nikki tried to push boundaries, but then she always did when you'd leave me with her. This time though I feel it's different."

"Yeah, I am going to have to talk to her about that."

"Ah, maybe she is just being a kid. It's fine. She was a little tired today. She didn't want to go to bed last night, and she was up later than she should have been tonight. So, when I put her down tonight, again, there was no bedtime story."

"That's okay. She will live without a story for a couple of nights. I know what she can be like when she gets cranky. I swear Brittany just lets her do whatever she wants when she is with her. I've also been noticing that every time she comes back from there, she never wants to sleep. She also gets demanding."

"Yeah, I have a feeling it's because she's ignoring her. You should have seen how she acted, Nikki was trying to tell her something and she wouldn't even look at her."

"Well, I'll address that when I have a chat with Brittany. I also need to mention it to my lawyer."

"How did things go with Max?"

"Okay, nothing that we couldn't correct. He also sends his apologies for not making it to our engagement party."

Ainsley shrugged. "It doesn't matter, but you can tell him thank you."

I watched her drag her fork around her plate, moving pieces of carrots and asparagus around, not really eating. "Did you hear anything from the venues?"

Ainsley let out a deep sigh. "No, nothing. Nor from the caterers. Carly and I went to all of them today as well. I think I am just going to look up some different places."

"Sure, never hurts to do that. We could always try contacting the one we used for the Christmas party. It's always an option."

"I'll do that. Oh, you should have seen Nikki at the mall. We went into the bedding store, and she found the bedding she wanted immediately. That was until she spotted three others that she liked as well. I spent twenty-five minutes letting her try to decide on the one she wanted, only to end up deciding for her by bribing her with a set of purple sheets," Ainsley said, hiding her face in her hands and laughing.

I let out a laugh. I knew how Nikki could be. "Well, I am glad you two figured it out and had a great time. I'm also glad that you decided for her, otherwise you might still be there." I chuckled, setting my fork and knife down on my plate.

"We did. She's been asking to use everything since we got it. So, I compromised. I feared if I didn't, she'd never go to bed. I allowed her to use the heart-shaped pillow I got for her."

"Heart-shaped pillow?"

"Yep, she wanted it to go with her blanket." Ainsley laughed.

I was glad to see Ainsley appeared to be in better spirits than when I'd spoken to her the other night. I looked into her eyes; she looked tired, which I expected.

She reached for my plate, but I put my hand on hers, stopping her. "Why don't I clean everything up and you head down to the bedroom and get ready for bed?"

She looked at the dirty dishes in front of us. "The kitchen is clean. Everything is in the dishwasher. It will only take me a couple of seconds. Besides, you've travelled all day."

"And you've been looking after everything here."

She looked around. "Will you be in soon?"

"I'm going to pop these in the dishwasher and then I'll be right behind you," I said, taking her hand in mine and bringing it to my lips.

She looked at everything before reluctantly getting up and starting down the hall toward the bedroom. I took a few moments and wiped the counters down and put the rest of the food away, then I shut out the lights and headed down the hall to the bedroom.

When I walked in, the two bedside table lights were on, and the door to the bathroom was ajar. I placed my bag down on my nightstand and quickly got out of my clothes. I'd just hung up my suit and was just about to unpack my bag when Ainsley appeared in the bathroom's doorway.

I glanced her way and did a double take. Ainsley

stood before me wearing a very sexy black lace lingerie set I'd never seen before. My mouth watered at the sight of her, and my cock instantly hardened.

Her eyes locked with mine as she slowly made her way over to me. I'd never seen her eyes so full of want, need, and sex all at the same time. She trailed her fingers down my chest, stopping at the top of my boxers. "I missed you," she whispered, running her hand over my bulge.

"I missed you too," I said, my voice cracking at her touch.

She pressed her lips to mine and her body into me. I grabbed her. Picking her up, I carried her over to the bed and placed her down on the edge. She lay back on the mattress as my eyes roamed her body. "When did you get this?" I asked, my fingers tracing over the lacy material.

"Do you like it?" she asked, innocently looking up at me.

I gripped her thighs and pulled her to the edge of the bed. Standing between her legs, I pushed myself against her. "Does it feel like I don't like it?" I growled.

Instantly, the innocence washed from her eyes and in place of that I saw nothing but heat, want, and desire. I met her lips and kissed her hard, making my way to that soft spot on her neck. I felt her body weaken as I concentrated on that little spot she loved. When I heard that little moan, I pushed her body back onto the bed.

I looked down at her. Her eyes were begging me for more. I kneeled on the bed and held my body weight with one hand as I bent down and licked her nipple through the lace, then gently bit and sucked it into my mouth.

Arching her back, pushing herself farther into my mouth, Ainsley let out a moan that sent a wave through my body. I gripped my hardened cock, hoping that I could relieve some pressure. I repeated the process with the other and then ran my finger between her legs.

She looked up at me as my fingers danced over the now soaked piece of fabric that covered her.

"Don't tease," she whimpered.

"Teasing is half the fun," I whispered, using just enough pressure so she could feel me there.

I met her lips, my tongue washing through her mouth as her fingers gripped my back. "Slide up into bed," I whispered.

She did as I asked, moving into the centre of the bed. I kissed my way down her body and moved between her legs, pushing them open. I ran my fingers once again over that square piece of fabric, again pushing just hard enough I knew she could feel me.

"Don't tease me," she cried, gripping the blanket under her.

I smiled. I loved it when she begged me. I slid that little piece of fabric to the side and ran my finger through her wet center. She sucked in a breath and arched her back as my finger ran over the bundle of nerves again and again, before sliding two fingers deep inside of her.

"Am I teasing you now?" I whispered as I leaned down to her ear, gently biting her earlobe while fucking her with my fingers.

Her only response was another moan as my thumb circled the small bundle of nerves as my fingers curled inside her. Her hand gripped my arm, and she met my lips, kissing me hard as she moaned louder this time.

I could feel her tightening, so I pulled my fingers from inside her and pulled my aching cock from my boxers. She looked up at me and watched as I stroked myself, my eyes meeting hers.

I slid the little pair of panties down her body and threw them to the floor, then spread her legs open a little farther, lining myself up at her entrance. "You want this?" I asked, pushing just hard enough to enter her a tiny bit.

She bit her bottom lip and nodded her head.

I pushed inside, burying myself in her. Instantly, I met her lips as I thrust into her. Wrapping my arms around her, I held her tightly against me, kissing her as I slowed my pace. I rolled onto my back, pulling her on top of me.

She pulled the rest of the lacy garment over her head and placed it beside her, then she rested her hands on my chest. My eyes ran down her body. I placed my hands on her hips, slowing her and guiding her movement.

I watched as nothing but pure pleasure lined her face. I loved watching her. "Does it feel good, baby?" I asked, breathing heavily.

The inhale of breath between her closed lips told me all I needed to know as she continued at the pace I'd set for her. She closed her eyes, her head dropping back as she rolled her hips. "God, yes," she cried.

I sat up and wrapped my arms around her and guided her, slowing her down as I felt her tighten around me. She buried her face in my neck, her hot breath tickling me as she started moving a little faster.

She interlaced her fingers with mine as her breathing quickened, and her head dropped back as she screamed my name. As soon as she called my name, I couldn't hold back any longer, and I poured into her, holding her close.

AINSLEY

THE AFTERNOON SUN poured through the windows behind me. The office was buzzing today; the phone hadn't stopped ringing since we'd gotten in, and Spencer hadn't had a second to himself all morning. I got up from my chair and pulled the blinds down behind me so I could see my computer screen a little easier. I glanced at the clock; it was a little after two and I still hadn't heard from my father.

I'd placed a call to him earlier this morning, as Spencer had suggested. He wanted us to have dinner together, to clear the air, so I'd called and invited my father and Jane over tomorrow evening. Jane had tried to get my father on the phone, but he refused to take the call and instead she said she would talk to him.

I was about to get up and head down to the washroom when my phone rang. I grabbed it, hoping that it would be my father, but disappointment flooded me. It was the last venue I'd contacted. They finally returned my call to tell me they, too, had no availability for us. The other ones had left voice messages over the weekend. This one was our last option. I swallowed hard. I could feel the tears building as I put the phone down.

"Don't cry here," I muttered to myself. "It's unprofessional." I rubbed my temples, like I did when I had a headache.

I wiped at my eyes just as Spencer's office door opened and two men stepped out into the hall, with Spencer following. He didn't look over my way, thank goodness, so I covered my eyes and pretended to be working on something when the phone rang again. This time it was the caterer, and once again, they broke the news that they were fully booked right into the later part of the summer.

Completely defeated, I stood up and stretched just as Spencer rounded the corner. "What time is your doctor's appointment at?" he questioned.

I glanced at the clock. "In twenty-five minutes."

"Why didn't you send me a reminder?"

"I reminded you this morning over breakfast. You said you put it in your calendar."

"Give me five minutes," Spencer grumbled under his breath before going into his office and shutting the door.

I frowned. It wasn't like him to be so grumpy, especially toward me. Ten minutes later, we were in his car, heading toward the medical building five blocks away.

We now sat in the small exam room. My stomach felt uneasy as we waited for the doctor to come in. I pulled my phone from my jacket pocket and looked to see if I had missed any calls, hoping that my father had attempted to call me back, but still nothing.

"Hasn't called yet, has he?" Spencer questioned.

I shook my head and shoved the phone back into my pocket, then I slipped out of my coat, passing it to Spencer. "No. I don't think he will," I said, looking toward the floor and swallowing hard, hoping I didn't break out in tears.

"Hello." The door opened and in walked Dr. Pines. "Ainsley, how are we feeling today?" she questioned as she sat down behind the small desk and turned on the computer screen.

"Good, thanks," I lied.

Spencer glanced at me. I could tell from the look on his face he knew I wasn't telling her the truth, and I hoped he said nothing.

"Spencer, how are things?" Dr. Pines asked.

"Good, thanks."

"Good, so shall we get started?" She came around with a blood pressure cuff. "Just want to get a blood pressure reading first."

"The nurse already did that," I replied, looking at Spencer.

"Well, the first reading was a little high, so I want to take it again now that you've been sitting here for a while. Hold out your arm."

She wrapped the cuff around my arm. "Relax," she said as the cuff tightened. She watched, frowning. "It's higher than I'd like to see at this stage," she said, going back around to her chair and typing into the computer. "Have you been experiencing any stress?"

Spencer looked at me and waited for me to say something, only I kept quiet.

"Ainsley?" Dr. Pines questioned. "Have you been experiencing any stress?"

I knew Spencer would probably say something if I didn't, so I slowly nodded my head. "Yes. I'm also a little nervous."

"Nothing to be nervous about. I also noticed that your weight is a little low as well. Have you been eating okay?"

"Yes."

"Actually," Spencer jumped in, "she barely eats on a good day."

Dr. Pines looked over at me. "Ainsley, you need to eat. Especially now. I see from your family doctor that you've always had an issue eating, especially when you're experiencing stress."

I nodded. "Yes, that is true." In the time Spencer and I were apart after my father found us, I'd lost almost twenty pounds in a month. I still hadn't put all that weight back on and then I found out I was pregnant.

"Okay, so we will go over a healthy diet before you go today. Now, how about you lay back?" Dr. Pines said with a smile as she pulled a tray with a machine on it behind her. "I want to take a peek at this baby. If we are lucky, we may even hear a heartbeat. I'll just have you slip in behind that screen in the corner and put the gown on, open at the front."

I did as she requested and when I came back out, the doctor had already adjusted the table so I could lie down a little more. I walked over and climbed back up, Spencer coming over to my side and taking hold of my hand as I lay back.

She placed a blanket over my legs. "Now, we will just open your gown a little. You can leave your breasts covered."

I did as she asked. She squirted some cold jelly onto my belly. Then she took a wand and rubbed it over my abdomen.

She studied the monitor, moving the wand slowly over my abdomen. "There we go," she said, pointing to the screen.

"Is that it?" I asked, trying to see something that resembled a baby.

"That is it." Dr. Pines smiled, pointing to the monitor as she continued to move the wand over my abdomen, pressing a little harder than before. "Let's see if we can get a heartbeat."

A frown came to her face as she moved the wand, and I got a little worried. "Is there something wrong?" I questioned, lifting my back off the table.

"No, Ainsley, just relax."

Spencer tightened his hold on my hand and brought a kiss to my forehead, trying to comfort me, but I was growing increasingly worried that something wasn't right from the look on the doctor's face.

"Why haven't we heard the heartbeat?" I asked, alarm in my voice.

"Well, sometimes we can't hear it just yet. It's nothing to be concerned about," she said, turning the monitor closer to her as she continued waving the wand over my stomach at a slower pace. "We will set up another appointment for two weeks from now. Lots of times I can't get a heartbeat this early. Doesn't necessarily mean something is wrong."

She shut the machine off and passed me a cloth, and I quickly wiped up the jelly. Spencer held my hand while I got off the table and went and got changed. When I returned, I sat beside Spencer.

"Now, I'd like to talk to you about restrictions. First, I am printing out a healthy selection of foods that I want you to make sure you are eating. Also, a portion guide. I also want as little stress as possible for you. Do you know what some stresses are?" Dr. Pines asked, quickly making a note. "Is it family?"

I gave a small nod. "How did you guess?"

Dr. Pines smiled. "Well, you aren't the first couple I've had that have had such a difference in age. Plus, your family doctor filled me in on a few things."

I nodded again. "I see."

"So, I'd like you to limit those visits with the ones who are the primary cause of those stressors."

I nodded and looked at Spencer, who softly smiled and winked.

"Is there any reason that stress could harm the baby?" I questioned.

"Well, stress isn't good for any of us. I tell all my patients to limit their stress triggers." She smiled. "Also, I don't want you lifting anything heavier than twenty-five pounds."

My head shot up and my eyes met hers.

"Is that an issue?" she questioned.

"We are moving. I have to lift. I have boxes to pack and unpack."

Spencer cleared his throat. "We have a moving company coming to pack and move us. If need be, I'll have them unpack as well. Ainsley, you can supervise," Spencer replied.

"Problem solved," Dr. Pines said, smiling at me.

On the inside, I felt like screaming, but I sat there, listening to the things Dr. Pines said. I prayed this appointment was soon going to be over. I somewhat felt like I was being attacked, and I could feel the stress and worry piling on until I began feeling unwell. I swallowed hard as she finally stood up from behind her desk and handed Spencer a few pages that she'd printed.

"I want to see you in two weeks. We will have another ultrasound during that appointment. You can book at the front desk before you leave."

I nodded and took Spencer's hand. As soon as the doctor was gone, Spencer and I made our way out to reception. I was just as happy to call and book, but Spencer stopped at the small desk and waited.

Once the appointment was booked we headed out of the office. We were just about to the car when I felt my phone vibrate in my pocket. I removed it to see a text from Jane waiting for me. I stopped walking and my hand shook as I typed in my password.

"What is it?" Spencer questioned.

"Jane messaged me," I said, swallowing hard as I read the message. "Jane says Dad won't come for dinner." I swallowed hard, my eyes burning.

"Perfect. Just perfect," Spencer muttered under his breath.

"How is that perfect?" I cried.

Spencer looked at me. "Ainsley, I didn't mean it that way."

I looked down at my phone as the words Jane had written blurred in front of me. A tear slipped down my cheek and my throat got tight. "Limit the stress. Easier said than done," I whispered to myself.

Spencer wrapped his arms around me. "I don't want you worrying about anything," he whispered. "If your dad is going to be that way, let him. If he doesn't want to come to the wedding, that is fine. However, if he does, and he creates a scene, I will ask them both to leave."

Alarm filled me. "You will?"

"Yes, it is our wedding, and you are going to be my wife. I will not let him treat you like a child at our wedding or in our own home. Now, chin up. We are going to get your weight up, and the house will get packed, and things between you and your father will get straightened out. It's up to him now to decide which path he would rather take," he said, kissing my lips.

AINSLEY

Rain hit the large window, while I sat on the couch replying to an email. A large rumble of thunder followed by a flash of lightning tore my attention away from my laptop. It had been cloudy and rainy for the past three days, totally matching my mood.

I was just about to get up and check on the people who were packing things up in the house when my phone dinged with a message. I looked down and smiled.

ROMANTICALPHA42: How are things?

BABYGIRL89: Going well. They are just about done with Nikki's room.

I'd been working from home for the past two days

while the packing company Spencer hired came into the house and began packing things. They would pack up a room or two and then they would load things into their van and take them over to the new house and unpack.

BABYGIRL89: How are things going at the office?

ROMANTICALPHA42: Busy. As always.

BABYGIRL89: Great. I think Brittany called here today.

ROMANTICALPHA42: She's been calling the office all morning.

BABYGIRL89: Phone is ringing again.

ROMANTICALPHA42: Just ignore her. I'll be home in an hour.

I put my phone down and laptop on the table just as one girl who was packing came into the living room.

"We are just about finished with the basement and the little girl's room. Tomorrow we will tackle this room, the spare room, and the garage. Then on Saturday we will finish the last four rooms to have you completely moved in for moving day."

"That sounds perfect. Did you need me to come over to the new house with you when you take this load?"

"No, miss. Mr. Brooks went over where everything goes."

I nodded. "Thank you for everything."

"You are welcome."

I watched as she made her way back down the hall and turned into the small bathroom outside of Nikki's room and got busy while two of the others began taking boxes out to their van.

BABYGIRL89: You'll be happy to know that everything will be done by moving day. They are finishing everything up over the weekend.

While I stood there waiting for a reply, I heard a knock at the front door. I put my phone down and walked down the three steps, pulling the door open. My father stood there in the rain, soaking wet, with a sad look on his face. I was so shocked to see him standing there, all I could do was stare.

"You have a couple minutes for your old man?" he questioned; his hands shoved in his pockets.

I didn't know what to say. All I wanted was for him to wrap his arms around me and tell me everything was okay between us. When I didn't respond, he hung his head.

"I don't blame you. I'll be on my way."

I watched him turn and walk across the driveway. "Daddy, wait," I called.

He turned back around and came running over to the door. I stepped to the side, allowing him enough room to come inside. I shut the door behind him and immediately he wrapped his arms around me and pulled me in for the biggest hug he'd ever given me.

"Daddy, I am so sorry," I cried, hugging him just as tight for a moment before I slowly released my grip and took a step back.

"Ainsley, I'd like you to come back home." He muttered, "Please."

Shocked, I stood there staring back at my father. "Daddy, I'm not coming back home."

"Ainsley, please."

"No, Daddy. We are getting married, we are having a baby. Your grandbaby," I said, crossing my arms in front of my chest. I felt I had to remain strong and stand my ground. I was by myself in this for the moment, at least until Spencer arrived.

"Ainsley, I just want to talk."

"I don't need to come home for that. We can talk here."

He was silent for a moment, and he shifted his weight from one foot to the other. "I want to know why it is you both felt you couldn't tell me the truth?"

"Do you really have to ask that?" I questioned. "Dad, you haven't been the most understanding person about any of this."

"Understanding? You want me to be understanding?"

"Yes," I practically shouted, then remembered that I had the packers in the house.

"Ainsley, do you have any idea how shocking this has been? I mean, I come home in the middle of the night. Go to check on you and find my daughter in bed with a man that I trusted to look after you while I was gone."

"You're acting as if he was babysitting me. I'm twenty years old, Dad. I babysit his daughter."

"Fine, 'look after' is the wrong way to put it. However, I find you, wrapped in his arms, naked. A man my age. What was I supposed to say, that everything is all right, just keep fucking my daughter?"

My mouth flew open at his choice of words. My father had never spoken to me like that. "Dad, please."

"No, Ainsley, you are a grownup. Tell me what the hell was I supposed to think? Why else would a man my age have any interest in a girl your age? You were nothing more than something he could fuck."

My eyes filled with tears at his choice of words. Then anger filled me. "Did you ever think that the way you react to things was the reason we didn't tell you?"

"The way I react!"

"Yes, you found out about the baby through an invitation not even addressed to you. Then you barged over here and demanded I move back home without even asking us if it was true. You just assumed. I'm not coming back home." I crossed my arms over my chest and stood there staring at my father, reeling with hurt and anger.

My father looked at me, worry crossing his face. "I really hope you aren't making a huge mistake, Ainsley. I hope I am wrong."

Just then, the front door opened, and Spencer stepped inside to find me glaring at my father. Without so much as a word to Spencer, my father shoved past him and left the house. Spencer took one look at me. "What the hell was that about?"

I shook my head. "I don't know. I thought he was coming here to apologize."

"What happened?"

"I told him I wasn't coming home, and then he reminded me of all the reasons I didn't want to tell him the truth about the baby right away." My eyes filled with tears as I stood there looking at the closed door. "Do you ever think he will come around?"

"I don't know. I'd like to say yes," Spencer said, wrapping his arm around me and pulling me into his chest.

SPENCER

Once I'd gotten Ainsley calmed down, we went into the kitchen and prepared a meal together. I'd wanted to do whatever it took to get her mind off what had happened, and so far it had worked.

We ate in the kitchen as the dining room table was now covered in boxes and glassware. We'd just finished our meal, and I sat back in my chair and took a drink. "So, you said that everything will be done in time?"

"That is what they told me."

"Well, that went better than I expected. We should take a drive over to the new place tonight and check on things."

"Sure." Ainsley shrugged.

"All right then, give me a few minutes and we will head out."

I cleared the table and shoved the dishes into the dishwasher. Then we made our way out to the car. I pulled my seatbelt across me, while Ainsley did the same, and then I noticed she shifted uncomfortably in her seat at the same time she let out a small moan.

"What is it?" I questioned.

"Nothing, I just got a sharp pain in my back is all. I must have pinched something," she said, moving around while trying to get comfortable.

"You sure that is all?"

"Yes. See, it's all better now," she said, finally sitting still.

I drove off toward the new house, pulling into the driveway in ten minutes. I came around to Ainsley's side of the car and opened the door, helping her out, and together we walked to the front door while looking at the gardens. I slid the key into the lock and we stepped inside. Some rooms contained boxes and others had the furniture all set up. We headed upstairs to the bedrooms and found Nikki's almost completed.

"Wow, it looks amazing," Ainsley said.

"Yes, this company was highly recommended. They have done an amazing job so far, haven't they?"

I watched as Ainsley walked across the room and flipped the light on the inside of Nikki's own bathroom. "Wow, I really think Nikki is going to love this. What about you?" She was about to take a step when, once again, she flinched in pain, this time putting her hand on her abdomen.

"Ainsley, what is it?" I asked, rushing over to her.

"Just that same pain again."

I frowned, worried that something was wrong. "I think we should get back to the house. I think a hot bath and bed are for you."

It surprised me she didn't fight me but agreed. That worried me more. Concern lined my face; she took my hand and together we made our way back out of the house and drove back home.

Once home, I drew her a hot bath and got her settled, and then I headed into the living room to do some work. I'd just gotten off the phone with Max when I heard a bang come from the bedroom. I listened hard, but heard nothing, so I went back to what I'd been working on. I was just about to call Max back when I was sure I heard my name.

I got up and began walking down to the bedroom; halfway down the hall I heard Ainsley scream. I took off, shoving the bedroom door open, and ran into our ensuite to find Ainsley sitting on the bathroom floor, naked. Her legs and hand covered in blood.

"Spencer," she cried, looking down at her hand, then her legs. "I...I...I...don't know what is wrong."

Immediately, I dropped to my knees and grabbed the towel off the edge of the tub, wiping her hand. I reached and grabbed the towel that hung on the towel rack and covered her legs and pulled my cell phone from my pocket immediately dialing the emergency line.

Her body shook as she leaned against me, listening as I made the emergency call. I held her close, waiting for what seemed to take forever for the ambulance to arrive.

I'D BEEN WAITING in this damn waiting room for over two hours and had heard nothing. I paced back and forth frantically. I was just about to sit down when a nurse walked by the room.

"Excuse me," I called, and then repeated, "Excuse me."

"Sir?" She came back into view.

"I'm here with Ainsley Matthews. Has there been any updates?" I questioned.

"I'm sorry, sir, I don't know. I'm not looking after anyone by that name. I can check with the nurses' station and find out for you if you like."

I could feel my heart beating in my ears and nodded. "Thank you."

The nurse turned around and went back the way she came. I took a seat on the couch and picked up a magazine off the table, flipping through it, barely seeing anything. They'd taken her from the paramedics the second I'd walked through the emergency room doors. I didn't even have time to say anything to her, to let her know I was here, nothing. They just whisked her off as she lay on the stretcher, clutching her body, crying in pain.

I'd sent a message to Carly a little over an hour ago and still had heard nothing from her. I dropped the magazine on the table just as the nurse returned to the doorway.

"I'm sorry, sir. There have been no updates yet," the nurse said quietly and continued to walk down the hall.

I felt helpless, completely powerless at this moment. I always had control. I wasn't used to this. I leaned back in the chair and stared at the wall when I heard my name quietly called from behind me. I turned and looked over my shoulder to see Carly, Jon, and Jane standing together. Sadness lined all their faces, along with worry.

"How is she?" Carly questioned.

My eyes travelled from her to Jane and then to Jon, who looked more worried than any of them combined.

"I… I don't know. I haven't heard a thing," I said, the first tear escaping from my eyes. I covered my mouth and turned my back. I just needed a minute to calm myself and take everything in that had happened in the past few hours. I never cried, but when I felt a small hand on my shoulder and turned around to see Carly standing there, her eyes full of tears, my own tears fell.

She wrapped her arms around me, and we stood there, the pair of us crying. "I just love her so fucking much," I whispered, feeling as if my heart were being ripped from my chest. "I don't know what I'll do if she isn't okay."

"She is going to be fine. Don't talk like that. She is going to be fine," Carly cried.

I pulled away from her and saw Jon and Jane standing in the same spot they had been. Jon had his arm around Jane, and they both had tears in their eyes. Carly guided me over to a chair, and the four of us sat down together.

We talked for a while, going over what happened, each of them listening, and then I heard my name called. I turned to see Doctor Pines standing in the doorway. "Spencer, can I see you please?"

Carly softly smiled and nodded at me. "Go... we'll be here."

I looked at Jon; he nodded as I got up from my chair, feeling the weight of everything on my shoulders.

"We'll be here, Spencer," Carly called out again, reassuring me they weren't going anywhere.

I turned and looked at her over my shoulder. "Thank you."

I walked over to where Doctor Pines stood. "Walk with me," she said.

We began walking down the hall toward a bank of rooms and stopped at the first one where I could see Ainsley lying in the bed sleeping. "She's been asking for you."

I swallowed hard; I wanted to know what had happened, but I was afraid to ask. I was afraid to hear the answer, because somehow, I already knew the truth. Instead, I just stood there watching her.

"Do you want to know?" she asked. "Or would you prefer I let Ainsley tell you?"

"Is the baby… okay?" I questioned, the words getting stuck in my throat. I needed to be prepared in case the outcome wasn't good. I needed to be prepared to be strong for Ainsley.

Doctor Pines looked at me, a sullen look on her face. "I'm afraid not, Spencer. She lost the baby," she whispered.

My chest hurt as what Doctor Pines said registered in my mind. I looked through the doorway at the love of my life lying in the bed all alone. My thoughts drifted back to when she told me about the baby, how scared she was at how I'd react and how surprised she was when I didn't blow up. Then the complete look of excitement and happiness on her face.

"What happened? Do you think stress caused this?" I questioned.

"Most likely a chromosomal abnormality. I've seen this many times, and I have sent some tissue for testing to see if that is indeed the reason. Elevated cortisol can speed up the inevitable, but stress is not the cause, Spencer. While stress isn't good for her, or anyone for that fact, this is quite common to happen. About eighty percent of pregnancies end in miscarriage this early on."

I grew quiet as I watched Ainsley. "Will we ever be able to have children?" I asked.

"Yes, of course. She is perfectly healthy. I am going to set up an appointment for you guys to come in and speak with me at my office once the test results are back. I am not sure how Ainsley is going to take this. She knows, of course, but it's too early to tell how it may affect her psychologically. However, there is also a slight chance she won't be affected at all. Either way we can set her up with some therapy."

I nodded, still watching her through the window. I wanted to hold her, to make everything okay for her, but I knew that was impossible. This wasn't something I could put into a spreadsheet, tweak and fix.

"Go be with her. She has been asking for you since she woke," Doctor Pines said, placing her hand on my back. "I am truly sorry for your loss."

"Thank you," I whispered.

I stepped into her room, listening to the gentle beeping of her heart rate monitor. I made my way around the bed and gently took her hand in mine. I bent down and brushed her hair from her forehead and kissed her. She didn't move. I had just sat down in the chair beside her bed when a nurse came in and swapped out the almost empty IV bag, adjusted a couple of things on one machine and printed a report from another. She said nothing. She just gave me a nod and quietly left the room.

I brought Ainsley's hand to my lips and kissed the back of it, and she let out a small moan and slowly opened her eyes, blinking fast. She looked over at me. "Where are we?" she questioned, looking around the room.

"At the hospital, baby girl," I replied. "In your room."

It was then that her eyes filled with tears, and the once gentle beeping of the heart rate monitor got faster and a little louder. "Spencer, I'm so sorry, I lost the baby."

I wiped the tears that slid down her cheek and placed a kiss on her forehead. "I know," I said, swallowing hard. "It's not your fault," I whispered.

She tried to move closer to me but she couldn't, so I lowered the rail on the side of her bed. She was over far enough that I could lie beside her, so I carefully climbed onto the bed, sliding my arm under her and wrapping myself around her.

I'd just gotten comfortable when the door opened, and a nurse stepped inside. "Everything okay in here?" she asked, silencing the alarm on Ainsley's heart monitor.

I nodded, holding Ainsley tight against me. That was when I noticed that people from the hallway could see into the room. I didn't want them staring, watching us, as we shared this private moment together. "Nurse, could you please pull the curtain closed give us a little privacy?"

"Certainly, sir," she said, pulling the curtain over the glass window. "If you need anything, just hit the call button, okay," she said before leaving the room.

As soon as the nurse was gone, Ainsley shifted onto her side and wrapped her arm around me, burying herself in my chest. A guttural sob escaped her. Once again there was nothing I could do but hold her tight, allowing her to cry, to grieve for what we'd just lost.

A FEW HOURS had gone by. Ainsley was now sound asleep on her back. I slipped from the hospital bed and headed down the hall. I'd forgotten that Carly, Jon, and Jane were still there. I rounded the corner in time to see the three of them look up.

"How is she?" Carly asked immediately. "How is the baby?"

I looked at them, feeling empty. "She is okay. She, um…" I pinched the bridge of my nose and closed my eyes, "She lost the baby," I muttered. It was the first time I'd said those words. I'd heard them, I'd thought about them, a lot, but this was the first time I'd actually said them.

Carly covered her mouth as tears ran down her cheeks. Jane grabbed her and wrapped her arms around her, and she grabbed Jon's hand.

I stood there, watching as each one of them consoled the other, wishing that there was someone to console me. I turned around, sitting down on a chair away from them all. I buried my face in my hands as I listened to Carly cry. Jane was doing her best to calm her down.

I ran my fingers through my hair and let out a breath, and that was when I felt a firm hand on my shoulder. I sat there for a moment before looking up to see Jon staring down at me.

"I was wrong."

When I said nothing, he came around and sat down.

"I was wrong about you. About how you feel about her. I see it now."

It was wrong that it had taken this to get him to see my feelings for her. To lose a life in order for him to realize that I really, truly loved his daughter. I didn't have words. I wanted to shout at him but knew it would do no good. We'd all lost something here. It wasn't just Ainsley's and my loss; it was also Carly's, Jane's and Jon's.

It would take all of us time to heal. Heal from this, heal from the words that had been spoken. It would take us time to rebuild our relationships with one another. Everything now hinged on time.

AINSLEY

---

4 months later

SPENCER and I had spent the last four months working through what we'd lost. It had taken me a while to realize that it was nothing I had done. Doctor Pines had gotten the results back from the tissue samples she'd sent to the lab, and they confirmed it was a genetic abnormality that caused the miscarriage. Having that answer, along with an amazing therapist helped me to cope. Having Spencer at my side the entire time helped even more. We'd both taken time off from work, Max stepping up and running both sides of things for a bit while we worked through everything, including our relationship with my father.

During this time, Spencer had also dealt with Brittany. She'd appeared at our home to pick Nikki up, a month after we'd lost the baby, and spewed some horrible, hateful words at me. Then she'd taken Nikki back home with her. Two days later, we'd gotten a call from Brittany's neighbour who had noticed she hadn't been home but knew Nikki had been staying there. She'd left Nikki unattended for two days. Immediately, Spencer called his lawyer, and they awarded us immediate custody. Then we had a restraining order placed against her.

Nikki danced around the living room wearing her little flower girl dress as Carly and I watched her, laughing at her silliness.

"Ainsley, what flowers am I getting?" she asked.

I smiled. "Well, I am not sure what they will have. It might look something like this," I said, turning my laptop around for her to see one image from another person's wedding. The flower girl was carrying hibiscus flowers.

"Oh, those are pretty. Can we plant those in the backyard?" she asked.

"I don't know if those will grow well here, sweetie," I said, kissing her forehead. "We need to get you out of this dress though."

"Oh, but it's soooo pretty," she said, doing another spin.

"Come on, Nikki, let's get you changed, and then we can see Ainsley in her dress," Carly said, guiding her down the hall to her room.

I let out my breath, the flutters of nerves hitting my stomach. I looked at the bag that hung on the back of the walk-in closet door. I hadn't looked at this dress since I'd picked it up after the alterations had been done. I walked over and lowered the zipper. I looked at the beautiful dress I'd chosen almost six months ago and slipped the straps off the hanger. I worried about the weight I'd lost. It had been a struggle for a while to eat after I'd lost the baby. I had worked hard but I wasn't sure I'd gained enough back for the dress to fit any longer. I took off my shirt and my jeans and stepped into the dress and was surprised when it slid on like a glove. I reached behind me and raised the zipper as far as I could until I saw Carly standing in the door.

"Can you help me?"

"Wow, Ainsley, you look gorgeous," she said, coming over and raising the zipper the rest of the way. I turned around and looked at my friend, who, for the first time, had tears in her eyes because of something like this. "Spencer is going to bust when he sees you," she cried, straightening the lower part of the dress so that it hung straight.

"You think?" I smiled, looking at my reflection in the mirror.

"Wow, Ainsley, you are sooo pretty!" Nikki cried with excitement as she covered her mouth with her little hands.

"Isn't she though," Carly said, standing up and giving me another onceover.

We stood there for a moment, admiring my dress, when we heard a car door slam outside. I looked at Carly, my eyes bugging out of my head as panic filled me. "Is that Spencer?" I asked. I'd hidden the bag in the back of the closet, and we'd gone this long without him seeing it. I didn't want to ruin the surprise because he walked in after a long day at work to find me standing in it.

Carly ran over to the window and looked out, breathing a sigh of relief. "It's Jane." She giggled and ran down the hall to open the front door.

Moments later, Carly returned with Jane. One look at me and she smiled. "Goodness, Ainsley, you're breathtaking," she said, coming over and shoving my long hair off my shoulders.

"Thank you."

"Just wait until your father sees you in this dress. I think it might make him cry." She laughed.

I gave myself another look in the mirror and glanced at the clock. "Can you guys please help me out of this dress before Spencer gets here?"

"Of course," Carly said, coming behind me and unzipping the zipper, while Jane stood in front of me, taking the straps so the dress didn't fall to the floor. Together, they hung it back in the bag and zipped it up, slipping it behind the bag that held Spencer's suit while I got dressed.

"Everyone have their passports?" I questioned.

"Yes, your fathers just came in today," Jane said. "We were getting worried, but I got a notice from the post office. I just got it before I came here."

"I'm home," I heard Spencer call from the hallway. "Is it safe to come in?"

The three of us laughed. "Yes, of course," I called, throwing my T-shirt over my head.

Spencer rounded the corner, carrying a small bag and his laptop bag, and set them both in the corner. "Are we having a party?" he asked, looked from me to Carly to Jane.

"Just here, helping make sure everything is ready for tomorrow," Carly sang.

"And is it?" Spencer asked.

The three of us smiled, and I nodded my head. "Yes. Now, what is in that bag?" I questioned, curiosity getting the best of me.

"That," Spencer said, nodding to the bag, "is for our wedding night." He placed a kiss on my lips.

I felt my cheeks flush as Carly and Jane watched the exchange between us.

"Ohhh, what is it?" Nikki asked, running over to grab the bag, but Spencer grabbed it first, picking it up and placing it on the top of our dresser.

"It's not for a little person's eyes," Spencer said, grabbing her and throwing her over his shoulder. She let out a loud laugh as he tickled her before he placed her back down on the ground.

"I'm going to hit the shower and then get packed," Spencer said, heading to our ensuite shutting the door behind him.

Carly, Jane, Nikki, and I headed to the kitchen, where we sat down at the table to go over all the information for the trip. Spencer and I were to be married two days after we arrived, then we would be whisked away to a private part of the resort to spend our honeymoon, while the rest of the guests partied the week away.

"You're sure you'll be fine to watch Nikki?" I asked Carly.

"Of course. It's only for the wedding night, right?"

I nodded. "Yes."

"We can help too," Jane said. "We'd be happy to."

I smiled. "Thank you."

Things between my father and I, and Spencer and him, had changed in the days that followed the miscarriage. My father had been the rock that Spencer had needed, and he'd been there for me when I needed him as well. We'd had all the support we both needed, perhaps more. It was a welcome change, and soon Dad and Jane were visiting us more at the new place than they did when we lived next door.

"All right, who the hell is ready to party?" I asked, throwing my book to the side. I'd gone over and over all these plans for the last three months, to where there was really nothing left to plan.

"Yes!" Jane said, throwing her arms up in excitement.

Carly let out a laugh as she pulled Nikki close to her.

"I should get home. Your father will be home any minute, and I've got to get dinner ready and finish packing."

"Oh, me too," Carly said, jumping up out of her seat.

"Don't forget your dress," I said, running down the hall and grabbing her bridesmaid dress from the closet.

"I won't, don't worry. I also can't wait to meet Spencer's brother. You said he was single, right?" Carly asked, taking the dress from me.

I rolled my eyes and giggled. "Don't start."

AINSLEY

Carly had just zipped up the back of my dress when a knock came to her door. Jane walked over, pulling it open. The wedding planner stood there holding a small pillow that contained our rings for Nikki to carry, along with my bouquet.

She came right in, handing Nikki the pillow and showing her how to hold it, then she came over to me and placed the bouquet in my hand. I smiled as I looked down at the tropical flowers.

"Okay, so we are heading to the beach," she said. "Nikki, you will walk beside me. Carly, you will be next, and Ainsley, of course, you will be last. We will meet your father down there, and that is when the ceremony will begin."

I swallowed hard and nodded, hoping that everything would go smoothly.

"What about Spencer, Max, and Mike?" I questioned.

She smiled. "They are already down there. I just left them before I came here."

I let out a breath as she took Nikki by the hand. "Ready?" she asked, looking down at her.

Nikki nodded her head, and we began the walk toward my future. People turned their heads and watched as we made our way through the resort. Carly walked beside me, holding the back of my dress up out of the sand.

"You ready?" she asked, leaning into me.

"Never been more ready for anything in my life," I said, smiling at her.

"I'm thrilled for you," she whispered.

"Thank you."

Things between us grew quiet for a moment. Then she leaned in. "Can I tell you something?"

"Of course."

"I wanted to apologize to you. I really was wrong about Spencer. He really is a good man. I am so happy that you found him."

I laughed. "Found him? Well, in all fairness, I practically stalked the man." I giggled, thinking back to when I'd set up that ridiculous profile through his website just to speak to the man I lived beside.

"I know. I just wanted you to know that I was wrong. I never really gave him a chance."

"It's okay," I said, stopping and wrapping my arms around my best friend. "You've always been overprotective, and I know now that you were just looking out for me."

"I was."

We continued on our way toward the wedding gazebo we had chosen down at the end of the beach, finally coming to the end of the path. I glanced through the trees and caught sight of Spencer standing beside his brothers, talking. He looked so handsome in his dark suit. As I watched him, I noticed little things. He fiddled with his watch, then the button on his suit jacket. Then he laughed again at something Mike said before returning to the watch. Was he nervous?

I smiled, and then I heard Carly let out a little gasp as she, too, looked in the same direction. "Are you okay?" I whispered while the wedding coordinator spoke to Jane.

"Hmmm, yes," Carly said, a light blush on her cheek.

I glanced through the trees and saw Max standing there looking toward us as he spoke to Spencer. Then I turned and looked at my best friend. She was watching his every move, her cheeks flushed.

I softly smiled to myself, then nudged Carly. "I know what, or should I say who, you are watching." I giggled. "Perhaps a little crush going on here?"

"Maybe." Carly giggled.

They'd hit it off last night and spent most of the evening sitting at the bar, talking. When Max offered to walk Carly back to her room, Spencer and I glanced at one another.

I was about to lean in and say something when I saw the men take their positions, and then the Bohemian music began playing, and Nikki headed toward the gazebo carrying the little pillow that contained our rings.

As the music played, I took my father's elbow, and we stood together while Nikki and Carly started toward the gazebo. My father turned to me and smiled. "You look gorgeous, Ainsley. Just like your mother did the day we wed," he whispered.

It was the first time I'd ever heard my father reference my mother as being beautiful, and a tear escaped my eyes. "Thanks, Daddy. I'm so glad you are here."

"Me too," he whispered, leaning in and kissing my cheek. "I feel like I lost a lot of time with you because it was so hard for me to come to grips to hand you over to this man, but I know in my heart this is the right thing for you. I'm sorry for all you've lost."

A tear slipped down my cheek. My father wiped it away with his rough fingers. "I can't walk you down the aisle in tears," he said, leaning in and kissing me on the cheek. "It's supposed to be the happiest day of your life."

"It is, Dad. I am happy." I sniffled.

When the wedding coordinator signaled to us, my father looked over at me as I let out a breath. "Ready?" he asked me quietly.

"Never been so ready in my life," I whispered back.

Together we took the first few steps, and when I looked up, my eyes locked with Spencer's. All the memories came flooding into my mind. The first time I saw him over the fence in his backyard, the first time he'd turned those blue eyes toward mine and allowed them to run the length of my body, the first time his hand brushed my cheek and his lips brushed mine.

A flood of emotion waved over me as his eyes trailed my body. When we approached, my father leaned in and whispered something to Spencer, and then placed my hand in his. I took a step closer to Spencer. He looked down into my face. "You look absolutely stunning," he whispered to me as he leaned in and placed a gentle kiss on my cheek.

A gentle breeze blew as the wedding official began speaking. We stood listening to the words he spoke, each of us taking them in. Then he looked at us both. "It's time for the vows."

I swallowed hard. Spencer and I had written our own vows, and while I'd run over my words with Carly a hundred times, butterflies still floated around my stomach as I worried I may forget them.

I looked at Spencer as he took both of my hands in his. He looked at the ground and then up at me, looking me directly in the eyes.

"Ainsley, my love. It is with great pride I take you for my wife. We have proven to each other that together we can weather any storm that life presents."

I watched as he swallowed hard, his eyes looking a little glassy.

"In you, I have found my forever partner."

I blinked hard as my vision became blurry, and I reached up to dab under my eyes before I had tears and makeup streaming down my face.

"In a short time, you have become my lover, my companion, but most of all, my best friend. With you by my side, I know I will never be lonely again. I get to have you every day and night for the rest of eternity as my lover, my wife, and soulmate. You're my love and my light."

Spencer turned to Max and held his hand out. Max reached down and untied the ring from the small pillow that Nikki held and handed it to Spencer.

Spencer turned back to me and took my hand in his, sliding the ring partway onto my finger. "Ainsley, I give you this ring as a sign of my love, that it is forever, eternal and never-ending," he said, gently placing the ring on my finger.

I swallowed hard as I met his eyes. I took his hands in mine again, hoping that he couldn't feel them shaking.

"Spencer, I am so lucky to call you mine. You are everything that I dreamed of, and all that I will ever need. I'm so madly in love with you, and I promise that my love for you will only grow stronger with each day that passes. I promise to be your friend and partner every step of the way, no matter what we may face."

Spencer's eyes were glued to mine as I swallowed hard, willing my voice not to shake.

"Today I give myself to you in marriage. To share my life in good times and bad. When our love is simple and when it's an effort, through whatever may cross our paths, I promise to cherish you and always hold you in the highest regard."

I turned to Carly, waiting while she removed the ring from the pillow and placed it in my hand.

I turned back to Spencer and met his eyes. "I vow to be here with you and for you today, and all the days of our lives. Spencer, I give you this ring as a sign of my love, that it is forever, eternal, and never-ending." I slipped the ring onto his finger and met his eyes. He smiled down at me as I smiled up at him.

"I would like to take this opportunity to present to everyone Mr. And Mrs. Spencer Brooks. You may now kiss your bride."

Spencer took a step closer to me and wrapped me in his arms, pulling me against him. He brought his hand to my cheek and met my lips, kissing me for the first time as my husband.

AINSLEY

THE ROOM ERUPTED with laughter as Carly said a few words at the end of dinner. She took her seat beside Max and whispered something to him.

Spencer had arranged for all of us to share a private dinner in one of the resort restaurants. We'd just finished eating and were waiting for dessert to be served. I slid my hand into his and met his eyes.

"I love you," he mouthed.

"I love you," I whispered.

"Who's up for dancing?" Carly questioned, looking around the table. "It's a wedding. Hell, we must dance."

"Oh, well, I think we are going to retire for the night after dinner," my father and Jane said in unison."

"Yeah, us too. It's been a long day," Mike and Trina replied.

"Spencer, Ainsley?" Carly questioned, looking at us, "It's your wedding, you guys have to dance!"

We both looked at one another and shook our heads. "Not tonight," Spencer answered.

"Jesus, it's their wedding night, for god sakes. I'm sure they have far more exciting things to do than go dancing," Max quipped, pushing into her with his shoulder.

"Also, aren't you supposed to be watching Nikki?" I questioned, looking at my best friend. "She needs to get to bed on time." I giggled, knowing full well it was already way past her bedtime.

Carly looked at me, smiling. "Yes, she can go with me."

"We will take Nikki for the night," Mike said. "Carly, you go dance."

"You sure? She is welcome with us as well," Jane answered, my father nodding his head.

I looked over to see Nikki let out a yawn and put her head down on the table, her eyes fighting to stay open.

"We'll stop by on our way back to the room and get her pajamas and clothes for the morning," Trina told me.

"Carly has them." I nodded in her direction.

Trina nodded, "Okay, I will get them from Carly."

"No problem, I'll get them from my room. Yet I still want to know, who is going to go dancing with me?" Carly pouted.

"Max?" Spencer said. "Do us a favor and take Carly dancing."

Max turned to Carly and grinned. "Sure thing, boss."

Dessert was served, and once we finished, Spencer grabbed my hand in his. "Everyone, I just want to thank you for joining us on our special day. Now, if you will excuse us, I am going to take my wife back to our room."

Spencer

OUR SUITE WAS DIMLY LIT as we made our way into the bedroom. I closed the door behind me and looked over at Ainsley. Her eyes reflected that same want and desire as mine. I walked over to her and allowed my fingers to graze over the skin on her arms, watching it pebble at my touch.

She closed her eyes as I reached behind her, slowly lowering the zipper on her dress. She raised her eyes to mine as I removed my suit jacket and shirt, then my pants. She leaned forward and placed a kiss on my chest as my fingers caught the shoulder straps of her dress. My fingers slid down the length of her arms, and the dress fell into a pile on the floor.

She stood before me in the white lace bra and thong I'd gotten for her for today. "I've been waiting to get you out of that dress all day," I whispered as I bent and kissed her shoulder, then reached down and picked her up, carrying her over to the bed.

I placed her down on the bed, both of us moving toward the center. I leaned over to my side of the bed and opened the drawer, pulling out the surprise I'd gotten for Ainsley. I placed it beside my leg without her seeing it and then moved up and held my weight as I hovered over her. I placed a kiss on her chest and moved my way down, kissing the top of her breasts. I flicked the clasp open in front, her bra falling away.

Her nipples were already hard, begging me to take them in my mouth. I placed a kiss between her perfect tits as I allowed my hands to explore her body. I kissed my way down her body, running my tongue down her stomach, stopping at the start of her thong, allowing my fingers to play with the elastic.

I could feel my cock straining against my boxers. I opened her legs and once again held myself over her, allowing my cock to press between her legs with just enough pressure as I kissed her neck. I took one of her breasts in my hands, squeezing it, letting my hand play with it, and ran my thumb over the hardened nub.

"Take it in your mouth," Ainsley said quietly, arching her back.

I rolled her nipple between my thumb and forefinger, and then sucked it into my mouth, grazing it with my teeth. A loud moan escaped her as I repeated that on the other side.

"I love these. So sensitive, so beautiful," I said, taking them both into my hands and rubbing my thumbs just under her nipples.

I kissed my way down her stomach, stopping at the elastic once again, and slipped them off her body. I forced her legs open, looking down at her slick, wet pussy. "So fucking wet," I hissed as I brought my lips to her center, lapping and sucking as I slid two fingers inside of her.

I listened to her moans as I continued, placing my hands under her ass so I could fuck her with my tongue. She moaned even louder when I continued flicking my tongue against her clit.

I could tell she was close, so I stopped and knelt before her, removing my boxers. I rested my one hand on the back of her thigh, angling her just right, while I gripped my cock with my free hand, giving it a couple pumps before I lined up with her entrance. One swift movement, and I was buried inside of my wife deeper than I'd ever been.

"Oh God, Spencer," she cried out as I thrust myself even deeper into her.

"What do you want?" I asked, gripping her waist.

"Make me come," she begged.

I repeated the short, deep thrust again, then reached for the little finger vibrator I'd gotten. I slipped it onto my finger and placed one hand on the back of her thigh again, holding her in place. I hit the little switch, and a buzzing sound filled the room.

"What's that?" Ainsley questioned breathlessly.

"You'll see," I whispered, thrusting myself deeply into her before placing the little vibrator against her clit.

"Oh, fuck…" she screamed as I held that vibrator against her clit while I continued pumping into her.

"Let yourself go, baby," I said, reaching up and taking her nipple between my fingers and squeezing it.

I could feel her beginning to tighten as her body stiffened. I pulled the vibrator off her clit and began pumping into her hard and fast. "Spencer…" she screamed. I wrapped her in my arms and continued fucking my wife.

I felt her pussy clenching my cock as she came. I felt my balls tighten and allowed myself to let go, pouring myself into her.

Breathless and exhausted, I fell onto the mattress. I covered my eyes with my arm, my body covered in a sheen of sweat. I swallowed hard and let my body come down while Ainsley lay beside me, doing the same.

Ainsley

I LAY there listening to him breathe. He'd been quiet now for twenty minutes, sometimes even lightly snoring. My eyes travelled over his muscular frame. Even though he'd just given me one of the best orgasms he'd ever given me, I wanted him again. I was ready.

I nuzzled into his neck, pressing my lips to his warm skin. "You awake?" I whispered.

"Barely," he muttered. "That was so fucking hot."

"Yes, it was," I said, leaning down and kissing his chest. When he didn't move, I looked down to his cock. My fingers trailed down his abs and over his hips, his cock beginning to stir at my touch. I looked back at him. His eyes were still closed.

I took a moment and took his cock in my hand, then I slid down, bringing his cock to my lips. I licked his shaft, running my tongue all the way up, letting my tongue hit the rim of the head before taking his cock all the way into my mouth.

He let out a deep breath as his fingers slipped into my

hair. "That's it, baby," he said, his voice throaty. "Fuck, suck me."

I took him all the way to the back of my throat, my hand working him, the other cupping his balls. The more I sucked, the harder he fisted my hair. I pulled my mouth from him, running my tongue once again from the base of his cock all the way to the tip, in time to lick the drop of pre-cum that was waiting for me.

I crawled up his body and straddled his hips, reaching between my legs, grabbing his cock and lining him up with me. I slid down onto his cock, taking him in. I loved hearing the guttural groan that escaped him as I lifted myself up and slid back down.

His powerful hands gripped my hips, and he took control, guiding my movements as his eyes washed over my breasts. I loved how he watched me, how his eyes skimmed my naked body. He sat up, still working my hips. He sucked my nipple into his mouth, letting his teeth gently graze over it.

I could feel a flood of heat between my legs as he moved to the other one and repeated that again before he laid back. He adjusted the pillow behind his head so he could watch me as I rode him.

"That's it, baby. Ride my cock."

He reached for that little finger vibrator again, and I felt my excitement build as I watched him slip it onto his finger. He pushed me back, raising his knees up behind me for something to lean on so he could place it once again on my clit.

This time he'd turned the vibration up higher, and the second it touched me, I tightened around him. "God, Spencer, I can't."

"You can," he said, as he pulled it away for a moment, then placed it against me again for only a second before removing it again.

"Please, Spencer…" I cried.

"Please what? Please do it again?" he asked, placing it against my clit for only a brief second.

I could feel my orgasm building each time he did that, and it faded as soon as he pulled it away.

He allowed me to stay on him for only a couple seconds more before he lifted me off his cock and flipped me around so I was on my knees. He pulled me back and slid himself into me from behind, fucking me hard.

"Yes…" I cried as he slammed into me. He reached around, placing that little vibrator on my clit while he continued at an unrelenting pace. I pulled at his hand, begging him to remove that little vibrator, but it was useless. He refused. He held himself deep inside of me as I felt an earth-shattering orgasm rip through my body, while Spencer emptied himself into me again.

AINSLEY

Two months Later

"Hey, you meeting me for lunch or what?" Carly's voice erupted over the phone.

I smoothed down the sides of my skirt and fixed my shirt, turning to look over at Spencer, who stood with his pants down around his ankles, his shirt on the back of his office chair. We still hadn't seemed to pass through the honeymoon stage yet.

"I forgot about lunch," I mouthed to him. A smile came to Spencer's face as he reached around and rubbed my swollen clit, torturing me.

"Yep, Carly, sorry. I got, um… sidetracked. I'll be

there in ten minutes," I said, closing my eyes as the feeling of release built inside of me again.

"Why are you out of breath, anyway?" she questioned. I heard her breath hitch. "Oh my God, you're not."

"No, I um… I ran to my desk from the washroom. I was expecting a call from a client."

"Uh-huh," she said.

"Look, I'll be there shortly."

"Hurry," Carly sang.

I put the receiver down on the cradle and turned to look at Spencer, who stood there with a smug look on his face.

"What?" he said, licking my arousal off his fingers.

"Nothing," I said, feeling completely frustrated again.

"Hey, I told you not to answer that." He chuckled.

"Well, I wasn't supposed to forget lunch. You distracted me again."

"Is that so?" Spencer said, coming over to me, running his hands over my bare arms. "Give me another five and I'll do it all over again," he whispered, biting my ear.

"No deal. I've got to go." I giggled then climbed up on my toes and pressed a kiss to his lips. "I'll see you at home?"

"SORRY I'M LATE!" I cried as I rushed over to the table where Carly sat.

"Jesus, it's about time. It's not like we have tomorrow, you know." Carly laughed.

Carly was headed to Denver. She'd been hired at a school there and was starting in two weeks. I'd gone with her to find a place and to help get her settled, and tomorrow she started on her new adventure.

"So, did you call Max and tell him you'd be in town starting tomorrow? I mean, he said to call once you got there," I questioned.

When Carly and I had gone to Denver, Spencer had arranged for us to stay at Max's apartment. Max had been more than welcoming, taking the day off to show us around the city, and then he'd told Carly that there was no reason they couldn't hang out together until she got settled and met some people. I knew he was probably only doing it because Spencer had told him to; nevertheless, I thought it was nice.

"Yeah, we've been messaging back and forth. He said he'd meet me at the airport if I wanted."

"Awesome."

We took a couple of minutes to order, and then I slid the bag I was carrying into my purse.

"What's that?" Carly questioned, looking at the rolled-up bag.

I had told no one, not even Spencer, but the last few mornings I'd woken up I'd not been feeling so hot. This morning had been the worst, and I'd thrown up right after Spencer left for work.

"It's nothing," I muttered.

Carly gave the same look she always gave when she knew I was hiding something. "Ainsley?"

I let out a breath. I'd been dying to tell someone. "Okay fine," I said, looking around the restaurant as if I were guarding a state secret. "Say nothing, but I bought a pregnancy test."

Carly's eyes lit up. "Oh goodness, really. You think you're pregnant?"

"Shhhh…" I said, bringing my forefinger to my lips. "Yes."

"Oh God, I hope so," she said, rubbing her hands together in excitement. "You better tell me what the answer is as soon as you know."

Spencer, Nikki, and I had just returned home after driving Carly to the airport. It was late, and Nikki was sound asleep in the back seat. Spencer carried her in, and we put her to bed.

"What do you say we take a bottle of wine and hit the hot tub?"

I paused. "That sounds great. I'm just going to head down to the bedroom and get changed. I'll meet you out there?"

"Sure, I'll get the wine and towels."

I wandered down the hall to the bedroom and pulled the bag containing the pregnancy test from my dresser drawer. Carrying it into the bathroom, I locked the door behind me. My stomach fluttered as I stared down at the box. I'd just picked it up to open it when Spencer knocked on the door.

"Ainsley, I need my robe."

"One minute." I shoved the box under the sink and took a breath, calming my nerves before opening the door and handing him his robe.

He smiled, then kissed me.

"I'll be right there."

"Take your time," he said, wrapping the robe around his already naked body.

I waited for him to leave the room and listened hard until I heard no noise before opening the cupboard door. Staring down at the box for a few more seconds I decided to open it and remove one of the tests. "Moment of truth," I whispered to myself.

A few minutes later, I stared down at a positive result, my heart beating wildly in my chest. Excitement built inside of me as I wrapped the test in some paper and threw it into the garbage. I slipped out of my clothes and wrapped my robe around me, then slipped my feet into my slippers.

I wandered down the hall, stopping outside of the bedroom that was going to be our nursery. For the first time since the miscarriage, I opened the door and stepped inside. Spencer had the room painted as a surprise before we'd moved in, and he'd put together the crib together, which sat against the wall. That was as far as we'd gotten, and now, the room was empty. I walked over and ran my fingers over the edge of the crib, looking down, thinking of what could have been.

A tear slid down my cheek as I stood there. I wiped it away and took a deep breath. "Even though we never got to hold you, I loved you more than you'll ever know," I whispered to the empty room. "You'll be here forever in my hearts and thoughts."

I took a deep breath, turned, and made my way to the door. I looked back over my shoulder before I pulled it closed behind me and took a moment, wiping the tears from my eyes. I made my way to the back door and saw Spencer already sitting in the hot tub, a glass of wine in his hand. I went to the cupboard and grabbed some water first, and then joined him. Setting my glass on the edge of the tub, I crawled in.

"Water? I was sure you were going to want some wine. I figured it would help calm you down after that crazy display of tears you and Carly shared tonight."

I laughed, thinking about how we had clung to one another in the airport as if we'd never see one another again. "I will, in time," I said, sliding over and placing myself on his lap.

"I think Carly was on to us this afternoon," I said, laughing. "She kept giving me a knowing look."

"Oh, I am sure she was."

"I mean, there is only one reason someone would sound as breathless as you did. Actually, thinking about it is turning me on." He chuckled, reaching under the water and pulling me into him.

"You sure it's not because you have a naked woman in your lap?"

"That could have a bit to do with it." He chuckled, meeting my lips. "What took so long? Everything okay?"

It took me a moment, but I nodded my head as I thought about how to tell him.

"You sure?" he questioned, worry creeping into his eyes.

I smiled. "Everything is perfect, Daddy," I whispered, kissing his lips.

When I pulled away, I first saw a look of confusion and then a glimpse of understanding in Spencer's eyes. "Seriously?" he questioned.

"Yes. Yes. Yes. Yes…" I cried, growing happier by the minute. "We are going to have a baby."

Spencer looked at me, tears in his eyes. "You okay?" he asked, holding me tight. "I mean, are you okay with this?"

I nodded, another small wave of sadness coming over me. "I'm going to be okay. It is going to take me some time again, but I couldn't be more excited."

He pressed his lips to mine. "Please tell me one thing."

"What's that?"

"Please tell me I know before Carly."

I giggled. "Yes, that was what took me so long."

"Thank God," he said, pulling me in again for another kiss. "I can't wait to make lots of babies with you," he said against my lips.

Spencer grew quiet, then cupped my cheek with his hand and slowly brought his lips to mine, his tongue washing through my mouth. What started out as what most people would call infatuation had turned out to be the best move I'd ever made.

Spencer Brooks was the most attractive man I'd ever laid eyes on... my father's best friend... the man I babysat for... and now, my husband.

Want more of Spencer and Ainsley?
GRAB THE BONUS SCENE

To get your FREE bonus scene visit
https://geni.us/SpencerBrooksBonus

ABOUT THE AUTHOR

USA Today Bestselling Author S.L. Sterling was born and raised in southern Ontario.

An avid reader all her life, S.L. Sterling dreamt of becoming an author. She decided to give writing a try after one of her favorite authors launched a course on how to write your novel. This course gave her the push she needed to put pen to paper and her debut novel "It Was Always You" was born.

When S.L. Sterling isn't writing or plotting her next novel she can be found curled up with a cup of coffee, blanket and the newest romance novel from one of her favorite authors.

In her spare time, she enjoys camping, hiking, sunny destinations, spending quality time with family and friends and of course reading.

Catch up with me on social media!

Join my Reader Group

Sterlings Silver Sapphires

No social media? No problem, stay up to date with my Newsletter

Visit my Website

Follow S.L. Sterling

Did you know that bookbub has a feature where you can follow me and it will send you an alert when I release a book or put a title on sale? Sign up here and make sure you stay in the loop.

Bookbub:
https://geni.us/SLSterlingBookbub

Website
https://www.authorslsterling.com

Facebook
https://geni.us/SLSterlingFB

Twitter
https://geni.us/SLSterlingTwitter

Instagram
https://geni.us/SLSterlingInstagram

Tiktok
https://geni.us/slsterlingtiktok

Reader Group
https://geni.us/SapphiresReaderGroup

Goodreads
https://geni.us/SterlingGoodreads

Newsletter
https://geni.us/NLSignupBackMatter

GET A FREE BOOK

Sign up for my newsletter and I'll send you a free book.

https://geni.us/NLSignupBackMatter

His to Hold

Finding Forever with You

Vegas MMA

Dagger

The Doctors of Eastport

Doctor Desire

Doctor Right

Doctor Frost

All I Want for Christmas (Contemporary Romance Holiday Collection)

Willow Valley

Memories of the Past

The Holiday Dilemma

Letters from the Heart

My Darling Christmas

Scars on my Heart

The Happy Holidates Series

Pop Tarts and Mistletoe

Champagne and Fireworks

Summer Nights and Fireflies

Vancouver Dominators

Inside the Penalty Box

Ten Minute Misconduct

Crossing the Red Line

Two Minutes for Holding

Playing the Neutral Zone

Through the Five Hole

www.ingramcontent.com/pod-product-compliance
Lightning Source LLC
Chambersburg PA
CBHW031240310726
48971CB00004B/1099